DANCE OF THE TIGER

"Like all good novels, this one transcends categories. It has elements of allegory, of fantasy, and of myth. It is also a kind of detective story, complete with a challenge to the reader. Every few pages brings a new shock of surprise or laughter, of delight or recognition . . . Read the book!"

—*Washington Post*

BJÖRN KURTÉN

DANCE OF THE TIGER

A NOVEL OF THE ICE AGE
INTRODUCTION BY
STEPHEN JAY GOULD

BERKLEY BOOKS, NEW YORK

Originally published in Sweden as *Den Svarta Tigern* by ALBA, Stockholm.

This Berkley book contains the complete
text of the original hardcover edition.
It has been completely reset in a typeface
designed for easy reading, and was printed
from new film.

DANCE OF THE TIGER

A Berkley Book / published by arrangement with
Pantheon Books

PRINTING HISTORY
Pantheon edition published September 1980
Berkley edition / September 1981
Second printing / October 1981
Third printing / September 1982

ISBN: 0-425-05184-6

A BERKLEY BOOK ® TM 757,375
Berkley Books are published by Berkley Publishing Corporation,
200 Madison Avenue, New York, New York 10016.
The name "BERKLEY" and the stylized "B" with design
are trademarks belonging to Berkley Publishing Corporation.
PRINTED IN THE UNITED STATES OF AMERICA

To the crew of Stängesholmen, with love

CONTENTS

INTRODUCTION

by Stephen Jay Gould

This book is, first and foremost, just what a fine novel should be—a good story filled with insight into human character and the ways of nature. However, it contains another dimension that may not be detected by readers unfamiliar with the professional literature of anthropology and human paleontology. (But fear not; no one will miss the power and appeal of Kurtén's book in the absence of such knowledge. I merely argue that even a passing acquaintance with it will enhance enjoyment—hence the rationale for this introduction.) For Kurtén's novel is set in the midst of one of the most momentous and mysterious events of human prehistory, an event that has sparked debate among scientists for a century: the rapid replacement of Neandertal man in Western Europe by humans of modern aspect (often called Cro-Magnon, after the site of first discovery) about 35,000 years ago during a temporary thaw in the great glacial age.

When Darwin published the *Origin of Species* in 1859, he breathed scarcely a word about human evolution, limiting himself to a simple prediction based upon his theory of natural selection: "light will be thrown on the origin of man and his history" (in subsequent editions, he became a bit more courageous and wrote "much light"). Darwin's circumspect silence made sense, for in 1859 the fossil record of human evolution was virtually blank. The first decent human fossils had been unearthed in 1856, and the dust hadn't even settled over this discovery and its meaning when Darwin wrote.

These first fossils were found in a cave of the Neander Valley (*Tal* means "valley" in German) east of Düsseldorf in Germany. Twelve years later, another fossil skull was discovered in the rock shelter of Cro-Magnon in southwestern France. It cannot be distinguished from a modern human skull (in fact its bearer, at five feet, eleven inches, was a bit taller than the average for American males today), and it is classified as belonging to our species, *Homo sapiens*. Neandertals, on the other hand, had heavy brow ridges, a face that jutted farther forward than our own, and generally thicker and heavier bones (hence the squat appearance of Kurtén's Whites). What, if anything, had Neandertal man to do with our evolution?

This question touched off, and still inspires, one of the great debates about human prehistory. As evidence accumulated, it became clear that the Neandertal peoples had been the sole human inhabitants of Europe from at least 100,000 years ago until about 35,000 years ago. (Piltdown man once posed a challenge, but this curious creature with the human skull and the apish jaw proved to be just that: a fraud concocted from the jaw of an orangutan and the skull of a modern man.) Neandertals manufactured a distinctive kit of tools—the "Mousterian" culture—and practiced ritualized burial of the dead complete with flowers in the grave, as fossil pollen in burial sites at the Shanidar Cave indicates. Then, about 35,000 years ago, the Neandertal peoples disappeared—how rapidly we do not know; indeed, this is the essence of the debate. They surely did not pass by imperceptible stages into modern humans, but they may not have been abruptly dispatched either. In any case, European fossils after this Rubicon belong to our species: Cro-Magnon, or *Homo sapiens*. The Cro-Magnon peoples manufactured different tools, often considered more complex and advanced—the "Aurignacian" culture. They also introduced such artifacts as statuary—the "Venus" figurines—and the sublime and mysterious cave paintings of France and Spain.

What happened? Did Neandertal evolve rapidly into Cro-Magnon on the spot? Did the Cro-Magnons migrate into Europe from elsewhere and simply murder their indigenous competitors? Did the two cooperate and interbreed, with Cro-Magnon traits eventually prevailing by natural selection? Kurtén presents a hypothesis, framed as a mystery of sorts, that combines at least two of these traditional arguments.

Before we can reach any decisions about this troubling issue, we must resolve one fundamental question: who were the Neandertal peoples, and what was their genealogical relationship to us? And here we run into impediments imposed by some traditional prejudices of Western thought, particularly the false image of evolution as a ladder (the *scala naturae* of the ancients) stretching from primitive incompetence to advanced complexity. The conventional image—indeed the caricature—of Neandertal man developed from this notion that anything before us, and replaced by us, must be primitive and inferior.

Marcellin Boule of Paris (1861–1942), the leading human paleontologist of his day, created this caricature with his famous reconstruction of the Neandertal skeleton from La Chapelle-aux-Saintes, discovered in 1908 and by far the finest specimen then available. Boule depicted Neandertal man as a stoop-shouldered brute with a lumbering body and a heavy head slung forward in the style of King Kong. His Neandertal lived in caves and walked on the outer edge of his foot, while his big toe jutted out in the almost prehensile (branch-grasping) posture of his arboreal forebears. In short, Boule's Neandertal quickly passed into folklore as something we all recognize only too well: the "cave man" type of Alley Oop.

This *idée fixe* of Neandertals as brutish and primitive lay behind both contradictory ideas that dominated traditional interpretations of their relationship to us. They might be viewed—as Boule chose to see them—as an irrelevant side branch of surviving relics, only distantly related to us and just as well departed. Or for those truly wedded to the ladder and uncomfortable with the very concept of side branches, Neandertal became a primitive, and thankfully superseded, stage in human progress. From Boule's notion, we have the image of Cro-Magnon victorious, sweeping into Europe and exterminating the brutish aboriginal; from the ladder notion, we derive the idea of a primitive Neandertaloid stage giving way, by gradual evolutionary perfection, to the modern sapient.

But Boule was dead wrong—so wrong that we must attribute his error to an *a priori* conviction rooted in the venerable metaphor of the ladder and its equation: old and replaced equals primitive and incompetent. Boule's specimen had arthritis; hence its slight stoop. Actually, Neandertals walked just like us, erect and full-footed. Their brain exceeded ours slightly in size, probably a correlate of the heavier body it served, not a mark of superior intelligence. Most Neandertal fossils do come from caves, but this is an artifact of preservation: bones from open sites rarely survive. Neandertal man was beetle-browed and did have a large face, but shall we in our hubris equate a personal aesthetic of appearance with intellectual and moral worth?

In short, most anthropologists now view the Neandertal peoples as members of our species: as a distinctive European variety usually designated as a separate subspecies, *Homo sapiens neandertalensis,* while we are *Homo sapiens sapiens.* Very few experts today—though I can think of one or two—hold that Neandertal simply evolved into modern man in Europe. Most agree that the Cro-Magnon peoples migrated into Europe, ultimately, in all probability, from Africa, where the earliest fossils of *Homo sapiens sapiens* have been found. But they did not arrive as godlike moderns, meeting and quickly dispatching semi-gorillas. The encounter between Neandertal and Cro-Magnon—and this is the key point of my introduction—was a meeting between equals, a confrontation between two groups of *human* beings. And yet it was unlike anything that has happened since, unlike even the most stereotyped and racist image of white explorers meeting backward natives in jungles of the Dark Continent. For all modern human groups are recent and only slightly differentiated products of a common ancestry as *Homo sapiens sapiens.* The Neandertal peoples were human beings, but the gap between them and us (genealogically, at least) was far greater than that separating any two human groups today. We are now all brothers; this is biology, not political rhetoric. Neandertals were human, but different. Herein lies the fascination of that European encounter some 35,000 years ago—and herein the urge to novelize. For a meeting of two truly different human groups is more wonderful than all science fiction.

Dance of the Tiger is set in Scandinavia, as the Cro-Magnon peoples enter Neandertal territory during a thaw in the great Ice Age. Kurtén's account of this contact transcends mere good storytelling and character development. For this novel, written by one of the world's premier professional paleontologists, is filled with scrupulously accurate science and the kind of intuitive feel for natural history that no commentator or "science reporter" can attain, as it requires a lifetime of devotion and daily doing.

Kurtén has managed to insinuate into his story—in a way so subtle and natural that we can scarcely recognize he is teaching as well as novelizing—every fact and theory that I know (and several, undoubtedly, that I don't) about Neandertals, Cro-Magnons, human evolution during the Ice Age, glacial geology, and ecology and behavior of the great Ice Age mammals, including mammoths and saber-toothed tigers. Many deal with highly theoretical and speculative issues. Kurtén's Neandertals use only two vowels in their speech, in conformity with Philip Liebermann's claim based on a reconstruction of the Neandertal vocal tract (a hypothesis that I do not myself accept). They also have a strange fascination with and liking for the facial features of their Cro-Magnon invaders. Here Kurtén has joined an anatomical fact to an ethological theory. Cro-Magnons were relatively neotenized with respect to Neandertals, which is jargon for the fact that they retained, as adults, many facial features reminiscent of children. Neandertal children did not have the beetle brow and projecting face that the adults attained, whereas Cro-Magnon children *and* adults had smooth brows and small faces. Konrad Lorenz has argued that the characteristic features of childhood act as "innate releasing mechanisms" for feelings of affection—an obvious adaptation, since we must nurture our infants. But Lorenz also points out that we can be fooled into liking other creatures that happen to retain juvenile features, not because they are really sweet and cuddly, but for evolutionary reasons of their own. Human commerce has capitalized on this bit of biology; researchers for the doll industry determine what humans regard as cute, and the Disney artists have made Mickey Mouse progressively more juvenile in appearance to match his transition, during fifty years, from a nasty, rambunctious fellow to the inoffensive creature whose name has become a synonym for insipidity. Did Cro-Magnons "fool" Neandertals in the same way—not by being really "nice," but by evolving, for other reasons, features that elicited this impression? I don't think I'm giving away too much in stating that this reasonable speculation provides one piece to the solution of Kurtén's mystery. But for the height of creative amalgamation of science and story, read Kurtén's masterful account of the fight between saber-tooth and mammoth. It is virtually a treatise on ethology and anatomy, but you'd never know it while held by the power of his prose.

Let me, as a scientist, make a claim that may seem curious. I believe the Kurtén's novel is a more appropriate place than the professional literature itself for discussing many of the truly scientific issues that swirl about the Neandertal–Cro-Magnon debate. Evolutionary biology has been severely hampered by a speculative style of argument that records anatomy and ecology and then tries to construct historical or adaptive explanations for why this bone looked like that or why this creature lived here. These speculations have been

charitably called "scenarios"; they are often more contemptuously, and rightly, labeled "stories" (or "just-so
stories" if they rely on the fallacious assumption that
everything exists for a purpose). Scientists know that
these tales are stories; unfortunately, they are presented
in the professional literature where they are taken too
seriously and literally. Then they become "facts" and
enter the popular literature, often in such socially
dubious form as the ancestral killer ape who absolves us
from responsibility for our current nastiness, or as the
"innate" male dominance that justifies cultural sexism
as the mark of nature.

Yet these stories have a role in science. They probe the
range of alternatives; they channel thought into the con-
struction of testable hypotheses; they serve as tentative
frameworks for the ordering of observations. But they
are stories. So why not treat them as such, get all the
benefits and pleasures, and avoid the wrangles that arise
from their usual, inappropriate placement?

Kurtén, for example, probes the results of different
social systems by depicting Neandertals as matriarchal
and Cro-Magnons as patriarchal. No evidence supports
this assignment; each group could have been either or
neither. But the speculative exploration of conse-
quences, in this literary setting, is scientifically provocative as well. In another case, I felt enlightened—
and embarrassed. Kurtén depicts Neandertals as
white-skinned, Cro-Magnons as dark. Until reading
this, I had never realized that my unquestioned picture
of Neandertals as dark arose from standard reconstructions, Boule's trap of seeing everything ancient as
primitive, and from the racism that sadly afflicts us all
and leads white people to associate inferiority and
darkness. Kurtén's reconstruction makes much more
sense, since Neandertals lived in glacial environments

and light skin may be an adaptation to life in middle to high latitudes. Yet any scientist would be rightly dubbed a fool if he published a professional paper on "the skin color of Neandertal deduced from general evolutionary principles."

But the greatest appeal of Kurtén's novel arises from his proper treatment of both Neandertal and Cro-Magnon as people of fully human intelligence and feeling. They, in other words, are we—as we might have been in a world unfamiliar and so impossible to re-create. Scientists study structure by examining its behavior at, or beyond, the limits of its usual functioning. We seek odd adaptations—tiny shrews, gigantic whales, swimming seals, flying bats, thinking humans—in order to understand mammalian design (10,000 rats get us nowhere). We study deformed embryos, not from morbid fascination, but because they help us to infer the rules of normal development. May we not hope to understand ourselves better through a literal insertion into prehistory? I know, as abstract intellectual propositions, the theories that Kurtén discusses. But Kurtén has taught me something by giving them a human face. How would it feel to meet an alien being whose speech included beautiful sounds I couldn't make, who could draw the likeness of an animal on a rock? How would I respond to impending extinction, to a world where such pedestrian facts as twinning and poisonous mushrooms became aspects of magic and sources of power?

Björn Kurtén, who teaches at the University of Helsinki, is unquestionably Europe's finest evolutionary paleontologist. He is, with George Gaylord Simpson in America, the founding father of an important scientific movement that united Darwinian theory with empirical studies of fossil vertebrates. He is an expert on the mathematics of population structure, demography, and the growth and form of organisms. He is a leading student of fossil bears—amusing, since Björn means "bear" in his native Swedish (no inconsistency: many Finns are ethnic Swedes). He has written several books on mammalian life during the Ice Ages. He has now proved on paper something else I always knew about him, that he is also a man of rare insight and compassion. It is always heartening—and not so rare as some people think—to find such an exemplary combination of human and intellectual qualities in one person.

A CHALLENGE TO THE READER

About 35,000 years ago, during the Ice Age, men of our own species—which bears the proud name *Homo sapiens*, Man the Wise—entered Europe. Presumably they came from the southeast, for we know that typical sapiens lived in East Africa almost 100,000 years earlier. It was in the millenniums between 50,000 and 30,000 years ago that men of modern type spread into all the habitable corners of the Old World.

Until then, Europe was the home of another type of man, the Neandertal.* With the advent of sapient man, he vanishes from sight. You never find them together. So it looks as if *Homo sapiens* replaced Neandertal man.

What does "replaced" mean? What happened when and if they met? A great War of Races? general jollification? or something in between?

In William Golding's admirable book *The Inheritors,* the Neandertals are inarticulate but charming children

---

* The spelling "Neanderthal," besides suggesting an incorrect pronunciation, is obsolete since the German spelling reform of 1905.

of nature, who are destroyed ruthlessly by the brutal
invaders. In other stories they appear as terrible savages, also destroyed ruthlessly by the noble sapients.
Relentless enmity is the common denominator.

On the other hand, there are some finds—in Israel,
for instance—which suggest hybridization between
sapient and Neandertal men. If this is correct, which is
by no means certain, at least some sapients and Neandertals regarded each other as human beings. As shown
by Ralph Solecki in his *Shanidar: The First Flower
People*, Neandertal man sometimes did behave in an
engagingly human manner. He took good care of his
aged and incapacitated, and there is evidence, from
fossil pollen grains, that the dead were honored with
flowers. To be sure, there were grislier ways of honoring
the dead—eating their brains, for example. As Professor Alberto C. Blanc has pointed out, though, the
step from the ritual cannibalism of Peking and
Steinheim man and the Monte Circeo Neandertals to the
Holy Communion of Christianity is not all that long.

So perhaps the two kinds of men did not always con-
front each other as enemies. Then why did Neandertal
man, who had evolved and lived in Europe for perhaps
half a million years (actually, the first evidence of man
in Europe, at Chilhac in France, dates back 1,800,000
years), vanish so quickly? In perhaps as little as a few
thousand years?

The main theme in *Dance of the Tiger* is a model that
could account for this disappearance. One among many
possible models. As it can be neither proved nor dis-
proved at present, it does not attain the dignity of a
theory, nor even the slightly shakier status of a hypothesis, but remains simply a model. It is not science; you
may call it paleo-fiction if you like. And I challenge you
to discover the model, which is a combination of three

different factors. Taken together, they would ensure the speedy extinction of Neandertal man even in the most peaceful coexistence. Like every honest detective story this one is full of clues, and some red herrings. You can reach the answer from them. So go ahead—puzzle it out. I'll return to it at the end of the book.

Apart from this, why write a novel about prehistoric man?

In the last three decades, it has been my privilege to be immersed in the life of the Ice Age. More and more, I have felt there is much to be told that simply cannot be formulated in scientific reports. How did it feel to live then? How did the world look to you? What were your beliefs? Above all, what was it like to meet humans not of your own species? That is an experience denied to us, for we are all *Homo sapiens*.

Are these people interesting to modern, civilized man? Most of us probably regard prehistoric men as uncivilized savages not worth our notice. But this is fallacious. Humanity is old, very old. Even in protohumans three million years ago, the anthropologist finds something that looks very much like Broca's area in the brain, the center of speech. Our ancestors of 30,000 years ago were of our own species and blood. They were superb artists and artisans, daring hunters, and skillful sailors. (They got to Australia!) The notion that "primitive men" are some kind of inferior race has been shown to be nonsense by students from Charles Darwin on. So many of our behavior patterns are innate and immediately understandable by anybody, regardless of race, culture, and language: the smile, the frown, the kiss, the embrace, the eye-greeting. More than that, the love of our fellow man, the sense of pride and of humor, the joy of creation, the urge to solidarity. They are all universals. We may have original sin, but assuredly we also have original virute.

So how these people, our own forebears, might have lived about 30,000 years ago is also one of the themes of this book. It is based on facts, as much as they exist. The writer of a historical novel has his troubles with the *Zeitgeist*, the spirit of the time. Still, the ambitious author may draw upon thousands of documents. The manner of speech, the clothes, the main events, the expressions of the day, can be rendered with convincing authenticity even if you choose to put yourself in the Carthaginian suburb of Salammbô.

In a prehistoric novel you must use more varied ingredients. A cave painting here, some footprints there, perhaps a population of skulls (which shows that the aged were well cared for). The material for *Dance of the Tiger* was collected in a geographic range from Shanidar Cave in Iraq to Kent's Cavern in southern England and spans at least 30,000 years. Admittedly, this is mildly anachronistic, like showing Theodore Roosevelt in animated conversation with the Great Mogul Akbar. But there are limits, so the Neandertals of Veyde's Island are nicer than the cannibalistic Neandertals of Krapina, Yugoslavia, who lived about 50,000 years earlier.

Most students now agree that Paleolithic man possessed the faculty of speech. Faced with the problem of rendering those long-dead words in my story, I see only one solution: to use modern language throughout. These men spoke the modern language of their time. It should be dated only by its substance of culture and religious belief, not by spurious archaisms.

Again, there is more to it. I suspect that our view of men who live in close contact with nature is colored by the romantic image of the taciturn Red Indian, the epitome of the Noble Savage. In contrast, my experience of the men of forests and lakes is that they are loquacious to a degree, with a great fund of small talk; they carry their hearts on their sleeves. Aloofness is simply a mask put on before a stranger. A large vocabulary is characteristic of the so-called primitive languages of today, and probably has been so for millenniums. To find a really primitive language I suspect you would have to journey back in time to the beginning of the Ice Age.

A note at the end of the book will detail some of the factual basis for the story.

PART ONE

VEYDE

THE HUNT BEGINS

And I saw the beast.

Revelation 19:19

The mammoths broke cover, soundlessly, at the place foreseen by the human mind. One by one they emerged from the forest, big animals at the head of the line, smaller ones next, and an immense bull bringing up the rear. As if under orders, adults and young alike pointed the tips of their short trunks upward, suspiciously sniffing the lazy airs that wafted across the bog. But the wind brought no message to them other than the heady scent of labrador tea and ripening cloudberries. Nothing was heard except the faint whirring of countless dragonflics, intent on their rounds over the surface of the bog, a mist of glittering specks under the hot sun. A dozen gazes focused on the column.

The mammoths started to skirt the bog, cleanly outlined now against the sky. The silhouettes of low hindquarters, humped shoulders, and peaked heads gave an impression of top-heavy power and might. The great curved tusks gleamed, bright white against the black fur. A stomach rumbled; and a curt command was heard.

In seconds, fires crackled into life. After weeks of fair

weather the land was dry as tinder, and the bracken and
sedge burned with a roar. Yelling figures threw spears.
The terrified animals squealed. Shying away from the
fire, they stumbled toward the bog.

This was the climax of days of planning and tracking,
from the moment the small band of hunters had known
of the mammoth herd. It was early in the year for mammoth, and the Chief was skeptical when the breathless
scout panted out his news. Shelk, moose, deer, even
bison could be expected. But mammoth?

"Chief, there's no doubt about it," said the man. "I
saw the fresh tracks and dung. There are seven or eight
animals, moving east."

"Where are they now?"

The scout pointed to the northwest. "Less than half a
day away, Chief. We could bag them, couldn't we?"

"We will be a long way from home before we find a
good place to strike," said the Chief. "We're not
properly equipped for mammoth. And to get the meat
home! Still . . ."

An eager group had now gathered around the Chief,
and the excitement was unmistakable. A mammoth
hunt during the summer was unusual. Mammoth and
caribou left these parts in the springtime for the
unknown northlands, where people said there were no
trees and no men. Only Trolls and worse. The first
mammoth appeared in early autumn, but the real season
was later, when the herds came thick, just before the
freezing of the bogs where it was best to trap them. But
by then it was often too wet for fires. Without fire to
drive the quarry, a mammoth hunt could be very risky
indeed. Now, in late summer, after a long dry spell, the
chances were good for a successful hunt. The Chief
reminisced.

"It's true we've had a few mammoth hunts in the

summer, usually when it's been dry for long times. The last one was many winters ago. Perhaps they can't find enough to eat up north. Still, we don't have mammoth spears."

The only arms the party carried were light atlatl javelins. Much heavier equipment was needed for mammoth. These men were not a hunting party but a trading group, on their way back from the Summer Meet. There, under the first full moon of late summer, northern hunters exchanged furs, ivory, and castoreum for precious flint and amber from the south. Neighboring tribes met and shared news and gossip. Rituals and dances were performed, and marriage contracts made between heads of families. The successful conclusion of any business was celebrated by a drop or two of black wine out of great bison horns.

Back home, the women and children of the clans, not permitted to take part in the Meet, went out to gather the rich harvest of berries in the bogs and forest.

So this group was trekking homeward, laden with riches acquired by successful barter, including some excellent flint work, hard to come by in this land of granite and quartzite. For a few days they had journeyed with a neighboring clan, amiable people who lived on the northern shore of Big Lake. Now they were heading south. The going was slow, for their goods were heavy. Four days, at this pace, separated them from their home at Trout Lake. They would meet their womenfolk on the way.

The Trout Lake Chief was tall and lean. He had black hair, bronzed skin, and a sharp-featured, lined, but good-natured face. He had lost count of his years, but was in his early forties. He trimmed his beard short. His real name, Ferret, was long forgotten, much to his relief. His renown was associated with a very different

animal. As a young man, he had killed a black tiger, a
feat unknown in the memory of his tribe. True, this particular tiger was old, had broken one of its teeth, and
had lost its mate. Nonetheless, it was a real black tiger,
the only creature besides man with the courage and cunning to destroy the mighty mammoth. So the black tiger
became the totem of the Trout Lake clan, and the
Chief's eldest son, who was in the trading party, was
called Tiger.

The Chief fingered the tiger tooth which hung on his
breast. That and the tattered black loincloth, his only
garment in the summer heat, were tokens of his unforgettable hunt. The story was often told—too often,
in the view of some of the younger men.

"We can't carry all these goods on a mammoth
hunt," he said.

"Let's cache it and mark the place," suggested young
Tiger, his black eyes shining. "We can pick it up when
we come back." The others agreed, and the Chief gave
way, as they knew he would.

The party began making preparation for the hunt,
hafting the heavy spearheads, collecting all the hand-
axes for dressing the meat, and making sure there were
enough fire-balls—the clay balls filled with glowing embers, which kept the fires alive.

"We must split into two parties," said the Chief.
"One to track the mammoths, and one to go ahead and
mark the place."

Everyone knew which task was more important.
Tracking mammoths without frightening them into a
run was not always easy. But to anticipate where they
were going to go, to be there before them, was a
challenge they relied on their Chief to meet.

If the party had been larger, they could have raised
enough fires to drive the mammoths into the nearest

bog. In this weather, with only a dozen men, the fires might get out of hand and the mammoths panic. For this hunt, the strategy must be different. They would have to follow the mammoths until they came to a manageable spot. Then all the men would draw together for the attack.

"To the east, where the mammoths are heading, is unknown country, all the way to the Great Water," said the Chief. "We must take them before that, or they might swim away."

"The land to the east is Troll country, isn't it?" asked Tiger.

The Chief nodded. As far as he knew, there were no men in that land, only Trolls. Years ago, from the top of a hill, he had seen the Great Water to the east and south, where the world ended. What he had to do now was form a picture of this unknown land in his mind, predict which way the mammoth herd would travel, and decide exactly where to strike. There was no time to lose.

"You, Dhole, will track the mammoths. I'll give you two men. Two others will be liaisons. The rest will come with me."

Orders given, the men dispersed to their tasks. There was a general feeling of exhilaration. Somebody was already talking about mammoth tongue with cranberry sauce.

Tiger was the youngest of the party, sixteen winters old, or "three hands and a finger," as he would have put it. He had been initiated into manhood in the spring, had stood up well, and was proud of it. Nobody knew he had seen the place before. It was winters ago. He had gone out to pick berries for his brother Marten, who was ill. Half a day from home, he had come upon the boulder by the rock face. It was in a small glade at the edge of the wood, hidden by juniper and rose thickets. He had not known then what it was, and something had told him he'd better keep silent about it. But he did investigate the traces of charcoal on the boulder before leaving the place.

When they took the blindfold from his eyes, he recognized the place at once. Now the boulder had turned into a black tiger, with patches of fur and a scimitar tooth put cunningly in place. Another black tiger was drawn on the rock wall. Tiger had stood with his back to the wall, facing the hail of clay pellets without flinching. Afterwards he drank the pungent berry potion, sweetened and strengthened with honey, sweet gale, and yarrow; wonderful dreams came to him. He was a man now, a hunter, an artist, one of the best marksmen with the atlatl. He was the fastest runner, too, and on this hunt, his first for the great mammoth, he would use his speed, for the Chief had made him one of the two liaisons between the mappers and the trackers.

The mammoth hunt went on for days, while the Chief, wily and versed in the mammoth's ways, worked out his plan. The herd was moving slowly, and was located without much trouble. Deciding where to strike was a more difficult matter, but at last the Chief was satisfied. He found a wide bog, hemmed in on the western side by a stretch of low hills with a single narrow pass. Here, all the marks showed that mammoth herds had traveled through before. Here, along the flank of the bog, he would deploy his forces.

So intent were the men on their task that they spared little time to take heed of other activities in the forest. Not one of them knew that they, the mammoth-watchers, were also being watched, that a second, more cunning hunt was about to take place.

Tiger, running along on his business, practiced

throwing his spear at likely targets, thick pine-trunks, make-believe mammoths. Otherwise he concentrated only on the mammoth tracks and the urgent messages he was carrying. He did not notice the occasional shape freezing into immobility behind a bush or a tree, or the watchful eyes registering his movements.

THE LAKE AND THE CAIRN

A shadow is the thing which is generated when you posit yourself between it and the sun.

Anonymous

Years later, at the age when men turn to survey their own tracks, and in the far distance see the landscape of their youth as illuminated by a setting sun, Tiger would speak of the memories crowding his brain. He would relive his boyhood at Trout Lake, remembering it as an undisturbed procession of summer days, winter days, glittering and sparkling. Foremost in his mind was always his brother Marten, one year younger and his companion as far back as he could remember. Together they had roamed the lake and the forest, every day bringing new discoveries, new experiences, new excitement.

His earliest memories were of the house, sturdily built, with walls made of wooden posts and mammoth bones, lined with moss and covered with mammoth skin. It lay a good distance from the shore, sheltered from the north wind by a long wooded drumlin ridge. There were six or seven of these buildings clustered together, but the Chief's was the biggest. Inside was one great room with a fireplace. A small window to the south, overlooking the lake, was covered in cold

weather by a pane made from mammoth gut. There
were two gables, each with a lean-to; one for hunting
and fishing utensils, the other for stores. The former
was the Chief's responsibility. Tiger and Marten loved
to creep into it, fingering the spears and javelins with
their beautifully worked points and admiring the fishing
harpoons made from bone, with small stone barbs.

The larder belonged to their mother, Oriole, for as
soon as game or fish was brought home, it became the
responsibility of the women. On long hunting expeditions the men would butcher their quarry and
prepare the meat themselves, but anything felled near
Trout Lake was hauled back entire and turned over to
the women.

When the hunt was taken care of, men were free to do
what they liked. Many did work in stone, ivory, or antler, making weapons and ornaments. On fine days there
were often exhilarating games: racing, fencing, or field
games using a football made out of a horse's stomach.
Then there was music—tomtoms, a flute or two—and
men began to sway or dance as the rhythm swelled. All
the animals were evoked. The drums imitated the stately
movements of mammoth and elk or the swift rush of the
horse. The children weaved like fishes between the dancing men. Sooner or later even the busiest women
gathered to watch, sometimes taking part themselves.

In general, though, the women knew few idle hours.
There were always skins to be scraped and chewed,
tanned, and sewn into garments. There was hair to be
spun into thread; sinew to be made into twine. The harvesting of berries, fruits, roots, leaves, and edible seeds
was women's work too. In this they were supposed to be
helped by the children, but the boys often played truant,
going out in small bands to fish and hunt for themselves. Early on, the boys also began to share the artistic

interests of the men. They learned the art of stonework, of shaping bone and ivory, and learned to record the shapes of the wild beasts in tracings and engravings.

The lake was the center of their world. Like everything else, it had its spirit, and Tiger knew that spirit. Perhaps it was in a dream, but he had seen it, rising like a frozen mist out of the lake and collecting itself into a shape greater, more awe-inspiring, than anything he had imagined. Then he knew that the spirit of the lake must be the Guardian of the mammoth. Immense and powerful, white like the hoarfrost, the spirit carried spearpoints on his tusks. Tiger saw that he was also the Guardian of the black tiger, for the two were one. Tiger and mammoth formed the upper and the nether shape of the mist. To Tiger, it seemed right that Trout Lake was the abode of this spirit. It meant that the Guardian was a friend to the Trout Lake people and would permit them, like the tiger, to hunt the mammoth and eat its flesh.

The lake was for fishing. There were crayfish, easy to catch, but not much to eat, except for the tails and claws. Small trout could be taken barehanded in the becks that fed the lake. In early winter, when the ice was still thin, pike could be stunned with a blow as they glided underneath. But the ice was often treacherous. One of the older boys fell through, and the lake never gave him back. They knew then that the spirit of Trout Lake was angry. The Chief offered his finest mammoth tusk, and the lake received it and was appeased.

The great time for fishing was early summer, when the nights were short and light. That was when the salmon came up the river to spawn, fighting their way up the rock-filled cataracts Trout Lake spilled into. They came in vast numbers, as their Guardian decreed, and very little sleep was had by anybody for a whole moon while the tribe caught and stored the fish. Early summer was the best hunting season. Bears, wolves, lynxes, and foxes were also keen on the salmon, and with eyes for nothing but the bounty of the river, they were easily bagged. This was a time for feasting and for filling the larders, which had been depleted during the late winter and spring. The spirit of the lake was in his best mood, and the villagers responded with their traditional rituals of love and gratitude.

The lake was for rafting and swimming, too. Tiger taught Marten to swim, and they both taught their little sister, Godwit. These three were the only surviving children in the Chief's family; several others had died in infancy. Yet there were always many children in the village by Trout Lake, for men and women took pride in their families, and the grief of frequent death was fought by bringing forth new life.

The lake was a mile long, and half as wide. By day it was deep blue, a festive mirror for the sun. By night it was dark and dim, reflecting the moon and the stars. When Tiger walked along the shore, the moon would follow him above the trees on the other side of the lake, always at the same place by his shoulder. He told Marten about his discovery, and they walked together, watching the moon and its obedient reflection, while owl-calls broke the stillness, and distant snorts revealed the presence of elk in the gathering dusk. Always full of mischief, Marten ran in the other direction, shouting, "The moon is going with me! The moon is going with me!" Tiger, much offended, ran after him and gave him a buffeting. But sure enough, there was the moon in its proper place, and the two boys could not agree about whose moon it was.

Then a light breeze whispered in the trees and rippled the surface of the lake, breaking the moon's reflection into a long path of dancing light fragments. The boys stood still, experiencing the wind. They knew that the great trees, tired of their long stillness, had started to wave their branches. The breath of the forest walked the lake. "Now the animals will come," whispered Tiger.

They lay in wait behind a boulder, but the only animal they saw was a lynx, moving like a shadow through the alders. For a moment its round, unblinking eyes stared at them. Then it was gone, as silently as it had come.

After a snowstorm, the lake was a virginal white sheet. Soon, though, it was crisscrossed by animal tracks, and Tiger and Marten would read the story of what had happened in the night. Once they found the carcass of an elk that had been killed by a wolf pack. The boys scared off the wolves and worked hard to drag the half-eaten animal back home.

As they grew bigger, the boys took longer excursions. Exploring new parts of the forest, they looked around warily. They did not fear wolves or hyenas, though it was true that the Guardian of the hyenas was reputed to be wicked. Perhaps he was just a ghost pretending to be a hyena, not the real Guardian at all. In the stories, he always came out badly in the end. Trying to trick others, he got tricked himself. So maybe he was not really dangerous.

The spirits of the trees and rocks were always kind. If you broke a branch or chipped a stone, all you had to do was tell them you were sorry. They would calm down right away.

The boys were a little afraid of Trolls and ghosts, even though the Chief assured them there were none around. It was always comforting to come up on a ridge and see, far away, the blue sheet of the lake.

There was a cairn on the crest of one ridge, and they decided to make this their house. They would move here and live as hunters forever. Perhaps someday, when they bagged a bison or a mammoth, they would invite the tribe to a feast.

Among the boulders Marten picked up a broken spear with a curious stone point. He knew it must be very old, for the shaft came apart in his hands and the point fell off the moldering wood. "Look, Tiger!" he said. "If we make a new shaft, we'll have a real heavy spear. I bet you could kill a mammoth with it."

Tiger ran up to him. "That's treasure," he said, for he remembered stories about buried Troll treasure. "Let's roll the boulders to the side and see if there are more."

The two boys heaved mightily, sweat breaking out on their foreheads. Finally, the boulder rolled away. There was something underneath, and Tiger started scraping at the soil. Suddenly he stopped, in terror and disgust. It was the skull of a man, yet not quite a man. He had a bony face with two owl-like, round eye-sockets staring blindly beneath the heavy ridge of his brows. A few teeth were left, and the skull seemed to grin at them with a wide-open gape, as if ready to devour them.

Tiger and Marten ran away in a panic, and stopped only when they had reached the forest. Trembling, they looked back to find out if the terror was stalking them, but there was nothing to be seen.

"It was a Troll," said Tiger.

"He was lying down under the rock," said Marten. "Do you think he was waiting for us? Do you think he will come after us now that we've taken away his rock?"

This possibility had struck Tiger at once. "Maybe not now while it's light," he said.

"But tonight when it gets dark?"

"Yes, then he may come." It was a dreadful prospect.

"We'll be safe in the house," said Marten.

But Tiger had already come to a decision. "No," he said, "We'd never be safe. There's only one thing to do. We must go back and put the rock on top of him again, so he can't get out."

Tiger turned to go back. Marten hesitated, but when his brother had walked a few steps, he caught up with him. In silence they climbed to the crest again, watching for the Troll, but when they came to the cairn, the skull was in the same place.

"He's just dead," said Tiger. "He's not going to harm us. That's what the Chief would say. He only wants us to put back his rock, so he can sleep again."

The boulder slid back easily.

"I'll make a new shaft for his spear, and we can give it back to him," said Marten.

"That's a good idea. Then he'll know we're friends."

They made the new shaft as fine as possible, using twine to fasten it to the point. Proud of the result, they slid the spear under the rock and covered the place with stones so nothing could be seen.

"Now he'll be friendly," said Tiger.

"Poor old Troll," said Marten. "Think of him lying there, never having any fun."

"I know," said Tiger. "Let's come here every day and play. And let's keep it a secret. Then he'll know we are watching and won't let anyone disturb him."

So the shadow passed from Troll Cairn. They came back, not every day, but often. They went to Troll Cairn by devious routes, intent on keeping their secret. Once a terror, the Troll became a friendly spirit. In this place, Tiger was Chief and Marten henchman. They hunted, bringing their catch of squirrels, hares, birds, and once a fox to the cairn for dressing and cooking. And they always slipped a few pieces of meat, or berries in season, into the cairn for the Troll.

It became a place of benevolent magic. Often Tiger felt that the Troll was somewhere about, resting comfortably on his new spear, enjoying their play, but always ready to turn a terrifying face toward any danger that might threaten them. So it was that Troll Cairn, and the image of the Troll who had lived at Trout Lake in ancient times, became associated with Tiger's happiest memories. Yet when older men talked about the Trolls, their stories were far from reassuring. Tiger and Marten would prick up their ears, but though the men were always ready to bandy the most blood-curdling tales, only a few had actually seen living Trolls, for most of them had come from the far south with the Chief a few winters before Tiger was born.

The boys' father, Chief of the tribe, never said much about Trolls, and only smiled at the stories. In his presence, their terror was quickly dispelled. He was an unbeliever, or at least that was the image he presented. Of course, he would spit three times if a hoodie crow flew across his path. If a cuckoo was heard from the south, he would refrain from hunting until the spell had been broken by another calling from the north. His automatic response to a thunderstorm, or some other display of the forces of nature, was a quickly mumbled incantation to the Black Tiger. But if asked about this, he would doubtless have answered that they were nothing but sensible precautions, like refraining from sitting down upon an anthill or standing in front of a charging rhinoceros.

He distrusted what he called sorcery, and that was why there had never been a shaman at Trout Lake. In his youth he had had a violent quarrel with the shaman of his clan. It had happened after the killing of the black tiger. Arriving home with the trophies of the hunt—the tiger skin and the single scimitar tooth—he had been dismayed by the shaman's insistence upon ownership of the tooth. This would have been right and proper if there had been two tusks; for the custom of the clan was that the hunter took one and the shaman the other, in acknowledgment of his spiritual help. But this tiger had only one tooth, and the Chief was outraged at the idea of giving it away.

He had been a very stubborn young man, and had voiced his rage before the whole clan. The memory still aroused the Chief's wrath. "I soon told off that old good-for-nothing," he would say, getting up and striding back and forth under his own roof, his head bent to keep clear of it: the Chief was a tall man. "He couldn't cure the old Chief who broke his leg in two places when we went on that mammoth hunt with the Falcon Hill boys, and he died within a moon. When we ran the rapids of Little River, he was so drunk with black wine that he lost his hat and his spear. Some medicine man!" The business had ended with the Chief and a party of friends going north to start a new settlement. "The Shaman cursed us when we went off, and said we would all be dead in a winter and a summer. That was fifteen winters ago, and look at us now! No good to anybody, he was, and the next summer at the Meet I heard he was dead. So there you are. No curses or spells for us, thank you!"

That was how the clan of Trout Lake came into being. Trolls had lived there before, but they were long gone, and the new settlers soon made friends with the Biglakers, their neighbors to the north, intermarrying to further the friendship.

THE HUNT ENDS

A icel jor que la dolòr fu grans
Et la bataille orible en Aliscans

Chanson de Guillaume d'Orange

      The only time Tiger actually heard his father talk at any length about Trolls was near the end of the mammoth hunt, when they were far away from their usual hunting grounds. The land was new to the Chief, and on that last evening before the strike he had betrayed some uneasiness.

"We may be in Troll country already," he had said. "We are getting close to the coast where they live."

"There are some bad stories about them," murmured one of his men.

"Mostly old wives' tales," said the Chief. "I believe the Trolls are more afraid of us than we of them. Still, in their own land, you never know. Of course, they should be easy to spot. They are white, you know."

"You've seen them, then?"

"I have," said the Chief.

"You never told us, Father," said Tiger, and everybody turned to listen. The Chief pulled his beard, his face wry.

"Well, you remember we moved into this land winters ago. Back south there are no Trolls any more,

19

though there may have been in the days of my grand-father—but he too had moved in from much farther south, maybe even from the Land of Flints.

"Long ago, just after we'd settled at Trout Lake, I went out to scout some of the land to the east, and met a party of Trolls. There were just three of them, one ox and two bitches. You might have thought they would resent me for being in their land, but they didn't show any fight. They were trying to talk to me. Of course they can't make the sounds of Men. And they were grinning all the time, flinging their hands about their faces. They looked funny, but they were armed, all carrying big spears with very crude points made out of this kind of rock." And he pointed to the elephantine granite hogback beside which they had put up their camp. Tiger nodded knowingly.

"You don't mean the bitches carried spears?" interrupted one of the men.

"They did indeed. And very hefty they were, too, broadbodied and almost as tall as the ox, though much shorter than we. But there was certainly no fight in them—rather the other way around." The Chief smiled a little. "I tried to talk to them—civilly, as we talk to strangers to show we mean no harm—and gave them the open-hand sign. But they only grinned more, and all of a sudden ran off.

"I've thought many times about what happened next, and I still don't know for sure. It could be that they put some spell on me after all. Thinking they might gather more Trolls, I went the opposite way. But it was late in the evening and I didn't go far before lying down to sleep.

"That night I dreamed that one of the Troll bitches followed me and came down on top of me to make love. And as if I had been hard at it all night, I didn't wake up until the sun was high in the sky. So it may be true that Troll bitches can cast a spell and make a man tired from love's labor without him even knowing what he's done.''

"Maybe it wasn't a dream," said one of the men, smiling.

"Whatever it was, I was none the worse for it," observed the Chief. "But strange it was, and I put it down to sorcery. That's why I've kept out of Troll country ever since."

"She came down on top of you?" asked one of the men.

"Yes, she rode me—in my dream," added the Chief hastily. "I once heard that Troll bitches are keen on men, but that they have wolf teeth in their vaginas, and when you're through they bite off your cock to keep you from giving pleasure to other women; but that's all rubbish. Neither is it true that they suck you dry and never let go until you're dead. I was none the worse afterwards."

"Well, I heard some Troll stories at the Meet," said another man. "Do you remember the people from up north? They seemed to know a lot about Trolls."

"Ye-es," said the Chief with some hesitation. "They haven't been at the Meet before—must have moved in from somewhere else. They kept rather to themselves, didn't they?"

"I talked to one of them. He didn't say much at first, but we had a hornful of wine, and he became quite genial. Lynx, he was called, and Shelk was the name of his chief."

"Oh, Shelk!" cried Tiger. Everything at the Meet had been new to him, but that man had made an impression. "He had that amber necklace . . . and a bracelet of bear teeth. He did look high-and-mighty."

"If Lynx was right," said the first man, "Shelk must be quite a wizard. He told me that Shelk could be in two places at the same time and often was."

"That's foolish talk," declared the Chief.

"Yes, but I wasn't going to say so. That fellow looked like one who takes offense easily. You're right, though, about them being newcomers. He told me they'd moved in from the southwest and didn't know much about this country. In fact, he asked a lot of questions and was grateful for the information I gave him. He told me they didn't want to trespass on our hunting grounds or those of the Biglakers, so I told him our landmarks."

"So they have moved in up north?" asked the Chief.

"That's right. He said it was getting crowded where they came from. To the north there are only Trolls, so they thought it would be a good place."

"And what are they proposing to do about the Trolls?"

"He said they are vermin and should be killed off. In fact, they had already cleaned up some Troll settlements."

"I don't like that," said the Chief decisively. "The Trolls are bound to make trouble if their territory is invaded. So far we've had no trouble. Let them alone is what I say."

The Chief shook his head gravely. But Tiger was thinking about something else. Abruptly he said, "There was something about the Shelk. He looked a little bit like a Troll himself."

The Chief laughed. "Don't be ridiculous, Tiger. The Trolls are short and white, and beardless. Shelk was tall and black like us, with a big beard."

"But there was something about his eyes," said

Tiger, and he cast back his mind, trying to remember what had suddenly made him think of Troll Cairn and that long-dead face which had looked up at him from the ground. The eyes . . . But the dead Troll had no eyes, only the empty sockets beneath a scowling brow. That was it! Shelk had a brow like that. Tiger shuddered a little at the memory of that imperious frown.

The remarkable stranger had not been Tiger's foremost interest at the Meet. He was a man now, and it was time to find a woman. He knew that his parents had been discussing it, and he had guessed whom they had in mind. The Big Lake Chief, Wolf, had a daughter named Hind. He had seen her once before, two summers ago, when he was in a gathering party with his mother and some other women and children from Trout Lake. They had met up with gatherers from Big Lake. Though Hind was shy and timid, their eyes had often met.

Now he was older. When they stopped in at the Big Lake settlement on their way to the Meet, there was music-making and dancing, and many girls had their eyes on him. But Tiger saw only Hind. She, too, was grown up, and strikingly beautiful, with large brown eyes and a slim, high-breasted figure. She was very provocative, dancing past Tiger, turning her back to him, smiling with mischievous eyes over her shoulder, and with a quick bend forward baring for a moment her trim brown buttocks. They had stolen away briefly and kissed, pressing their eager bodies to each other.

Yes, it would be Hind, Tiger thought, when he saw his father in grave discussion with Wolf. He watched them laugh and clasp each other's hands, and knew there would be a wedding later in the summer. He would go to Big Lake with his parents and Marten and little Godwit. There would be a great celebration, with flutes, tomtoms, dancing, eating, and drinking. Hind would be his woman, to take back to Trout Lake, where he would build a house for her.

At the thought of it, he had taken off into the woods to run a race by himself, to feel the air rushing by and the power of his own body. He swam in a small stream to cool off, then lay on the bank to dry, until the stings of the myrmicids drove him away.

Now the campfire was dying, and Tiger's thoughts were called back to the mammoth hunt by a dispute between two of the men. One had insisted that he, too, could be in two places at the same time. When he was asleep, he could go to places that might be days and days away from where he was.

"So that's what you do," said the neighbor. "That's just what I thought. You'll sleep through the mammoth hunt too, unless we do something about it—dreaming about mammoth tongue with cranberry sauce."

The man blushed—it was he who had talked about that particular delicacy—but persisted. "I believe there's a part of me that travels about when I sleep, though nobody else can see it."

The Chief realized that the conversation had been inconclusive and that his men were anxious. He chose his words carefully.

"One Shelk is quite enough," he said. "If he comes in two parts, I want neither. But he's far away now. As for you, I want you all in one place tomorrow; no wandering in dreamland. Tomorrow's the day to strike, Trolls or no Trolls. But they have done us no harm all these years, and if we leave them alone they are not likely to start now. To be safe, though, everyone keep on the lookout for Whites in the forest. And if you're going to sleep on sentinel duty"—he smiled at the dreamer—"be sure to wake someone else first."

The man grinned and went to tend the fire. "You won't catch me asleep, Chief," he said confidently. "And I hope you're right about tomorrow. The fare has not been too good these days."

The Chief also rose, and raised his arms high, uttering the ancient prayer to the game:

"O great Guardian of the mammoth! If it is your wish to deliver your cattle into our hands, give us the sign, keep the tryst. For what we must do, we ask your forgiveness, with all our heart.

"And now some sleep," he added, looking around.

All the men except the sentry, who walked the perimeters of the camp, were soon dozing. The moon was down and the forest very dark. The sentry took the little moon-stick carried by the party, and made a mark for the night. The stick would tell them the phases of the moon, by which they lived as much as by the changing seasons.

Among those sleeping soundly was Tiger, who would return to the trackers at dawn with plans for the assault. He was no longer afraid of Trolls. No, the only danger was losing the mammoths; and the Chief would take care of that.

Indeed, everything was working out according to plan. The mammoths were just where the Chief's craft and experience had told him they would be. His men had reached their stations in time, the trackers being summoned by Tiger at the last moment. The fires had blazed up simultaneously all along the line, and now the mammoths were swerving toward the bog. The spears had found their targets, and though none of the mammoths had been mortally wounded, they were all in a panic to escape. Already one or two animals were knee-deep in the bog, sinking helplessly. A couple of young clung to them, still able to move but afraid of leaving their mothers, and shrieking incessantly. Others retreated more slowly, squelching at the edge of the bog.

Only the big bull in the rear refused to budge. Hooting and blowing blasts of air through its trunk, stirring up a cloud of dust and dry leaves, it was working itself into a fury.

Some of the hunters were already in the bog, closing in for the slaughter. Everybody was intent on the prey, utterly unaware of the long line of men now emerging from the edge of the forest. Crouching, silent, they took up their positions and chose their targets.

Suddenly the bull seemed transformed into a gigantic incarnation of rage and destruction. Its black hair rose all over its body, making it look twice its size. Ears flapping out, tail swinging high, trunk above its head, tusks forward, it charged through the flames and towered in front of Tiger.

The boy flung himself to the side, seeking the shelter of a young pine tree. But nothing stopped the momentum of the mammoth; its seven tons of bone, muscle, and ivory snapped off the brittle pine like a reed, and it thundered into the forest, plowing a trail of broken bushes and small trees. Tiger was pinned beneath the fallen tree.

Sensing disaster, the Chief turned around and raced back. "Tiger, Tiger! Are you hurt?" His eyes were seeking the spot where the tree had fallen. At the edge of the forest, the men in line had already risen to launch their missiles. They were in full view, but the Chief never saw them.

Tiger tried to answer his father, and found that he had no voice. He could not move, but felt nothing, for the shock had numbed all sensation. He watched the long, agonized run of the Chief, the white tiger tooth on his breast dangling with each bound. Suddenly something like a stick was standing straight through the running body, which lost its life in mid-air. The body swung with the impact and its own speed, and vanished from his sight with a thud reverberating through the noise of the slaughter. The boy closed his eyes, and at last the physical pain overwhelmed him.

THE LAND

Now I see for a second time
Earth in fresh green rise from the sea;
The cataracts fall, the eagle flies.

Völuspá

     The land had only emerged in the last few thousand years. Obeying the commands of sun, wind, and water, the great ice that had once covered it had retreated to the fells of the far north. There it was collecting its strength to reconquer its empire. For now, every summer was warm enough to divest the ice of its power. It was holding its own, but it could not advance; and its strength was spent in great rivers coursing south, bountiful and awesome, cascading through narrow gaps, broadening into lakes and estuaries.

Relieved from the weight of the ice, the land was rising from the sea, and plants, animals, and men invaded it. It was now a land of forests, bogs, and lakes, richly stocked with game. To the north it was bordered first by a belt of dwarf birch and bogs, then by the tundra, and finally by the ice. To the southeast lay the sea, which had once been a gigantic freshwater lake and was now a brackish water body, linked to the oceans by narrow straits. Its contours shaped by the ice, the land gradually dipped into the sea, in a fleet of thousands of islands large and small, down to single ice-polished rocks

among the seaward skerries. And far away to the west
lay the real salt sea.

To the sparse groups of men entering this land, it was
a world of wealth and beauty beyond measure. The pine
forest, gay with the soft browns of its rough-scaled
trunks and the persisting green of its crowns, stretched
endlessly. It was a forest of infinite variety, from the
windswept, stunted firs of the outer islands and the
sharp dry woods of esker and granite hills to the mighty
pillars of the lowland grand forest, secure in their
massed strength. There were also the wetlands, where
the pine became scrawny and dwarfed once more,
fighting for its life amid willow, alder, and birch, and
the bogs, where the pine died. But the somber spruce
had not yet invaded the land, and perhaps would not do
so at all, in this age; its domain was half a world away to
the east.

In early summer, the pines blossomed into the light
green of their new shoots, as if dressing for a festival.
Mammoth and caribou had left the country much
earlier and the great bird migration was at its peak. But
it had started long before, perhaps when the silent
woods awoke with the chirping of innumerable chaf-
finches, whirring in myriad flocks close above the
treetops, which still carried a melting mantle of snow; or
with the august spectacle of hundreds of cranes in sleek
formations flying in from the south at a dizzying height.
Serenely they flew in search of the wetlands and lakes
where the excitement of courtship and nesting awaited
them. Then came the explosive awakening of spring:
now the hepaticas in timid stands amidst patches of
melting snow; soon the white carpet of wood anemones
covering the floor of the forest.

Bison, elk, and the tremendous shelk, its palmed
antlers up to a fathom in length, could be hunted when

the mammoth was gone; and the sturdy little horse, and the stag with its many-tined antlers too. But the sweetness and variety of the berries of forest and glade, beach and bog, made them the most coveted food. And to those versed in their lore, the mushrooms of late summer offered excellent fare.

In the autumn, bird-song died, and the skies were darkened by the southward flights. With the first snow, herds of mammoth and caribou reappeared. After the darkness, rain, and sleet of autumn came the silvery luminescence of winter nights and the crisp, clear cold of winter days. And so, following the rhythm of the seasons, the men who lived off the land measured their past in winters and their future in summers.

Into this land came a people raven-haired and dark of complexion, carrying the inheritance of a long line of ancestors from sun-scorched steppes far away. They called themselves Men; others called them Black. Their marks of dominance were a proud stature, jutting chins, high foreheads, manes of swept-back hair, long exquisite necks, a breadth of shoulder and a narrowness of hip. The flowing beard of the adult male was a wondrous sign of his rank. The women were smaller, and graceful in youth; in maturity they, too, developed the tokens of their station, in splendid volumes of breast and haunch, belly and buttock. The man's role was to hunt, fight, beget sons, and seek the mystery of communion with the powers of the unknown; the woman's, to bear and rear children, gather the harvest of forest and meadow, and obey the man who chose her to be the mother of his sons.

These men brought with them their new, full-toned speech, elastic and expressive beyond compare. They also brought their inventive technology, symbolized by the atlatl, or throwing-stick, which could catapult a javelin with superior speed and penetration. They brought their dreams and hopes and their passionate affinity with the beasts of game, which they sought to record with all their skill and love.

They strove to catch and render in undying images those transient animal shapes that burn into the retina and are seen again in exquisite detail and precision when the eyes are closed: animals in repose, in action; the sights before the hunter in that fleeting moment at the point of the kill, when endurance, skill, and cunning are to be rewarded. In that moment, javelin poised, muscles and sinews already exploding into the throw, the strength and beauty of the beast are forever impressed upon the hunter. By recording this image, he pays off his debt and receives absolution, for the taking of a life is a crime, which must be atoned for.

So the hunters flocked around the master draftsman, who swiftly conjured up the sought image with unerring lines. They traced the pattern laboriously, again and again, sharing in the mystery and atonement. Just as the atlatl and the spear were the tools of the hunter, so the charcoal stick, the engraving point, and the dye became those of the artist. The tribesmen sought fulfillment in animal portraiture as a complement to the hunt and took the names of four-footed or winged beasts, exulting in the splendor of their totems.

The mystery of fertility was equally significant. A man must be not only a hunter and an artist but a father of sons. Here the women participated in like degree. Man's pride in his phallus and his sperm was equaled by his pride in his fertile woman, who received his sperm and gave him sons in return. A man without sons was no man. So his art, too, encompassed that revered symbol, the Mother of Sons, and the tokens of fertility, the phallus and the cleft fruit.

A thousand years earlier, the men of the past had made this place their home. Twenty thousand generations in the snowbound lands of long winters and brief summers had bleached their skin and hair to a light fairness. The equality of men and women was reflected in similarity of stature and body build. The mark of dominance in the full-grown man or woman was a wonderful pair of eyes, shaded by the perpetually frowning superstructure of their jutting brows. In their myriad tales and stories, remembered from generation to generation, the boldness and power of their eyes were likened to those of the eagle. Birds were deities in their myths. They revered the birds' song with its glissando of vowels and tones, hopelessly beyond their own tongues. They themselves, humble earthlings, took the names of flowers and trees. But each flower and each tree had its own bird in the Land of Dead Men, and the belief that transformation awaited them when they died was central to their lives.

So awesome were the eyes of the Whites that it had become a token of deference for them to pass their hands over their faces, hiding for a moment the brilliance of the eyes and the somber menace of the brow. Partly in compensation for that trait, the White society had become ritualized through and through, with tact and politeness as the prime code of behavior. They called each other "Miss" and "Mister"; they used polite circumlocutions when giving orders, and were ready with profuse apologies at the slightest suggestion of wrongdoing. So their great strength was balanced by their habits of deference and politeness.

Among the Whites, women chose their mates and descent was reckoned along the maternal line. They gloried in their ancestors, whose exploits and adventures they were ready to tell and retell. Story and myth were their art. Women and men found affinity not only with the living members of their clan but with those of earlier generations who walked unseen by their side, throughout their lives. To these women and men of the past, they could turn for advice, encouragement, and precedent.

The Whites were the oldest settlers of the land. Millenniums ago the entire continent to the south had been in their hands. Now only a small remnant of their race lived here, on the northern outskirts. The Blacks had settled the great interior, where the forest abounded in game and the lakes and streams in fish. They had spread along the coast of the Salt Sea in the west, where they found the inexhaustible riches of the ocean. The Whites still lived in the frontier lands of the north and along the brackish-water seaboard.

The Blacks had known of the Whites for a long time, and called them Trolls. Concerned with their own lives and passions, they took little heed of the older race. In broad daylight the Trolls seemed to be inferior beings, comical sometimes, or faintly sinister, making odd gestures with their hands about their faces and jabbering in a weird tongue utterly unlike human speech. Yet at night, the sight of these stumpy figures with their large pale faces and hooded eyes seemed to touch something buried deep in the Black man's being, as if recalling an age-old experience of unreasoning terror. Somehow the Trolls were like the ghosts that might haunt a man in a nightmare. They seemed to bear a menace of secret witchcraft, of deep cunning, perhaps even wisdom, of a kind denied to Men. They evoked unspeakable mysteries older than time.

To the Whites, the Blacks were godlike, tall and eloquent, with a speech as varied and flexible as that of the birds. And there was something else. No White could look at the clear brow of a Black without feeling a mysterious tenderness, such as a child might evoke in the heart of his parents.

While there was much to differentiate them, there was more that the two races had in common. They lived off the same land. They lived by the same laws, which governed rigidly the patterns of their thoughts and emotions, their actions, and their reverence for the numinous things in their world. Everything was alive to them, not only trees and bushes, birds and four-footed beasts, but the flying clouds, the moving streams, the caressing or whipping winds, the lakes and the seas in their placidity or foaming anger. Forever mutable, these must have life and sentience. Even stones and rocks possessed a mysterious life, which sometimes seemed to gather and become transfigured into strange formations where their spirits took shape—an august profile, a pair of shadowed eyes, a hand, a paw, a sexual organ, a resting body, the whorled gut of a ripped-up animal. The stillness and permanence of these forms, the assurance that they would always be there, enduring beyond the transmutations of things that grow and fade, invested them with a sublimity of their own. Men and women found security in them. An ageing man could return to the sanctuary of his youth and say: Here I am, changed, old, marked by my years; there you stand, indestructible, eternal; it is good to be near you again.

Man had to live in concert with all things. Every animal, bird, and plant had its own Guardian, big or small, against whose will there could be no appeal. Guardians spoke to men in the whisper of the rain, the voice of the thunderclap, the rush of the rapids, the nightly call of the owl. The eyes of the Guardians watched men with intense concentration in a glittering star, with sudden wrath in a flash of lightning, with veiled, inscrutable watchfulness out of the depths of a hollow on the face of a cliff.

But the rule of the Guardians was essentially benevolent, and the animate world was good. It gave men the things they needed; and in return, they offered ritual and prayer to complete their compact with the powers. Nor did the Guardians lack humor. They would stand for chaffing and impertinence with a glint in their eyes. But the sins of gluttony and extravagance they did not excuse. If a man took more than he needed, robbed others of the necessities of life, or killed indiscriminately, he broke his compact with the powers, and no ingenuity could help him escape their retaliation.

So the Whites and the Blacks, the men of the past and the men of the future, lived in a compact with the same powers, though they often interpreted the mysteries, of which the world was so full, in different ways. One might see the Star-Hunters' bridge of ice and snow in the wintry night sky; the other might see the pathway of the birds of the soul, soaring toward eternity. One might hear the voice of the mammoth's Guardian in the thunderstorm; the other might hear the boom of the Great Swan's flapping wings. Yet that is the world of appearances; the central compact is the same.

MISS SUNDEW'S CLOUD-BERRIES

Lotte ist todt, Lotte ist todt, Julie nah' am Sterben—
Schwere Noth, schwere Noth, da ist nichts zu erben!

Viennese street song (eighteenth century)

"Mother!" called the girl. "Here is another God. And he is alive."

The girl's full name was Miss Woad daughter of Angelica Parnassia-granddaughter Torchflower–great-granddaughter, and so on, but she was called Miss Woad for short. Tiger, using his own language, would soon call her Veyde; and that name, which she could hardly pronounce, was later adopted by others. She knew the life stories of her mother, grandmother, great-grandmother, and so on, through ten or more generations; she also knew those of her father, maternal grandfather, and maternal great-grandfather; she did not know her own age, which was about seventeen. One year ago she had had a child, a girl, who died a few weeks old. Since then she had been barren, and last winter her man had been lost on the ice.

Her blond head was barely visible above a tall clump of scorched juniper. One night had passed since the slaughter at the bog, and the reek of smoke hung in the air, blending with the intense fragrance of the bog and the stench of death. The fires had burned themselves out in the stillness without touching the woods. The remains of slaughtered mammoths and men seemed to be everywhere.

Miss Woad's people called the bog "Miss Sundew's Cloudberries," after a female ancestor (Woad could have recited her life story if asked to), and they had harvested it every summer for untold generations. The place, which the day before had been aglitter with the luminous wings of myriad dragonflies, was darkened now, not by soot but by ravens. They feasted in hordes, and some were so full they could hardly fly. Two golden eagles were intent on a mammoth cadaver which had been neatly skinned and fleshed on one side, then flipped over to expose the other, but left with most of the meat. Several other eagles circled above, majestic in flight, their straight broad wings dark against the blue sky. Winged scavengers arrived from ever farther away, and now there were even gulls all the way from the coast in the southeast.

Woad's party had been drawn to the place by the noise of the hyenas, who were unable to keep a secret. Their hysterical laughter, ranging in pitch from the self-confident boom of the leaders to the shrill falsetto of the underdogs, could be heard in the far distance. They had retreated to the pines now, and were slinking about, betraying their anxiety with occasional twitterings.

As usual, Woad's call led to the appearance of her mother, Miss Angelica daughter of Parnassia, and several others: old Mister Silverbirch son of Tansy, Miss Silverweed daughter of Buttercup, Mister Marestail son of Tormentil, and young Mister Baywillow son of Angelica. They hovered in the background while Miss Angelica bustled in, composed and authoritative.

Some thought her firmness bordered on acerbity and mumbled that she ought to be called Miss Cowbane, af-

ter the poisonous herb akin to the benevolent angelica.
To her people, her authority was vested in every feature
of her face and body: in her large, vivid blue eyes, over-
shadowed by proud eagle brows—the "brows of command"; in her full, round face; in her broad chest with
its firm, big-nippled breasts; in her flame of pubic hair,
disclosing good-sized labia; and in her strong arms with
broad yet sensitive hands. She carried a big sealskin bag
across her shoulder, and wore a seashell bracelet. Like
her people, she was naked. To them her beauty had not
faded, and her current husband, Mister Marestail, loved
her dearly. He was a few years younger than she.

Saddened by the scene of havoc, she looked down at
the boy, who was lying unconscious, pinned by a fallen
pine tree.

"Are you sure this is not one of the Devils, Miss
Woad?" she asked.

"Of course I am, Mother. Just look at him!"

Clearly the boy was young, still beardless. He was tall
and dark like the Gods, but so were the Devils. His
young face, now helpless and covered with grime, struck
them with a sudden wistful feeling of unattainable
beauty. His eyes, with long lashes, were closed. They
knew that if he opened them, they would be dark like
the moonless night.

"I think you are right, Miss Woad," said Miss
Angelica. "If he were one of the Devils, they would
have carried him away."

"I wonder why they left him alive?"

"They probably thought him dead—or thought he
would die anyway. And so he will, if we leave him
here."

The girl and her mother exchanged glances. Then
Miss Angelica smiled. "We will try.

"There is no question that this is the work of the Devils," she said, indicating the scene of the tragedy. "We first heard of them earlier this summer, when they killed some Whites in the north and took many others prisoner. But this slaughter is worse than any I have heard of. Those murderers are enemies of the Gods, just as they are our enemies, so we must save this boy and bury his people with honor. We must also take care of the meat they have left. But first we have to know if the Devils have gone away for good; we cannot risk their returning. Mister Baywillow, would you have the kindness to check their trail?"

The young man passed his hand deferentially over his face. He did not look like the others: he was a full head taller, with chestnut hair and brown eyes. His skin, too, was darker, and became rich with the sun. His shy bearing contrasted with the eaglelike ridge of his brow, which suggested latent strength. Now he set off at an easy run, vanishing soundlessly into the forest. To his trained eye, there was no difficulty in following the tracks of the Devils. Miss Angelica watched him fondly, then turned to old Mister Silverbirch. Her manner underwent a distinct change, and she passed her hand over her face.

"Would you be gracious, Mister Silverbirch, and look at the young God? Can you tell us how badly he is hurt?"

The old man was already beside the boy. "We must get the tree off him, Miss Angelica," he said.

"Please, Miss Woad, would you ask some of the men here to assist?"

"With pleasure, Mother."

Gently they lifted the tree and flung it aside, muttering, "Excuse me, Miss Woad," "Please, Mister

Silverbirch,'' and other civilities. The tree had fallen on
the boy's legs, which were badly bruised and bleeding;
the left leg had an ugly twist.

"He is alive, Miss Angelica," said the old man. "His
leg must be straightened out. I should like to have some
plantain for the wounds, but we have to go back to the
coast for that. I will need a strong stick and some straps.
Then we must make a litter."

"We will do this first," said Miss Angelica. "We
must care for the living before the dead. Mister
Marestail, I wonder if you and Mister Alder would be
kind enough to see to the litter. Miss Rosebay and Miss
Silverweed can take a party to start working on the
meat. Miss Woad and I will see to the dead."

Much to the annoyance of the ravens, who took wing
in a noisy black cloud, the meat-collectors went to work
on the fallen mammoths, most of which had been very
sketchily dressed. The real delicacies—tongue, brain,
and liver—were gone, but much of the red meat was
left, and would keep perfectly well if smoked without
delay. "They must have departed in a hurry, Miss
Silverweed," said Miss Rosebay. Miss Silverweed,
wielding a big hand-axe and splattered with blood from
head to foot, agreed.

Meanwhile, Miss Angelica and Miss Woad looked for
the corpses of the Gods. They started at the far end of
the bog to head off the hyenas, who promptly vanished
into the forest. Some of the dead had already been attacked, and one or two mostly eaten. A number of them
still carried ornaments, mostly necklaces made of teeth,
which did not look particularly valuable. "The Devils
probably carried off the best pieces," said Miss
Angelica. The two women carried the corpses to the
edge of the bog, where they meant to bury them.

Though they did not know the dead men, it was sad work for both women.

Untouched by scavengers, the last corpse lay on its face, quite close to the wounded boy. Its wounds showed that it had been killed instantly by a light javelin.

"That is one of the Devils' weapons," said Miss Angelica. "They fly faster and farther than ours, with a magic which makes the arm longer and stronger." Turning the body over, she gazed with wonder at the great tiger tooth that had been concealed beneath it.

"Look, Mother! I never saw such a thing before," cried Miss Woad.

Miss Angelica's lips moved though she made no sound. She stared at the dead God, looking from his face to the tooth and back again. "Mother?" repeated Miss Woad, and finally Miss Angelica became aware of her again.

"It is a tiger tooth," she said. "There have been no tigers here for a long time. I saw a pair a very long time ago, when I was younger than you are now, Miss Woad. And once, also long ago, I saw a tooth like this." Again, she searched the face of the dead God.

"We will take the tooth," she said, "and give it to the young God." Very gently she lifted the head of the dead God and took off the tooth, which hung on a simple necklace of twined mammoth hair. "Now, please, go and see how old Mister Silverbirch is getting on, and bring the men to help with the grave. I will keep watch." The girl strode off obediently, with a glance over her shoulder at Miss Angelica, who knelt by the bodies. But she could not see her mother's face.

Mister Baywillow returned, saying that the Devil party had left for good. The dead Gods were then buried, each with a generous piece of smoked meat to sustain him on his journey to the Land of Dead Gods. For surely there must be such a place, just as there was a land for Dead Men. Big boulders were rolled down from the esker overlooking the bog and placed upon the graves to keep their contents safe. Finally, yellow loosestrife, red campion, and other flowers in season were scattered over the graves, and the dead were honored in an epic song by Mister Silverbirch, who made up a remarkable catalogue of their feats. His tales astonished all who listened, and would have astonished the principal characters even more.

Woad's people had cut the mammoth meat into strips, treated it with fragrant juniper smoke, and piled it on runners. It was late in the afternoon before the party set out, heading due southeast and pulling their runners easily through the low bilberry bushes that covered the floor of the forest. Two of the men carried the litter with the young God's unconscious body.

Tiger awoke and felt he was leaving one nightmare to enter another. He shivered with cold and a dull pain ran through his body, gradually collecting itself in his left shin. He tried to fight it, but the pain barricaded itself like a patient enemy, preparing to strike again. Tiger realized that he was being carried, and looked up to see stars in the gathering dusk, visible in the openings between the pine crowns.

Why was he being carried? Something had happened: that he knew with a terrifying certainty, but he could not remember what it was. He must be hurt. Were they carrying him home? Tiger looked for his friends, but could not see them clearly in the dark. There were shapes around him, but they seemed odd, uncouth, hardly human.

The odd sensations waned, and Tiger fell unconscious once more. Time passed. The shooting pain came back. He groaned and looked up.

He was staring into a big, hideous face, which grinned down at him like a madman. A Troll, thought Tiger, too weak to be surprised.

It was dark, but there was a fire near by. He felt its warmth on one side. On the other, the cold of the night assailed him. The swaying had stopped. He felt his body covered by something furry—a bearskin.

Again he stared into the large pale face, still showing its teeth in a fearsome grin. He's going to kill me, thought Tiger. And with that idea, memory returned, with a violence which drove out his physical suffering. The image of his father, transfixed by an atlatl spear, stood before him. That picture would be with Tiger for the rest of his life.

They killed him, he thought. Now they are going to kill me. And the idea came almost as a consolation. Yet there was still fight in him. Closing his eyes, he raised his voice in an incantation:

"O Black Tiger, Mammoth-Killer, stand by! I need your help!" He was surprised at his own rasping, unsteady voice.

Nothing happened. The Troll chuckled, and Tiger opened his eyes again, to find the strange figure bending over him still. It was a Troll ox with a broad nose, an enormous mouth, and light grey eyes under heavy browridges. There were deep wrinkles around the eyes, and the head was completely bald. The Troll passed its hand over its face, and the gesture was oddly reassuring to Tiger.

Then the Troll turned and uttered something in a surprisingly high-pitched voice. In a moment several more of the big pale faces were looking down at Tiger. The

Trolls were all talking, gesturing, passing their hands over their faces. The bald Troll raised his hands and started talking slowly.

Tiger stared at him without understanding, and the Troll passed his hand over his face many times before trying again. Suddenly Tiger realized that he was hearing something like his own language, only so distorted that he could hardly recognize the words.

"Ah spahk Man talk," the Troll was repeating. "Ah spahk Man talk."

"You . . ." mumbled Tiger, "you speak my language!" With the image still torturing him, he had a ready accusation. And yet, something made him turn it into a question: "Did you kill my father?"

He had to repeat it twice before the Troll understood. Finally, he shook his head vigorously.

"Na kall, na kall," he said. "Troll na kall. Black man kall."

Tiger tried to understand. "I don't believe you," he said in a whisper. He looked around. "I saw the javelin hit him . . ." Then his eye was caught by the Troll spears stacked close to the fire, and he remembered an echo of the Chief's voice—yesterday? a week ago?—"Big spears with crude points . . ." He saw Marten with the spear-shaft coming apart in his hands; himself, making a new shaft.

With a sudden exertion, Tiger rose up on his elbow, ignoring the spasm of pain that immediately shot through his body. He looked around the camp, barely visible in the flickering light of the fire, and a curious gleam came into his eyes. Yes, there was the fire, the stacked spears, the packs of meat, and other supplies on the runners. The Chief had been right. His own recollection was right. The Trolls had no atlatl javelins.

Tiger tried hard to remember the day of the hunt. He

felt that he had forgotten something important. Suddenly, he was reminded. Among the Troll oxen and bitches, all short and sturdy, with large pale faces and almost white hair, he now saw someone different—one dark face among the Whites. As if drawn by Tiger's gaze, the face moved closer.

"Shelk," said Tiger.

The tall dark Troll responded at once. "Shelk?" he repeated.

And at that single word the other Trolls looked at him with awe. Already, Tiger perceived his mistake.

"No, you're not Shelk," he said. "You're much younger. But there is something . . ."

"Shelk?" said the young man again, as if trying out the sound of the word on his tongue.

Weary, Tiger returned to his own problem. Shelk! He remembered the stranger's arrogant face and bearing, his rich amber ornaments, his retinue of hardened hunters, and his eagle brows, shadowing dark and penetrating eyes. Yes, the shape of the face and the brows were the same, but in the eyes of this young Troll there was only innocence and wonder.

Tiger's people had known violence, but in a restrained form. They dealt death swiftly and competently to the animals of the hunt, and in this act they felt that they fulfilled the demands of the mystical bond between man and beast. No hunt was consummated without a ritual of participation and love, without celebrating the quarry as a chosen animal and honoring its life, which sustained the men whose tryst it had kept. Building their houses from mammoth bones, men talked proudly of the splendor and might of that animal, thus ensuring long life and prosperity to the structure.

Clashes with their fellow men occurred too, but they were always conducted in a way that combined a minimum of bloodshed with a maximum of excitement. Each warring group chose one man, and the outcome of a single combat decided the issue. In early summer, soon after Tiger's initiation, the right of his people to the hunting grounds west of Trout Lake had been challenged. The question had been settled by a man-to-man fight, without arms. The Trout Lake Chief emerged victorious against the champion of the other party, and that settled it. No one was seriously hurt, and reconciliation followed at the Summer Meet.

The image hovering before Tiger's eyes was utterly different, beyond the experience of his people, just as it was beyond the experience of the Troll tribe. One thing could never be justified: that was the deliberate shooting of an atlatl spear into the body of a fellow man. Yet the image of his father's death rose to his mind's eye again and again.

The atlatl was a sacred hunting weapon, used sparingly, and with the greatest compassion for the suffering of the animal pursured. Who had heard of manhunts except perhaps in stories of the distant past and far-off lands?

With swift certainty, Tiger decided that this was Shelk's doing. That proud stranger and his followers were new to these parts. Who could tell from what land of terror they had come?

Tiger sank back, oblivious to the rising excitement in the camp.

"I knew it!" said Miss Angelica. "You can speak the birdtalk, Mister Baywillow! My son, you are a child of the Gods!"

"What is Shelk?" asked Baywillow. "Do you think he meant me?"

"Shalk," repeated Silverbirch, unable to pronounce the correct vowel. "It is the name of an animal in birdtalk, but I do not understand why he should call you that.''

"Please do ask him, Mister Silverbirch," begged Miss Woad. "He understands you."

"Yes," said Silverbirch, with pride. "He understands me, though I do not speak the real bird-talk." He turned to Tiger, who lay with half-closed eyes. "Shalk?" he asked, pointing to Baywillow.

Tiger shook his head. "No, he isn't Shelk. I thought he was, but Shelk is older.''

"A Black man?" asked Silverbirch.

"Yes, a bad Black man. He killed my father.''

Silverbirch nodded. He understood.

"Yar nahm?" he asked.

Tiger smiled at the old Troll's strange rendering of his language, and told him his name. Suddenly it was repeated almost perfectly by the dark young Troll: "Tiger!''

The two young men's glances met, and something passed between them.

"He is not Shelk," repeated Tiger. "Shelk is the man who killed my father.''

Again Silverbirch nodded, then turned away to search for something among the supplies stacked on the runners. When he returned, he closed Tiger's hand around the great tooth of the black tiger.

"Fatha?" he asked.

Tears came to Tiger's eyes, and the Trolls gathered closer to comfort him, stroking his cheeks, his forehead, his body, with their strong hands, until Tiger fell into exhausted sleep. That was the last he remembered for a long time. He was unconscious that night, all through the remainder of the journey, and for days afterward.

VEYDE'S ISLAND

So enamored is the traveling wind of the tree that stands
with its root in the earth and grows.

Johannes V. Jensen, Myter

Where the land dipped into the sea, the eskers
and ice-worn knolls, all striking to the southeast, jutted
out as points and islands—a once-drowned landscape
now emerging from the deep. The inner skerries, sheltered from the onslaught of the sea, were densely
wooded, much like the mainland. Farther out the
trees were wind-beaten and stunted. And beyond these
islands were hundreds of islets fringing great water
bodies where rocks now awash were slowly emerging.

Miss Angelica's party walked a well-beaten path to
the far shore of one of these points of land, from which
they rafted themselves to the nearest island, their
home. They had chosen the island because it had a good
spring; fresh water was often hard to get on the islands.
The nearest point of the island was not far from the
mainland promontory, as if the long ridge of hills had
made a small dive into the water, then emerged again in
another headland. Though short, the crossing could be
dangerous enough in a strong southwestern wind. In
that direction lay an open bay, on which heavy seas built

up easily. Then the waves would crash through the narrow channel, towering and breaking as they met the drag of the shoaling bottom. But on this day the weather held, and the water glimmered in drowsy stillness, broken only by long lines of ripples where indolent cat's-paws ruffled the surface. Great flocks of scoters with their young dotted the bay, and white-fowl still patrolled the sky, though it would soon be time for their departure.

The Troll's island, irregularly shaped and at most a couple of miles long, was wonderfully varied. Forests covered much of the land, but they were interrupted by rocky hills sheltering wetlands which supported patches of crowberry, labrador tea, and cotton grass. Coves dissected the coastline, in some places almost cutting the island in two. Water shallow enough to be waded separated it from neighboring islands, so that one could easily tread for miles from one island to the next, never having to swim. To the south, the island drew out into a long, narrow moraine. West of this, commanding a view of the sea, was the bluff where Miss Angelica's people had pitched their tents.

Much later, Tiger himself would navigate the raft, made of pine logs of varying length, tied together with leather thongs and supported by crossbars. Of that first voyage he had no memory. His first hazy impression was of waking up inside a small conical tent, made from skins stretched over poles that leaned together, leaving a smoke-hole on top. A small seal-fat lamp burned in the middle of the tent, and the open door-flap admitted the murky light of an overcast late-summer day. A Troll girl sat beside him, her pale features and white-blond hair shimmering in the dusk. When she saw that he was awake, she smiled, scooped up something in her hand,

and held it before him. Berries—bilberries and cloudberries. He managed to swallow the handful, then dropped back into a doze.

For days, he was alternately chilled and feverish,
faintly aware of the Troll girl waiting upon him and
feeding him, first only berries, then pieces of fish and
meat. When he shivered with cold, she lay down beside
him, sharing her own warmth; when he was hot and
thirsty, she offered him water out of a skin.

When he tried to ask her name, she did not understand, but went at once to fetch the old Troll who
spoke such a peculiar version of Tiger's own language.
Silverbirch did not know how to render the girl's name,
but she suddenly pointed to the roof, where he saw a
dried woad plant, its trusses of seed-pods hanging like
pendants. Tiger understood, and spoke her name in his
own language: "Veyde!"

That plant was man's friend. Soaked in water, it gave
off the deep blue of a summer's lake. In many pictures
had Tiger contrasted the ochre-red of life with the
blueness of the woad. When you scattered the seeds over
fertile ground, new plants would sprout. If the Trolls
had the woad, perhaps they were human.

For a long time Tiger was too ill and weak to move,
but he became used to seeing Veyde at his side, and took
comfort in her presence. Gradually he began to recognize the other Trolls. There was the old interpreter,
whose name, he learned, was Silverbirch. There were
curious, blue-eyed children who could only peep in
through the flap-door and grin at him because Veyde
would not allow them in. And there was the tall, dark
young Troll called Baywillow.

Tiger soon came to be especially glad of Baywillow's
visits. Only a few years older than Tiger, he listened intently as Tiger spoke to him in the Black tongue and

skillfully imitated his words, which none of the other Trolls could do. Veyde learned to pronounce Tiger's name and her own after a fashion, but Baywillow took to the new language as if it were a dormant skill, needing only the catalyst of Tiger's presence to return it to memory. Smiling his shy smile and often passing his palm over his face, the young man sat on the floor at Tiger's side, cross-legged and hunched as if to hide his height. He repeated Tiger's words carefully, making sure he got them right and understood their meaning. Sometimes he stood up and raised his arms, as if giving thanks.

But there were times when Baywillow was away, sometimes for several days. To ease the tedium, Tiger tried to understand and repeat the words of Veyde and Silverbirch, but the language was difficult, full of queer and uncouth sounds that were hard on Tiger's tongue. He soon found that it was not a language you could whisper in. The pitch of the voice was an integral part of the language, and the varied modulation compensated for the monotony of the vowels—just ah and oh. Indeed, the Whites seemed to have a perfect ear for music, and were able to discern very subtle variations in pitch. The language was necessarily spoken with great deliberation, quite unlike the sophisticated patter of the Blacks. It seemed full of the mammoth's bones. Tiger came to learn it well, but the road was full of pitfalls, and he seemed to stumble into all of them, much to Veyde's amusement. Old Silverbirch, shocked by her rudeness, admonished her with a stern brow, gesturing to Tiger to apologize for the insult. Tiger loved these exchanges, which made him laugh and forget the pain in his leg.

Occasionally the other Troll oxen and bitches (Tiger still thought of them more as animals than as humans) would look in. At first he found it hard to tell them apart. The only exception was the authoritative Miss Angelica, who always looked long and hard at Tiger, then held a low-toned consultation with Veyde, and left as abruptly as she came in. One day, feeling more sure of himself, Tiger forestalled her.

"See you tomorrow, Miss Angelica," he ventured, carefully patterning his words after Veyde's. Miss Angelica smiled.

"It will be a pleasure, Mister Tiger," she answered graciously.

Then came the day when Tiger first crawled to the entrance and looked out. The sight overwhelmed him. The tent was pitched high on a bluff overlooking the sea to the south. (In winter, they would move to houses in the shelter of the woods.) Never before had Tiger seen the sea, and its immensity came as a revelation to him. The perfect straightness of its far edge was a mystery beyond all others. For the first time in his life, Tiger saw a straight line. He had climbed hills as a boy and looked out over the endless panorama of forest, but always there was the undulating line of hill and vale, the tussocky contours of distant trees. Here was the sea, barely ruffled by a gentle breeze that built a lane of glittering sunshine to the end of the world. Here he looked into eternity.

Later he came to know the sea in its varied moods and seasons, but he never forgot the exhilaration of this first view. There were rocks and islands in the sea; there were distant flocks of ducks and mergansers, and white-winged seagulls. Early autumn had already turned the occasional rowan trees a rusty red, but the alders still formed a belt of light green against the background of dark pine woods on the larger islands hemming in his view to the right. Here and there a birch gleamed yellow. Tiger lay motionless in the opening of his little tent, remembering the story of his father's first view of the sea. So this was it!

When his legs healed, Tiger would even walk on the sea, a frozen waste. He would trek for days from island to island, or just walk straight out into the whiteness, with nothing but sky and ice for company. Then he would look back to his landmarks, watching them shift with the increasing distance until at last, afraid of getting lost, he turned homeward again.

During the spring thaw the sea was treacherous. The ice broke into great sheets that churned against each other and built strange jagged structures that froze again overnight. Then black cracks widened between the floes and the spring storms broke up the remaining ice, grinding it into round patches that formed an intricate pattern on the endless surface. And finally the blue summer sea returned, warm enough for swimming and for navigating the raft and the little coracle that Silverbirch had built.

That coracle, made from sealskin stretched over a frame of pliant branches, became Tiger's favorite plaything. It was very small, and folded flat; distended, it was not even big enough for two grown people. It was almost as wide as it was long, and Tiger's first attempts to navigate it began with him and the coracle spinning round and round. But he learned to propel it in one direction, using a leafy bough for a paddle. When the wind was in his favor, he would stick the bough in the prow of his skiff and drift along, shouting excitedly to the onlookers.

Running along the shore, the children begged to be taken aboard, and Tiger carefully hoisted the smallest girl into the skiff, paddling around with hardly any freeboard. These excursions usually ended with a swamped coracle, and Tiger returning to shore with a very wet but delighted child.

The coracle gave Tiger one unforgettable memory. It was early in the spring, and the ice had melted enough for him to paddle around. Looking to the northeast, he saw a mirage such as he would never see again. It was as if the surface of the earth had buckled up into a towering, distant mountain, on which were dark outlines of faraway islands against the white of the surrounding ice. It was like a bird's-eye view, and the map was inscribed into his visual memory for the rest of his life.

Tiger continued to gaze at the image, but it became hazy and finally vanished. He tried to explain it to Veyde and Baywillow, but they had never seen such a thing. They told him about the ordinary mirages, which lift rocks and islands over the horizon. Soon they would be familiar to Tiger too.

Tiger became an established member of the little clan on Veyde's Island. He spoke the White language tolerably well (he had long since ceased to think of them as Trolls), and his friend Baywillow spoke his own language far better now than old Silverbirch. Tiger walked with a limp, for his leg had not set quite straight, but he ran as fast as before. He had regained his old skill with the throwing-stick, and Silverbirch had taught him the sling. This came naturally to him, and he bagged many a hare and bird. He had taken part in many sealing expeditions, had taught his new friends what he knew about fishing, and was now one of the best providers on the island. He was also going to be a father.

It was when he learned this that he ceased to look upon Veyde's people as Trolls and saw them instead as human beings. He was well on his way to recovery the

day Veyde straddled him for the first time, seeking that
fulfillment for which she had yearned since the moment
she saw him pinned by the tree at Miss Sundew's Cloudberries. Using artful fellatio to rouse him, she rode him,
body erect, head back, her eyes fixed on the soot-black
roof of the winter house, as if she could see right
through it into that sky of birds where she would
ultimately go.

Tiger needed coaxing, for Veyde was so utterly unlike
anything he had experienced that he had found it hard
to think of her as a woman. He closed his eyes until the
pleasure grew unbearable. Then he opened them, taking
in forever the sight of this woman who was straddling
him, her fair hair, her great smiling mouth, the swollen
tits over her barrel chest.

Then the sensation was gone, and new emotions
swooped down on him like a flock of ravens. Veyde
took him in her arms, and his went around her too in an
automatic response. But the only thing in his mind was a
terrifying question: What animal is this I am holding in
my arms? And for a second he felt that he had made
love to a bison cow or a wolf bitch. This image struck so
deep that Tiger lay still, in a struggle with this feeling,
while Veyde, oblivious, fondled him with immeasurable
gratitude and uttered endearments in her outlandish
tongue.

Tiger never told anyone of his terror and soon forgot
it himself. The two of them had moved into Veyde's
winter house, clustered with the others in the shelter of
the woods. The houses were built on a small eminence,
with good drainage so that they stayed dry. They were
dug down into the earth, and the walls were made of
rocks, lined with earth and moss. The wood-beamed
roof was covered with pine and juniper branches and
animal skins. The entrance was a short underground

tunnel. But when they moved into their summer tents in the spring, a few blocks of stone were removed from the wall and a thorough spring cleaning was done.

When he had mastered the White language, Tiger got to know the other members of Miss Angelica's tribe. The new couple's closest friends were Baywillow and Silverweed, who lived in the house next to theirs. Miss Silverweed was a genial but singularly absent-minded young woman who often lost herself in meditation, becoming oblivious to the events around her. Despite her fits of abstraction, she was an excellent hunter. But she was not much good at housework, and Tiger was amazed to see Baywillow busy with such chores as tanning hides and sewing clothes. At Trout Lake, and among the Blacks generally, this was women's work. Nonetheless, Tiger was an adaptable and impressionable youth, and he grew accustomed to seeing the women join the men on fishing and hunting expeditions. He even tried his hand at domestic work, and came to enjoy the sessions of hide-scraping, when stories were exchanged all around.

Storytelling was the favorite pastime of Miss Angelica's people, and some of the stories were terribly lurid and frightening. But Tiger soon noticed that these tales, which sent the audience into tittering hysterics, seemed always to be about distant relations or other clans. They were usually followed by a more decorous narrative about the tribe's own ancestors, as if the clan needed to return to safety after a brief trip into a wonderland of terror.

Tiger found the tanning business far less pleasant, because the Whites used rancid urine instead of wood-ashes and water to cure the leather. As a tailor, he was no success at all. The clothes he wore—sealskin boots and breeches, a blouse made from caribou skin, and a

lynx-fur beret—were the handiwork of Baywillow and
Veyde.

Old Mister Silverbirch was the local sage and doctor,
and lived with Miss Angelica and Mister Marestail. He
could have moved in with one of the women, for there
were more women than men on the island, but he did
not wish to. He still mourned his own woman, who had
been lost almost ten years ago. Silverbirch's polite and
circumstantial manner set the tone for the community,
but he never succeeded in quieting Veyde's gaiety and
her unorthodox behavior. Once she told Tiger, "Do you
know, I was almost killed by a falling tree one day
because Mister Silverbirch was too polite to shout at
me! He just said courteously, 'Would you be so kind as
to step out of the way, Miss Veyde, because Mister
Marestail is felling a tree and it is about to fall on top of
you.' I said 'What?' and he started saying the whole
thing all over again, when Miss Rosebay rushed up and
pushed me to the side. Whoosh, bang! and there was the
tree. Mister Silverbirch clicked his tongue at us and said
something about 'young people nowadays.' "

Poor Mister Silverbirch had been having great trouble
with his teeth of late. He had pulled out the worst one,
but he could not eat tough food unless he was mouth-
fed, so he preferred fish, which he could chew himself.

He doctored everyone else in the tribe too. When
Tiger's condition improved and he was able to walk
again, Mister Silverbirch often looked at him with a
proprietary air: here was living evidence of his skill as a
healer.

Unlike the other Whites of Veyde's Island, Mister
Silverbirch was a well-traveled man, born and raised on
the shores of the Salt Sea in the far west. He was orphaned when he was very young and was taken care of
by a Black girl. So he grew up among Blacks, learning

many of the crafts and a little of their language. As he
conceded sadly, his tongue was too stiff for the bird-
talk, and he never learned it properly.

"The Black people lived in a big camp not far from
the coast. They had come up from the south that
spring," he said. "When the girl brought me to the
camp, there was much excitement. All the people came
to look at me and touch me. I had never seen a Black
before, and was all in a whirl. Some of them looked
angry, others laughed. But the girl spoke for me, and I
was allowed to stay.

"I played with the Black children. Some of them were
friendly, but many of the boys took a dislike to me and
hurt me whenever they could. They called me a Troll
imp, taunting me for not speaking their language
properly. The girl who saved me—her name was
Squirrel—often had to save me again, from those boys.
I was lucky to be a good shot with the sling. I taught the
Black children to use it, and for that they respected me.
They tried to teach me the use of the throwing-stick, but
I never was much good at it.

"Among the Blacks, everybody has the name of an
animal or a bird, like you, Mister Tiger. They used to
draw a picture of their animal in the sand—"

"Yes," said Tiger, "I can do that."

"Please do, Tiger," said Baywillow. They were sitting near a cove where there was a small patch of sand.
Tiger found a stick and began to draw. First he drew the
long, undulating line of the head and back. Quickly he
sketched in the face, the ears, and the great scimitar
teeth. He made the eyes brood under heavy brows.
Finally he drew the long front legs, the shorter hind legs,
and the stubby tail. "My father taught me that," he
said. "I have never seen the black tiger myself."

"There is magic in your hand, Mister Tiger," said

Silverbirch. "I have seen the black tiger. That is how it looks. And that is how the boys drew their names— every one a different creature. The best of all was Stag. He drew it very big, with great antlers growing like bushes from its head. I could not draw anything but just this—"

And Silverbirch, with Tiger's stick, laboriously produced a small crescent. "The boys used to laugh at me for that. Stag laughed hardest and said that it was a grub. So they called me Grub. I tried to tell them my real name and showed them the birch, but this made them laugh again. Nobody could be named for a tree, they said. When my feet turned to roots and my fingers to leaves, they promised to call me Silverbirch. Until then I was Grub, except to Squirrel. She called me by my real name.

"Could you draw a picture of the birch?" he asked Tiger.

Tiger looked around. The idea was new to him, but he was a good draftsman, and he felt challenged. There were few birches on the island, but a small one was in sight. He looked at it long and hard to let the picture sink into his eye. Then he closed his eyes, trying to remember. After many false starts he finally produced a likeness of the tree. Old Silverbirch looked at it with great admiration. "There it grows, just like the real tree," he said. "Truly there is magic in your hand, Mister Tiger. Thank you."

But Tiger had already begun to draw something else. Suddenly Veyde raised her arms in delight: it was the woad plant with its many seed-pods. "There you are, my dear," said Tiger and threw away his stick. "Finish your story, please, Mister Silverbirch. What happened next?"

Silverbirch resumed his tale. "Now, Miss Squirrel

married a man, and he was one of those who disliked me. Nor did she like him—''

"Then why did she marry him?" interrupted Veyde.

"Because she had to. Here, a girl chooses her man, but among the Blacks—at least among those Blacks—the parents decide who is to marry whom. The man presents the woman's parents with a gift, and she moves in with him, becoming his property."

"That is true," said Tiger, who had never thought about it that way.

"So it was with Squirrel. I did not see her often any more, but I heard that her man was bad to her. He wanted a son, but she did not give him one. After a time he began to beat her, calling her a Troll bitch and making her cry. Then he took another wife. Meanwhile, I had grown to manhood. So had the other boys, and they began to play with the girls. I would have done the same, but the old folks would not permit it. I could see that some of the girls liked me, but they dared not defy their elders.

"But Miss Squirrel still saw me in secret. I told her how sorry I was for her, and that maybe it was all my fault. Then she put her arms around me to comfort me. So it came about that I loved her, and soon she was in a blessed state, her belly growing big.

"At this her man became very proud, for he thought it his own doing. He sent his second wife away and stopped beating Miss Squirrel. For a while everything was fine. Then came the disaster. Miss Squirrel had not one child but two—twin boys. They were dark like their mother, but they had the marks of our people in their faces. Her man was in a rage. He went to look for me and kill me, but I was a strong young man now. He found me in the woods, and thinking I was unarmed, came at me with his spear. But I had my sling and was quicker than he. My stone hit him in the forehead, and he never rose again.

"Now I had to flee for my life, for even my friends were against me. I hid in a tree and watched them hunt for me, listening to Stag boast about what he would do when he found me. They never did.

"During the night I crept back to the camp to see Squirrel and the two boys. She told me I had to go—quickly and far away. I wanted to take her and the boys with me, but she said no. 'They will only track us down and kill us all. I must stay. I will move back to my parents' house where nobody will harm me.' I left, and I never saw Miss Squirrel nor my two boys again. They must be grown men now, if they were allowed to live. And now you must see that it was not a happy thing, in Miss Squirrel's tribe, to mix the Black and the White."

They thought in silence about Silverbirch's tale. Then Veyde suddenly noticed Baywillow, who had been crouching in the sands. "Look!" she cried.

Baywillow looked up, somewhat bashfully. He had drawn a branch of the little tree for which he was named, showing a catkin and several elliptical, pointed leaves.

"It is very good," Tiger said, and Baywillow smiled. Veyde was thrilled. "Tiger, our child will be an artist too—she will draw the trees, and the animals, and the birds . . ."

Tiger slipped his arm around her waist. "What did you do then, Mister Silverbirch?"

"I ran east—into the forest. It was late summer, the berries were ripe, and there was plenty of game. I found my old home farther north, but there was nobody there, only some bleached bones. Then I came upon another Black settlement, but dared not show myself, in case they had heard something. Finally, I decided to leave the coast altogether, and struck out for the forest in earnest.

"I traveled for a long time without seeing anyone, Black or White. Autumn came, and I found a small White camp where I could spend the winter. By then I craved a woman, and when I did not find one there, I set out again in the spring, always heading east. I could tell you of many adventures, but I am growing tired of speaking and will keep my tale short.

"That was how I came upon the White camp up at Blue Lake, and found the woman who wanted me. Speedwell she was called, and her eyes were as deep a blue as the flower for which she was named. We lived at Blue Lake for many years, had children, and were happy. Then one day she did not return from the hunt. I spent that whole summer looking for her, but never found her, dead or alive. I knew she had to be dead. Otherwise she would have come back to me.

"The children were grown up by then, and there was nothing to hold me at Blue Lake. Everything that had been sweet like the wild strawberry when we shared it turned sour like the wolfsbane now that she was gone. I remembered the sea where I had grown up, and I knew there was another sea not far from Blue Lake. So it happened that I took up with Miss Angelica's people. I still remembered how to fish, to hunt the seal, and to build a coracle, which was new to the people here, who until then had used only rafts. That," Silverbirch concluded, "is my story," and Tiger heard it without any premonition of its importance in his own life.

Miss Angelica's mate, the dependable and silent Mister Marestail, was master stone-knapper for the tribe. He made most of the spears and harpoons, and his tremendous strength was called upon whenever there was a particularly heavy job to be done. Otherwise he was content to be Angelica's shadow, following her everywhere, whistling soft tunes, his heavy brows wrinkled as if he were concentrating hard on finding a way to lay down his life for her. Standing behind her, feeling the need for a moment's attention, he sometimes smacked her gently on the behind. She would then turn to give him a smile, and he would stand with cleared brows, a sparkle in his eyes.

Though Tiger did not articulate it, he certainly got the impression that in this community the women were more forceful and interesting than the men, Silverbirch and Baywillow being the only exceptions. It was customary for a woman to share her house with her man and children, but as there was a surplus of women on the island, two women often lived with the same man. Such was the case with Miss Rosebay, who lived in an apparently happy relationship with Mister Alder, a much younger girl named Marigold, and four children. But Miss Rosebay, well over the mature age of twenty, had started to eye one of the boys in the camp, young Campion son of Angelica, who would soon become a man. The possibility of this affair was the subject of many good-natured jokes.

These were the people among whom Tiger now lived. Many of their ways seemed strange to him, but he was impressed by their gentleness and generosity, and knew that he owed them his life. He was ashamed now to remember that his own people used to talk about Troll oxen and bitches, as if they were not human. Yet sometimes he could not help thinking of Hind, her graceful figure becoming more and more ethereal as the months went by. Then he would look at Veyde, robust, intensely alive and spirited, and his affection for her surged up.

So the winter passed on Veyde's Island. The last of

the ice was melting, and the air became filled with a glorious harmony of bird voices new to Tiger. The long-tailed ducks passed by in endless flocks, heading northeast along the coast. In the brilliant mornings of early spring, triumphant cadences were heard from a thousand throats. Crawling out of their tent to watch, Tiger and Veyde saw the entire bay dotted with resting birds. These were holy birds; nobody harmed them. And in the vigorous triad of their song, Tiger thought he heard something of Veyde's own nature. As if she had guessed his thoughts, she suddenly turned to him and said, "The long-tailed duck is my bird, the bird of the woad plant."

So it was that the spirit of the island, in Tiger's mind, took the shape of the long-tailed duck. He, and later others as well, called it Veyde's Island.

GOSHAWK

Et si destoupe mes oreilles
Quant j'oc vin verser des bouteilles.

Froissart

To all appearances Tiger had settled down as a happy member of Angelica's clan, but he had bouts of restlessness, and as he regained his physical strength, they began to worry him more. The image of his father transfixed by Shelk's javelin haunted him. Sometimes he tried to free himself by drawing the image in the sand, then smoothing it out. One day Veyde found him at this, and understood at once what was in his thoughts.

"Do you want to go back to your people, Tiger?"

"I think I would like to go back to Trout Lake, to see what happened to them," he said. "They have lost all their men. Only the women and children are left, and the winter must have been hard on them. Perhaps they got help from the Biglakers."

"Still, there is your mother, and your sister, and your brother . . ."

"Marten—yes," said Tiger. "I would like to find out what happened to them."

They talked it over. Veyde suggested that she come along too. "I want to see your family, Tiger. And we would be going soon anyway, to gather berries at Miss Sundew's Cloudberries and the other moors. Why not go to Trout Lake at the same time?''

"I wonder if there is any news of Shelk and his gang,'' said Tiger.

"We could visit Blue Lake, Mister Silverbirch's old camp. His children still live there and may have some news.''

So it was resolved, and on a clear, still day the islanders ferried themselves to the mainland. Blue Lake was two days from the coast. With old Silverbirch as a guide, the trip was easy. They found good game and the bilberries were ripe.

Silverbirch took no chances. When they drew near Blue Lake, he sent Baywillow and Silverweed as scouts. When they returned saying that all was in order, the rest of the islanders followed.

The tents of Blue Lake were set up along the shore. This tribe was more prosperous than Angelica's, and about thirty people of all ages were out basking in the afternoon sun, their labor's done for the day. Among them were Silverbirch's two sons and his daughter, who were overjoyed to see their father. They embraced him fondly and hurried to show him their children, whom Silverbirch admired one after another. Tiger looked around, and soon noticed several children with brown eyes and dark complexions. Baywillow, it seemed, was far from unique among the Whites.

Tiger soon had an explanation. The flap of a tent was thrown open, and out peered a somewhat bleary-eyed Black man, squinting in the strong afternoon sun. Seeing Tiger, he shouted a word of greeting and crawled out.

Tiger gave a start of surprise. He had never seen a fat man before. His own tribe had been lean; so were the people at the Meet. This man was obese. Tiger mechanically offered his hand in greeting; the man did the same, letting out an enormous fart. This seemed to be accepted behavior, for he continued to intersperse his talk with occasional discharges.

"Well, well, well," he said. "Here we have another Troll-lover. Are these your bitches? It's not a bad life, as I daresay you've discovered. All the bitches vie for my attention and call me a God. True, they're not what you would call really enticing. In fact, I sometimes find it hard to tell their faces from their bottoms. But you know all about this, of course. By the Great Mammoth, it's a good thing to have someone around who talks a civilized language. You are a very welcome guest, I'm sure, and I hope you will stay for some time."

Tiger managed to say that he would be off soon, but the fat man waved the news aside.

"You must stay with us for a while," he said. "Leave the hunting and berry-gathering to the Trolls. They are only too grateful to serve us. But I haven't told you my name. I'm Goshawk the Divine, God of the Blue Lake Trolls for many winters. I bid you welcome."

Tiger found it hard to suppress a laugh, for anything less like a goshawk would be difficult to imagine. But he had been well brought up and knew the importance of civility. He politely mentioned his own name and bowed. Goshawk, undeterred by Tiger's reticence, rambled on, delighted with this rare opportunity to speak in his own tongue.

"Yes, it's a good life," he said. "I get anything I want, from the first strawberry of the season to the favors of the most buxom female. Speaking of that, let's have something to eat and drink. Hey, you!" he yelled, snapping his fingers at random to the nearest group of Whites. He fell into White talk, and even Tiger could hear how atrociously he handled it. "Wine! Venison! Berries!" He turned back to Tiger. "My dear fellow, you shall have a real meal in no time. You look starved. No flesh on your bones, young man. Don't your Troll bitches feed you properly?"

"I'm fine, really," said Tiger, still at a loss about what to make of this fantastic figure. "But I'll be honored to eat and drink with you, sir," he added quickly, remembering his manners.

Goshawk produced another thundering fart and sat down on a boulder with some difficulty, hoisting one of his fat legs over the other. "I was just about to send my people out for the berry harvest," he announced. "And we're running a little short on venison. There should be elk at hand—I really don't take to horseflesh, do you? Sometimes in the morning there are several hands of elk on the other shore. I'll see that my people get one or two for you tomorrow. Why, here's the wine," he went on, as a young White girl came up with a wine-skin. "Do have some. Don't stint, now. This is made from sap, and soon we'll have berries to make a new brew. *They* don't drink it, of course. Strictly for Divine purposes. They'd go stark mad. But I'm glad to share it with you. Would you care for a bitch in your tent? There's quite a selection here," and he pointed at the group of people chatting with Silverbirch.

Tiger sampled the wine, which seemed quite a potent brew, and handed the skin to Goshawk, who drank more deeply. "What I'd like is some information about Shelk and his gang," he said. "Do you know anything about them?"

Goshawk wrinkled his brow at this distasteful topic. "You must mean those people who sacked a Troll village up north last winter. I really don't know much about them," he confessed, wiping his beard, "but I know my responsibility. We have scouts out most of the time, and we're not going to be taken by surprise. I'll give that Elk or Shelk something to think about if he makes the mistake of coming our way. But let's see now. I seem to remember hearing about him years ago. I believe they said he was a bastard—half man, half Troll. Is that so?"

"I think so," said Tiger. "I saw him once. He looks a little like my friend over there," he added, nodding toward Baywillow. "Heavy brows like the Whites but tall and dark like the Blacks."

"Yes, that must be the man, a bastard gone bad," said Goshawk. "There you are, don't you see? My responsibility, I mean—or ours, to be sure," with a confidential nod to Tiger. "But we can cope with Shelk. The people under my command are strong and capable. They will do as I bid them. We're not going to stand for any nonsense." Then Goshawk relaxed. "But really, I'm sure it was nothing but a temporary outbreak. Probably they have left for good now."

"Do you know where they might have gone?" pressed Tiger. "I want to find Shelk."

"You want nothing to do with him," said Goshawk, shocked. "And besides, nobody knows where he is. Always flitting about, you know. Now here, now there, sometimes in two or three places at once. *That's* what I've heard." And Goshawk turned his attention to the wine-skin.

Tiger tried to find out how he had come by this meager information, but Goshawk seemed reluctant to reveal anything of his past. Still, Tiger persisted.

"But where do you come from, sir? You speak like the people from the southwest at the Summer Meet."

For a moment Goshawk was silent, casting an anxious glance at Tiger.

"As a matter of fact, that's right," he confided. "However, it's been a long time since I saw the great Salt Sea. I have come a long way," he continued, relapsing into his grand manner, "and I was hailed as a divine being by the Trolls in every village. Troll bitches all over the world are now blessed with children of the Gods, thanks to my generous efforts. Just think of it, I shall have hundreds of grandchildren. The line of Goshawk will surely rule the world. But of course," he added graciously, "that of Tiger will prosper, too. In future generations, our blood will blend. By means of our divine sperm we will raise these backward Trolls to new heights, and the world will be a better place. I've thought it all out."

He took another swig, just as a smiling girl appeared with two chunks of grilled elk. Goshawk started to grab one, then remembered he was the host, and politely asked Tiger to take his choice. While they ate, Goshawk continued his discourse, now on his favorite topic.

"I know most men despise and even fear the Trolls. That's where they are wrong. The Trolls really know how to revere a man. I see a great future for the children of the Gods, the union of man and Troll. There is a divine purpose behind it, and you and I are its vessels. I *know* this because I have seen the token."

"What do you mean?" asked Tiger.

Goshawk lowered his voice. "There is something about the children of the Gods. I've found this out by thinking. As I told you, I'm a thinker!" He tapped his forehead. "For seven or eight winters I have lived in this village. I've seen many children born and many children die. And do you know what? The lives of the children of the Gods are charmed! Charmed," he repeated. "In all these winters, not a single one has died. See for yourself. Look around. There are fewer White brats than children of the Gods. That's because the Troll imps die like flies, but nothing harms the children of the Gods. Surely you must agree that this is a token. They *are* divine. A great new race of men is growing up before our very eyes.

"But you're not drinking," he said. "Do have some wine. There will be a good berry-brew in half a moon. Tell me, though, am I not right?"

"There is certainly something in what you say," conceded Tiger, though his inherited dislike of sorcery made him guarded.

"Good man!" said Goshawk. "And now, cast your mind back. You grew up among Blacks, just as I did. Did you ever see anything like this? I bet not. I bet my finest bitch you've seen brothers and sisters die, and playmates too."

"That's quite true," said Tiger sadly.

"You see! Now, I don't say these children of the Gods are immortal, but I do say they are of sterner stuff than Man or Troll. Clever little beggars, too. Do you know that many of them already speak our language? That, I've found, is simply beyond the Trolls. So you see our responsibility. They must be kept on the Right Way. They must learn from their mothers to revere their divine fathers, and from us, the ways and language of Men. I mean to share with them all the wisdom in my mind and heart. Remember this, my friend!

"But now, I feel it's time for a little nap. Won't do them any good if I exert myself. I'm responsible for this flock, you know. I keep watch over them day and night. Nothing escapes me, I tell you! However, do feel free to choose a bitch for the night. I shan't mind. I might try one of yours, later on, if you like the idea. Even reckoning, eh?" Goshawk was suddenly seized by a fit of hiccoughs, followed by other, more unpleasant eruptions. When he was able to speak again, he rose unsteadily. "Yes, yes, thank you, I feel fine. See you later. Make yourself at home."

He crept back into his tent. With a shudder of distaste as he glanced at the soiled spot where the divine Goshawk had been sitting, Tiger also rose, and walked over to his friends. "Any news?" he asked.

There was indeed news. Silverbirch had found a young woman named Sorrel, who had been a member of the White clan attacked by the Devils last summer. She had striking, greenish-grey eyes and a vivacious manner. She held a baby, one of God's children, to her breast. According to her, the tragedy had taken place in high summer, well before the berry season. The camp was attacked at sunrise and taken completely by surprise. Most of the men and many of the women were killed, but some managed to escape, and she was among them. Yes, she had seen some of the attackers. They all wore a headdress with a single great eagle feather. Yes, she had noticed the leader. He was a tall Black man with a long beard, but he had the brow of a White.

"Shelk," whispered Tiger to Baywillow. "So it's true?"

Miss Sorrel went on: "We waited a day or two after the Devils left before we dared return to the camp. There was nobody alive, and the dead had been left for the ravens and hyenas. We buried them, but many people were missing. I believe the Devils rounded them up and took them along, for nobody ever came back."

"Did anybody try to track them?" asked Tiger.

"Two of our men went after the party," she said, "but they never came back either."

"Which way were they going?"

"To the west, toward the hill country from which the Great River flows. We call it the Land of the Osprey. I have never been there, but they say the Great River comes out of a gap in the earth, raging like thunder, and there is a rainbow all day long.''

There was a flash in Tiger's eyes. He had heard about the great rapids. Veyde glanced at him, and he could see recognition in her eyes too.

"None of the survivors cared to stay at the camp," said Sorrel. "They wanted to go north and start a new settlement far away. But my man was one of those killed. I had relatives at Blue Lake, and decided to come here. I haven't seen the others since.''

Tiger was silent. He already knew the Whites' superstitious awe of the Blacks. How could he get any help from them? And yet something had to be done. His was not a vengeful nature. A happy boyhood and the friendly camaraderie among the Chief's men had made him an outgoing, pleasant young man. Until now, the image of his father run through by the javelin had been a nightmare. Sorrel's tale made it real to him, and he realized that he must do something. He wanted redress, retribution. But the most important thing was to rid the land of this menace. He wanted to live without terror. What could he do, though, alone, with only a handful of Whites who would not dare to raise their hands against a Black man?

Veyde interrupted his thoughts with a shout of laughter. He looked up in surprise.

"What is all this about?" he asked.

"Oh, they were telling me that they built a new winter house for Goshawk the Divine last winter," Veyde explained between peals of laughter. "It was a beautiful house, very strong, but they made the entrance too small. He is so fat that he got stuck. They had to dig him out, and it took a long time because they had made the tunnel solid with stone facings. Goshawk was very impatient.'' This Tiger could imagine.

"This is by no means a laughing matter," said Silver-birch sternly. "Your behavior is most unseemly, Miss Veyde." He shook his head, but the corners of his lips were twitching.

"Tiger, Mister Silverbirch says I am wanton and most unseemly," said Veyde gleefully, flinging her arms around his neck.

"I like you that way," Tiger assured her. "But what should we do now? I would really like to go on."

"Of course," said Veyde soberly. "Do you want to start right away?"

"If you feel like it—yes," said Tiger, who was now well versed in White etiquette.

So they set out, and as they trudged along, keeping to the eskers to avoid the boggy country, a thin veil of clouds spread over the western sky.

TROUT LAKE

Facilis descensus Averni.

Virgil, Aeneid

The summer days slipped by as Tiger and
Veyde journeyed to Trout Lake. For two days there was
a steady drizzle, then came days with showers and sunshine in rapid succession. Their first stop was Miss Sundew's Cloudberries, the scene of the tragic mammoth
hunt a year earlier. Tiger performed belated rites at the
graves of his father and friends. On the boulder
covering the Chief's grave, he drew a picture of a proud
ferret, his father's totem, and labored hard to engrave it
into the rock. Veyde, following the custom of her tribe,
gathered rosebay, now in bloom all over the glades of
the esker, and scattered it over the mounds. Then they
pressed on.

Tiger led the way, retracing the route along which he
had tracked the mammoths. As they passed one familiar
landmark after another, his anxiety grew. Veyde tried to
divert him with stories, but it was only when she began
to talk about the Land of the Osprey that she was successful. Tiger listened with grim interest as she told him
the tale of Mister Cornel, her distant ancestor, who

grew up by the Great River in the days, long ago, when it flowed in another bed.

"Now," she said, "the river runs through a narrow gorge, a whole day in length, and its raging water is white. No one can enter it and live. It will break every bone in a man's body and carry him out through the Gap a mangled corpse. Such is the terrible strength of the Gorge rapids, far greater than that of the breakers against the shores of our island in a southern gale. Yet from the end of the Gorge it is only a short journey, overland, to its beginning; for the Gorge bends back upon itself. And once through the Gap, the river becomes serene, a broad sheet of water flowing quietly east to the lake which you call Big Lake and we call Diver Lake."

"I have heard about the Gorge," said Tiger. "Some of the Biglakers have been there. They say you can hear the roar of the rapids one day away. As you come to the Gap, there is a rainbow like a bridge across it—a bridge no man can walk. But the sun never reaches the Gorge itself, so steep and high are its banks."

"In those days long ago, the Gorge was dry," said Veyde, "and trees grew on its floor. Each spring and autumn the caribou passed through in immense herds. Mister Cornel and his people lived by a lake just above the Gorge. From that lake, the river flowed to the east. It was a good place to hunt the caribou. You could lie in ambush in the Gorge and take the stragglers—not the leaders, for that would have scared the herd away.

"Now it happened that Mister Cornel's brother, Mister Rowan, who was very dear to him, got sick and died in the autumn when the skies were grey and dark and the rain fell. It was hard to find game in such weather. Everybody was hoping that the caribou would come. Each day Cornel patrolled the Gorge, looking for

game. Often he thought of his dead brother and wished
for a sign from him. The rowan is the tree of the osprey,
and he knew that his brother was now an osprey,
soaring on long wings in the skies of Dead Men.

"One day, as he walked the Gorge, he felt a shock in
the ground under his feet. It was as if the land itself had
shuddered under that never-ceasing rain. He had a
peculiar feeling that something was watching him, and
turning around, he saw a terrible black shape, with
glowing eyes and great gleaming teeth. A black tiger!

"Cornel the hunter became the hunted, just like the
caribou. The walls of the Gorge were sheer cliffs, and
the trees were too stunted and weak to support his
weight. Running was his only escape. And he ran!

"The tiger must have been hungry and searching for
food too. It pursured Cornel, and was soon close on his
heels.

"Suddenly the clouds parted, and a single shaft of
sunlight fell on the wall of the Gorge. At the same time
Cornel saw a great osprey swoop up the Gorge. Afterwards he said he could not understand why it was there,
unless it came as a portent, for ospreys stay by the
water.

"The clouds closed again, but in that one moment of
light Cornel had seen a narrow fissure in the wall. Halfway up, a little rowan tree grew, as if by a miracle. Cornel ran to the spot and managed to clamber up where he
could hold on to the rowan. The tiger tried to reach him,
but its claws slipped on the wall.

"For the moment, Cornel was safe. He looked at the
tiger, snarling and growling below, and in his heart he
thanked his brother for coming to his aid.

"But now Cornel heard a terrible roar such as he had
never heard in his life. Even the voice of the tiger
was lost in that incredible din. A great wall of water,

the height of three men, came storming down the
Gorge, carrying logs and trees in its wake. In a flash
it swallowed the tiger, too, and halfway up the cliff
Cornel hung on to the rowan tree for dear life. He was
trapped, for there was no way up, and to go down into
the raging cataract would be death just as certain as in
the tiger's teeth. The only thing he could do was hold on
and shout for help.

"Finally help came, for Cornel's friends knew he had
gone to the Gorge, and went looking for him. They
helped him up the cliff, but Cornel knew it was his
brother who really saved his life—by means of the ray
of sunlight from the sky, the osprey, and the rowan tree.
In a way the tiger had helped save his life, too.

"The river, which had flowed to the east, had suddenly broken south into the Gorge. It happened when
the earth shook. The level of the lake sank a couple of
feet, and the old river bed dried out. But south of the
Gorge the forest was devastated by the Great River; and
that is how it came into being."

"It sounds like a fitting place for Shelk," said Tiger.

They were now in country he knew well, heading
straight for Trout Lake. As they went on, new thoughts
troubled him. Would there be anybody in his village?
He wondered if they would recognize him. When he
left, he was a beardless youngster. Now he was growing
a beard. And what would they say of him, coming home
with a Troll woman? Surely, they would be grateful to
Veyde. Had she not saved his life?

At the thought of Veyde, he smiled at her and said,
"It is not long now. We just have to cross that ridge
ahead. From up there we can see the lake, and we
should be able to hear the voices of children. They
would be out playing on a day like this."

Veyde hesitated. "What do you think they will say

about me? I am afraid. Maybe I should stop here and let you go first.''

The temptation was strong, but Tiger forced it back. ''No, I want you to come with me. I want to tell everybody what you have done for me. There is nothing to be afraid of.''

So they climbed the ridge. The pines thinned out, and there, just as Tiger remembered it, the water of Trout Lake sparkled in the sun. There was the shore where he had played with Marten and Godwit. Reeds fringed the lake, and there was the patch of sandy beach they had often covered with pictures. Quacking indignantly, a few startled ducks took off. Why had they been so close to the houses? Tiger's uneasiness rose. There was no sign of life. He started to run, and saw a jet-black raven fly up from the houses.

''Maybe they are out for berries?'' said Veyde.

But the houses were in disrepair. There were holes in some of the roofs, and one house had collapsed, probably under the weight of the winter snow.

''They must have left last summer,'' said Tiger. ''The village has been deserted for a long time—''

Suddenly Tiger stopped. One of the posts, leaning crazily askew, was crowned by something round and white—a skull. The empty eye-sockets were turned toward them. Tiger walked to the post, took the skull, and sank to his knees. He stroked the forehead, the cheekbones, the crown.

''So you tried to fight them,'' he muttered. ''They attacked and you fought back, alone. There was no one to help you. Oh, why was I not here? You put up a show, at least. You fought back. I did nothing but sleep under a tree.''

Tiger pressed his cheek against the bony temple.

''These are your teeth. Have you not smiled at me a

thousand times? Now they have taken your head and put it on a stake for the ravens. They have left your body to the hyenas.''

Then he turned to Veyde. ''Veyde, now I have two reasons for revenge. This is my brother Marten, only a winter younger than I. He would have been a man this summer. The Devils must have come here after they attacked us at the bog. He fought them, trying to defend the women and children. They killed him, and they must have taken away the others—just as they did Sorrel's people.''

''But how did they know about this place?'' Veyde asked.

The question brought the truth home to Tiger. ''The Summer Meet. That's where they spied out the land. They talked to one of our men, asking where he lived, how many we were. There was a whole gang of them, and Shelk, in all his glory.''

''What is the meaning of it all?'' cried Veyde. ''Why are they doing these things? Why do they not leave people in peace? What is all this killing, and taking prisoners?''

''I do not understand it either,'' Tiger said. ''But whatever it is, it must be stopped, or no one will be safe any more. We must fight them, kill them, wipe them out!''

''But we are so few and they are so many,'' said Veyde. ''What can we do to them? They are Blacks. They have the arms and the skill. We are just Whites. Except you, of course. And Goshawk,'' she added.

Tiger laughed. ''Goshawk! What a thought! But there are strong men and women in his camp, and in ours. You Whites are different. With us, and with Shelk, only the men fight and hunt. With you, women do as well.''

"How about your friends—the Biglakers?"

"I doubt that they are there any more," said Tiger. "They lived much closer to Shelk. I suspect that they have been wiped out too."

They buried Marten's skull high up on Troll Ridge, beside the cairn. When Tiger told the story of the place, Veyde was sure that it must be the grave of Mister Cornel. After his adventure with the tiger, he had left the Gorge and settled by a lake just like this. They paid homage in the ways of their own people, Tiger engraving the likeness of a rampant marten on the boulder with which they covered Marten's grave. "Though I cannot do it as well as my brother," he said sadly.

Finally they decided to return to the cloudberry bog to find their friends from Veyde's Island. The time for harvest was drawing near. There they could decide whether to go to Blue Lake to engage the Whites for an attack on Shelk.

"We cached a lot of things before we started the mammoth hunt last summer," Tiger said. "I do not think Shelk can have found them. There were fine spearheads and other weapons which will come in handy."

On the way back Tiger found the cache, untouched. He made two shafts and hafted the finest points to them. Then they added the arms to their burdens and continued their journey.

That same evening the new weapons came in handy. Veyde and Tiger were sitting by the campfire when they heard the sound of heavy snorting. A great grey shelk appeared in the firelight, its eyes glowing with the reflections of the flames and its immense antlers luminous against the dark background. It seemed to be irresistibly drawn to the fire and hardly noticed Tiger, who gripped his spear and drew to the side, ready to attack. Veyde, with her spear, took the other side of the advancing animal, who came forward, inhaling the wood-smoke in long, luxurious breaths. Tiger and Veyde lunged with their spears, and the shelk fell, struck through the heart.

While they butchered the animal, Veyde and Tiger talked about its behavior. Tiger felt that it was an omen, that they would slaughter Shelk himself in the same way.

They stripped the head and found maggots in the nasal cavity. The animal, plagued by its parasites, had sought relief in the tang of the smoke. "I hope Shelk will be eaten by maggots, too," Tiger muttered, and he started to dress the shelk's tongue for smoking.

After the rains, the weather turned warm and sunny. Mushrooms were sprouting. Used to Veyde's foraging as he was, Tiger was still getting surprises, and one of them came when they were close to Miss Sundew's Cloudberries. With a hoot of delight, Veyde threw down her burden and kneeled to pick a colony of small mushrooms growing inconspicuously in the moss. At first sight, they looked like autumn leaves scattered over the forest floor.

"Do you really mean that these can be eaten?" asked Tiger.

"Yes, of course," said Veyde. "They are chanterelles. Have you never eaten mushrooms?"

"Never," said Tiger. To him and his people mushrooms were uncanny things, sprouting silently overnight like little ghosts, then rotting into slimy corruption. The Blacks were afraid of them.

"Well, these are among the best, but there are many others. Look at this." And she picked a big one with a rich brown cap, a green underside, and a fat stalk. She bit off a piece and munched contentedly. Tiger took a nibble. The taste was faint but pleasant, and soon he was eating with relish. They went on, looking for more.

Tiger found some odd white ones with a heavy, long stalk and a very small cap. The base was enclosed in a kind of sheath. Before he had a chance to taste this new delicacy, Veyde gripped his arms. Her grip was so powerful that Tiger flinched and cried out, "Easy, Veyde! You are hurting me!"

"Do not touch those, Tiger! They are death! They killed one of my ancestors!"

"What happened?" asked Tiger.

"It was Mister Coltsfoot," Veyde began. "He begat Miss Cowslip, who bore Miss Torchflower, who bore Miss Parnassia, who bore my mother. Coltsfoot was Miss Mayweed's man. They had lived together for three winters, yet they were childless. Both wanted a child and they begged Miss Crowberry, an old woman, to help them. She sang magic songs and incantations, and they prayed to the birds of the north and the south, but it was to no avail. Another summer went by, and still they were barren.

"Coltsfoot was in despair. No matter what they did, his seed did not take root in Mayweed. Late in the summer, they went out to gather mushrooms, and he saw this one we now call the death-cap. You see its shape? It is the shape of your own cock when it rises to do its work. Coltsfoot secretly gathered the mushrooms, and ate them far away in the wood. Right away, he felt his cock rise and knew that he would be able to beget a child at last. He and Mayweed were in their tent all that day, and he came into her many times. When she marveled at his power, he told her what he had done, and she was pleased and happy, as sure as he that now they would be blessed.

"He never ate anything else that day, and made love late into the night. When the waning moon rose he fell sick, and soon was mortally ill. All that he had inside was flowing out of him, and at last his guts came out too. He died in agony.

"Mayweed was indeed blessed, and next spring she bore Cowslip. Cowslip never saw her father, who died for her sake. We do not know if it was the death-caps that killed him or the exertions of his lovemaking, but since then no one has touched them. And you must not touch them, Tiger, for we are already blessed."

Tiger let the mushrooms fall from his hands and smiled at her. "No, we have no need for them," he said. "And are there other deadly ones, too?"

"Yes," said Veyde. "There is the fleabane, the red one with white spots. They say it is dangerous, though I never heard of anybody who ate one. You must stick to the safe kinds—the chanterelles, which are like autumn leaves, and these big brown cepes. I will show you."

She jumped up, relieved now that the danger was over. Later on, she taught him to recognize the good kinds: the stately parasol mushrooms with their tall, ringed stalks and a disk two hands across; the small brown ones with a peppery taste; the moist yellow-skinned boletes, which melt in the mouth; and the honey-mushrooms growing in bunches on tree-stumps.

Veyde was interrupted by a shout, and out of the forest ran Baywillow.

"I was lucky to find you," he said. "I came upon your tracks and followed you as quickly as I could. You must not go to the cloudberry bog. The Devils are ahead of us. They have taken Blue Lake."

"When?" cried Tiger.

"Three days ago. Just after we left for Miss Sundew's Cloudberries."

Baywillow told his story. "The day after you left Blue Lake, Silverbirch and his party went on to the bog. They spent a couple of days there, harvesting the cloudberries. Sorrel came, carrying her baby, and told us that the Blue Lake village had been attacked by a group of Blacks. She managed to escape because she was out picking berries and spent the night in the wood. Returning, she heard voices speaking in the Black tongue and knew something was wrong. She crept away quickly and ran to Miss Sundew's Cloudberries, where she knew she would find us.

"Sorrel thinks the camp was attacked at sunrise, for she remembers waking and hearing distant noises, which made her wary. And a good thing it was. She went to the island with Silverbirch and the others. I stayed behind to make sure you did not walk into the trap. I also scouted around Blue Lake, and the Devils are still there. They are behaving differently now. Last year they took their prisoners and vanished. This time they are staying longer."

"What happened to the people at Blue Lake?" asked Veyde.

"I believe most of them are still there. I saw women and children, and one of the men. I thought I might get a chance to talk to somebody, but there are many sentries and they will not let anyone out. I do not know how many they may have killed."

Tiger was thunderstruck by the enemy's new move. His mind was racing, but only in a circle. He had counted on the help of the Blue Lake Whites. Now they too had been overpowered. Was there no end to Shelk's resources and power? The little group of Whites at Veyde's Island was alone, without friends on the mainland. His chance to fight the terrible Shelk was gone.

Baywillow was grave too, but he never lost his air of

polite calmness. "What should we do now, Tiger?" he asked.

Tiger shook his head. In a dull voice he told Baywillow about their journey to Trout Lake, and what they had found there. The tall young man's face showed little emotion, but he gripped Tiger's hand.

"I think we had better go back to the island," said Veyde. "There at least we shall be safe."

"I agree," said Baywillow. "Miss Silverweed will be waiting for us with the raft, and once we take it, Shelk will find it hard to get across the channel."

"He can build another raft," said Tiger.

"We will keep watch," said Veyde. "In that way we will know if they are coming."

"Why should they come at all?" said Baywillow. "They don't know where we are."

"Shelk seems to know everything," muttered Tiger, "but I hope you are right."

"We had better move fast," said Baywillow. "Let me help you with your burdens. That is a beautiful shelk's tongue. What a good thing you are not pulling runners—they make too big a track. I told Mister Silverbirch to be sure everyone carries his gear on his back to make it harder for the Devils to follow them."

Tiger nodded, but the next day he realized that the precaution had been useless. There was a beaten track leading down to the shore, and nothing could be done to hide it.

THE TRAP

Darnach sluoch er schiere einen vvisent und einen elch,
Starcher uore viere und einen grimmen schelch.

Nibelungenlied

Silverweed was waiting for them with the raft,
and they paddled across to the island with some difficulty in the fresh southern breeze. "If this weather
keeps up, they will have a hard time crossing," said
Veyde.

From that day on, in fair weather or foul, the crossing
was constantly surveilled by one or two of Veyde's
people, from the hill opposite the mainland promontory. Tiger called the place Lookout Point. Summer
slowly turned into autumn, and still nothing happened.
There were many days of storms and heavy rains, and
most people moved to their winter houses. But Tiger
pitched a tent on Lookout Point and spent most of his
time there. He seemed to live in a dark dream in which
the mainland, glimpsed through the mist and driving
rain, became a world of malevolence, an evil shadow at
the edge of his own world. He felt better when another
squall blotted it out of his sight. He practiced shooting
with his throwing-stick and his sling, and all the time his
thoughts oscillated between his own losses and misery

on one side and the enemy's invincible power on the
other.

Veyde spent much of her time with him, though she
was now heavy with child and tired easily. Her presence
was comforting. So was that of Baywillow, who came
often. Veyde told stories, of which she had an inexhaustible fund. Baywillow brought sketching materials,
pieces of birch-bark and charcoal, and prevailed upon
Tiger to make drawings, which he would then copy with
growing skill. Some of Tiger's own misery found expression in the images taking shape under his hand. He
had always been a skillful artist. Now the lines of backs
and legs, antlers and muzzles, took on a sensitive and
spiritual quality new to his work.

For a day or two, Tiger toiled to reproduce the shelk
he and Veyde had felled on their way back from Trout
Lake. He showed the animal head-on, with its muzzle
raised to display the majestic sloping crowns of its
antlers. Then, with a savage stab, he thrust a spearpoint
into its forehead.

The others lost interest in the Devils as the menace
faded with the passing days. Now the weather changed.
They had a late taste of summer, with clear skies and
great swarms of migrating birds. One evening just after
sunset, the sky lit up with the most tremendous auroral
light Tiger had ever seen. He sat with Veyde on Lookout
Point, gazing with wonder and awe at the great shafts of
light across the sky. They radiated out from a point,
their ghostly colors changing all the time from blue and
green to red. Not a sound was heard.

"It is the Great Swan shaking her feathers," said
Veyde. "I have never seen her so excited. She is calling
her cygnets. They are coming from the far north to tell
us—"

"We always said it was the Star-Hunters shooting their javelins," said Tiger.

Veyde shuddered. "Tiger! I know her message. She is telling us they are on the way. She is warning us, Tiger! They are coming."

Tiger was seized by her mood at once. He, too, felt that something extraordinary was astir. He had never seen the aurora so early in the autumn. The northern lights belonged to the winter sky. Now, when the leaves were barely turning, they must be an omen.

"Go back, Veyde, and tell the others," he said. "I will keep watch. If they come, they will come in the night."

She left quickly, and Tiger looked out across the water to the mainland. Was there something moving? A black speck, far off, against the dull sheen of the water? He rubbed his eyes. Now, when it was too late, he realized that he had made no plans. What would they do when the enemy came? Run away? Or fight? He knew he could fight. But the others? He thought of Veyde's gentle people, so polite, so compliant. What would they do? What could they do?

In sudden agony he realized that he should have prepared long ago. What had he done this year? Nothing. He ought to have been planning right from the start. Then he might have had a chance—they might all have had a chance. But he had just drifted along with the stream of events. Still a boy, Tiger blamed himself for not having the foresight and experience of an old man. Now it was too late. He would have to fight alone, like Marten. He would be killed like Marten, too, and his head put on a stake.

What could he have done? He could have rallied the Whites and the Biglakers into a fighting troop. Wolf, his father's friend, would have helped. They could have resisted, even attacked. He used to have friends, but Shelk had conquered them all. None were left except the little tribe on Veyde's Island. And Shelk was coming to finish them. There was somebody out on the water.

For a year Tiger had lived in a dream. Now he was awake, and shame of his neglect burned into him. He could do nothing now. They would have to flee, but where would they go? In his mind's eye Tiger saw the map of the islands as he had seen it in the mirage. The Devils would track them: Tiger knew they were good at that. If he and Veyde's people fled north or south along the fringe of islands, they would be caught in the end. The children would make their progress slow. Their only raft was here. Using it would take them straight into the enemy's hands. Besides, the raft was too small to carry everybody.

Could they swim back to the mainland from another island, and escape in the forest? Perhaps, but for how long? Tiger thought of Veyde, so close to childbirth, and of the children. They could not swim so far. The water was already too cold. He could do it alone, save his own skin, but he would never abandon the others.

The raft was close enough now for him to see it clearly. It was big, and there were at least two hands of men on it. No one spoke, but he could hear the faint sound of the paddling. Somebody on board knew the sea. The flickering light still danced overhead. "O Black Tiger!" he murmured, but the rest of his tormented prayer was silent.

A hand gripped his shoulder, and he looked around to see Baywillow in the faint light. "Are they coming?" Baywillow whispered in the Black tongue, which he always used when they were alone.

Tiger pointed at the advancing raft.

"We're ready for them," said Baywillow. "Come with me."

"Ready?" said Tiger eagerly. "Will you fight?" It was beyond his expectations. Baywillow smiled. "If necessary, but it may not be necessary. Come."

Tiger followed him, his mind full of questions. Baywillow started to go along the path to the winter houses, then stepped to the side. "Up here," he said, and led Tiger up a steep incline. This was the highest hill on the island, flat-topped, with sheer sides. There were only a couple of places where it could be scaled. "They'll never take us up there," said Baywillow. "I have stocked the place with spears and rocks."

Hope! Tiger brightened. The great hill was indeed difficult to climb, especially in the dark. At the top he saw Veyde. The burning shafts of the aurora were still shooting across the sky, and for a moment they seemed to crown her head like a halo.

She was shaking. "Are they coming, Tiger?"

"Yes, they are almost ashore now."

Tiger realized that the plateau was full of people. "This is a good place," he said. "We can keep them out of here." There were boulders which would give shelter from the enemy's javelins. Yet Tiger felt there was something they had forgotten. "Yes, we can keep them out of here," he repeated, "but for how long?"

"As long as we like," said Veyde. "If they try to climb up, we shall heave spears and rocks at them."

"There are only two paths to the top," said Baywillow. "We can cover both."

But Tiger was thinking further ahead. "When all the rocks and spears are gone—what happens then?"

Veyde scratched her head. The idea was new to her.

"You are right, Tiger," she admitted. "I thought we would send a hail of spears and rocks at them, but I see we can't do that."

Tiger looked around. He remembered how his father had seemed to know exactly what the mammoths were going to do, and he began to see the first step of strategic thinking: putting yourself in the enemy's position. He tried to imagine what Shelk might be planning. Shelk would try to rush them. When he found that it was impossible, he would do something else. What?

Slowly the sickening answer came to Tiger. Shelk would do nothing. He would simply wait.

What if Shelk waited for days? For a whole moon? What would happen then?

"Veyde, have we got anything to eat and drink?"

"Of course," said Veyde. "Are you hungry, Tiger?"

"Not now! But we shall be very hungry if we have to stay here for a long time."

"We cannot stay long," said Veyde. "There is no spring here. You know that, Tiger. The only spring on the island is down near the winter houses."

Tiger turned to Baywillow. "This is a death-trap," Tiger moaned. "Shelk will just wait until we die from lack of food and water, or until we give up. He has all the stores from our houses and he has the spring. He can afford to wait. We cannot."

An odd smile appeared on Veyde's face. "I am not so sure Shelk can wait," she said. "I know what the Great Swan told me. We are her cygnets, and she will save us. I know that you are trying to think for us and help us, Tiger, but you are not to worry."

"Worry!" cried Tiger in a rage. "Save us! Who? The Swan? The birds? Nothing can save us! Not if we stay here! The only thing to do is to go down! Then at least we can attack."

"Shh," whispered Baywillow. "I think it is already too late for that. They must have found the houses empty and come looking for us. I believe they heard you, Tiger."

In the distance, someone said, "They must be close by. I heard a shout."

"Keep still, everybody. We'll hear them if they move." There was no mistaking the authority in that voice. It could only be Shelk.

There was absolute silence, which seemed to last for an eternity. Then one of the children whimpered.

"They're up there, on that hill."

"More fools they," said Shelk. "Sentries up. Make a ring around that hill. If anyone moves, give the war-yell." Tiger heard people moving about: Shelk's fighters taking their station.

Then Shelk raised his voice, speaking the language of the Whites to perfection.

"Come down, everyone. Give up your leader, the Black man you call Tiger, and I swear by the birds and by the Sun God that nobody will be hurt. I am the Guardian of the birds and the son of the Sun God, and you must obey me. Only then will your lives be saved, and those of your children too."

Veyde made an impulsive move for her spear, but Angelica gripped her arm and shouted, "Go away from our island. Do not show yourselves here any more. Go in peace."

Shelk laughed. Somebody kindled a fire. Angelica bent down and hurled a spear. An agonized cry came from the darkness, and the fire was hastily stamped out.

"For that, you shall be punished, Mister Tiger," said Shelk. Then he spoke in his own language: "All right, we'll starve them out. Here, you, are you badly hurt? Only a scratch? Good. Now we're all hungry, and these people owe us some refreshments. Go to the camp, Weasel, and see what they have. Get the best.''

The trapped men and women on the hill listened in silence. The children slept. Gradually the sounds from below died away, and Tiger realized that Shelk's men were sleeping too. But he knew there were sentries around the hill, ready to cry out at any movement.

Time passed, the aurora died away, and slowly the first light of dawn appeared. Tiger could see Veyde's face, drawn and grey.

''Tiger, I feel it will be my time soon.''

Tiger could say nothing. He put his arm around her, and Veyde rested her fair-haired head on his shoulder. Baywillow lay beside them, but did not sleep. His gaze never left the wood. Marestail kept watch on the other side. Old Silverbirch rested, with his back against a boulder. Angelica slept, her hand closed around the shaft of a spear.

When the first sun rays stung his eyes, Tiger realized that he too had slept. In his dream he had been back at Trout Lake, hunting a fox with Marten. With a shudder he remembered where he was. Around him all was silent. He looked down at the landscape he had learned to know and love. This was the highest point on the island, and the view was magnificent. Everywhere there was the flash of water, glimpsed between the trees and the rounded hills. To the south the sea was a smooth mirror in which the outer rocks lay like grey specks. The sun rose, great and red, in a mist thick enough for Tiger to look straight at the mighty disk of light. To his amazement, he saw black specks, like beetles, on the face of the sun.

There was a whizzing sound, and Tiger started as a javelin passed close by his head, hit a boulder, and fell back into the wood. He had ventured too far, and quickly withdrew. A voice came from below:

"Don't bother with that. We'll get them all in due time."

"I just—just thought I'd get the Black one. Then the others would come down." This voice was slurred, as if sleepy.

"Well, you should have aimed better."

"Master, I don't know what it is, but I can't see well."

"Go to the shore and wash your eyes. Hey, Cook! We'll need something to eat and drink. It's morning!"

"I don't feel well myself," said someone else. "I think those berries were overripe. I'll have to take a crap."

Tiger returned to his mournful meditations. If he'd only done something in time, they wouldn't be in this hole. He should have known that the enemy would never give up. What Shelk's ultimate objective might be he did not know. Something about a Sun God. More damn sorcery.

Veyde stretched. "What is going on?" she asked.

"Nothing much. They are just waiting. They know that we are going to starve eventually."

"Well, we are not starving now. I am going to have some food. See? I brought the berries Mister Silverbirch gathered."

"You seem to have left some behind, though," said Tiger. "I heard Shelk's men complain that they were overripe."

Veyde looked at him, opened her mouth, and then shut it again. It was Baywillow who spoke, in Tiger's language: "Finicky devils, aren't they?" Was there a hint of a snicker in his voice?

Veyde rummaged among the bags stacked in the middle of the plateau. The children woke up and were admonished not to go near the edge. And soon Veyde's people were eating with relish.

"Master, I can't see! I'm going blind! blind!" someone screamed below.

"What is happening?" asked Tiger. To his surprise he saw that Veyde's cheeks were aflame. There were tears in her eyes. "What are they saying, Tiger?"

"Somebody is complaining that he cannot see."

Tiger started moving toward the edge of the cliff. Veyde took his arm. "No, Tiger! Wait!"

Again someone screamed, "Master, I'm dying!" his words lost in the sound of furious retching. Soon another man screamed, and another. Shelk's men cursed and prayed, and retched.

"I told you they would not have time to wait," said Veyde. "They will all die. They will die as Coltsfoot died. I have killed them. They were going to kill you, maybe all of us. They killed your father and brother. Now they are getting what they deserve."

"She's right, Tiger," said Baywillow. "I didn't know if it would work, but it has."

The frightful noises continued. Tiger was stunned. Yes, he had wanted Shelk and his gang wiped out. But he had dreamed of a fight, where he himself put a javelin through Shelk's body. Finally he managed to ask, "How did you do it, Veyde?"

"The death-caps. They grow on the island too. I thought it out as soon as we came back here. I picked a lot of them and shredded them into small bits, which I mixed with one bag of the cloudberries. I hid the bag, so nobody would find it and get killed, but yesterday I put it in our larder with the other supplies. I was sure Shelk's men would eat the berries sooner or later, but I was not sure they would work on the Devils. I am glad they did. Because of this, we live, and are out of danger.

We are free of the Devils, Tiger.''

Tiger went to the edge of the cliff and looked down. What he saw made him sick with horror and pity. Shelk's men, invincible fighters the night before, were now crawling on the ground, retching and screaming in anguish. A couple of them, still on their feet, stumbled blindly into trees and rocks, falling and trying to get up again.

"Let us go down," said Tiger. "This is too terrible. Is there nothing we can do?"

"They are already dead," said Baywillow. "But let's go."

They found Shelk lying on his back, his face grey, his eyes closed. Tiger spoke Shelk's name several times, and finally Shelk opened his eyes, staring blankly into space.

"Shelk, I have revenge upon you," said Tiger.

The dying man seemed to regain a little of his strength and sneered, "You think you can kill me. You are wrong. I'll come back. I won't forget, and you'll never forget, either. I'll come back! You can expect me at any time. There will be no peace for you."

"I did not do this to you," said Tiger. "Of all my people, I was the only one who did not know. I wanted to meet you in a fight. Still, I have revenge upon you. You killed my father and my brother, and I am the eldest son. The revenge is mine."

Tiger lifted his spear, but Baywillow checked his movement and spoke: "No, Tiger, you're wrong." He turned to Shelk: "You killed *my* father and *my* brother, and *I* am the eldest son. The revenge is mine."

With his hand-axe, he broke Shelk's head.

PART TWO

SHELK

THE SACRIFICE

Úre aéghwylc sceal ende gebídan worolde lifes.

Beowulf

The man called Shelk walked slowly up the path which only three men were allowed to tread. His head was bent, his hands behind him. His mood was in keeping with the day, for a great wind soughed in the pines and spatters of rain fell from time to time. He was keeping a tryst; one which he had kept, without fulfillment, for as many days as he had fingers on both hands.

He was well dressed, in clothes of caribou skin and a close-fitting cap of wolverine fur; his boots were waterproof sealskin. His dark beard, already turning grey at the roots, hung down over his chest. His eyes were fixed on the ground in front of him. Shaded by a heavy brow, they formed the most impressive feature of his brown, weatherbeaten face with its broad, high-bridged nose.

He reached the little hut on the crest of the hill and stopped outside for a moment to look around. The hill commanded a great view of the lands to the north, where endless vistas of forest faded into the distance, obscured by sheets of rain. In front of him was Caribou Lake, where the waters of the Great River collected before their tempestuous run through the Gorge. The

Gorge itself was hidden by the trees, but the sound of the cataract in the distance hung in the air. Autumn was here. He stepped into the empty hut and kindled a fire.

When the fire began to blaze, he dropped a few rocks into it. He took a big wooden vessel and poured it half-full of water from a container that had once been a horse's stomach. He put honey and a bunch of dried meadowsweet, of which a stock hung from the roof, into the water. When the rocks were heated through he dropped them into the water to make a hot brew, which he stirred vigorously with a stick before taking the first draught.

"Ah," he said involuntarily, putting down the pot. He wiped his beard and looked out: he had heard something moving. For a moment he brightened, but the gloom returned to his face as he saw who was approaching.

It was a Black man, not as tall as Shelk, but broad-shouldered and lean, with a narrow face and a hawklike nose. He was moving rapidly, and the expression on his face drew Shelk out of the hut. The newcomer stuck his spear into the ground and rested on it for a moment, regaining his breath. Shelk saw his eyes fill with tears.

"What is it, Fox?" he asked. "I have been expecting bad news for days."

Fox sank to his knees. "My sons are your sons, Left Hand," he whispered.

"Yes," said Shelk, "you have been as a brother to me always—to us. And now . . ." He paused. "I think I knew it days ago when the Sun God rose so red and terrible and the beetles crawled on his face. I looked at him boldly. He was shrouded in mist and the deviltry was eating him. What have I done? Where are we at fault, Fox?"

"I don't understand it, Left Hand. All I know is that

Right Hand is no more. He is dead, killed by black sorcery, by a Black man whose magic is greater than ours."

Shelk laid his hand on Fox's shoulder. "Come in. You need a hot drink. Then you can tell me."

Inside the hut, Fox took a grateful draught of the meadowsweet tea.

"A Black man. Do you mean the leader of the island people? The man Goshawk told us about?" asked Shelk.

"I don't trust that fat man!" cried Fox. "When the messenger brought him here after the victory of Right Hand at Blue Lake, I wanted him killed. But you wouldn't have it."

Shelk nodded. His gaze wandered idly, without emotion, over the few furnishings of the hut. "Goshawk took the vow," he remarked.

"He speaks without reverence," said Fox.

"Dear Fox, it's just his manner of speaking. I believe he's sincere. But now, Fox, tell me. I know the plan. Viper was to be put in command of Blue Lake. Goshawk told us of a White village out in the islands, led by a Black man . . ."

"A Black man called Tiger," said Fox. "Goshawk told us that he was young but carried a tiger tooth on his chest, and so must be a great hunter and leader, perhaps from that clan at Trout Lake. What Goshawk didn't tell us is that he's a great shaman too, and that his magic would strike Right Hand and all his men!"

"All his men, too?" echoed Shelk faintly, rocking to and fro.

"He should have told us, Left Hand. I think he's a traitor."

"Come, come," said Shelk. "As I remember his tale, he saw Tiger only once, and described him as a civil and personable young man. How could he guess that such a man was a great sorcerer? And when this dreadful thing happened, Goshawk was here.''

That was indeed true. The last two moons had been a trying time for Goshawk. His wine-cellar empty, he had retreated to his winter house the day after Tiger's visit (the entrance having been widened to allow him to wriggle through), and had promptly gone to sleep. He stubbornly slept off the remarkable after-effects of his long bout, getting up occasionally to drink water and eat a little. He slept through the uproar of the attack on the summer camp, and two more days went by before he felt able to face the world again. Finally he crawled out, blinked soberly at the overcast sky, and started to walk down to the lake, of which he intended to drink a fair portion, as well as taking a refreshing swim.

He never got that far. When he emerged on the beach, he was startled to see two strange Black men converging upon him. In spite of his voluble protests, he was held in an iron grip and immediately brought to the terrible Shelk. That stern warrior was found back at the summer camp in conversation with his lieutenant, Viper, a young but balding Black man of enormous stature, with a full beard. Even though he over-topped the tall Shelk, the authority of the older man was evident. Both were fully armed. At the appearance of Goshawk and his captors, Viper looked amazed, but Shelk merely glanced at Goshawk in a nonchalant way.

To be apprehended in this fashion was not quite new to the divine Goshawk, whose earlier career had been chequered. Sober, he was a different man from the expansive, condescending lord of Blue Lake who had hailed Tiger as a guest a few days before. He had figured out what had happened, and now intended to marshal all his shrewdness to save his skin. The fact that one of his captors was prodding his back with a spear

was no doubt unpleasant, and the austere bearing of
Shelk did not bode well, but after all, he had been in
trouble before and had always managed to scrape
through. So he bowed civilly to the conqueror and ex-
pressed his regret that he had not been present to
welcome him upon his arrival.

"Welcome!" barked Shelk. "Are you responsible for
these people here? They tried to fight us."

"No doubt they were very startled, sir," said
Goshawk. "Of course, if I had been here nothing like
this would have happened. We are pleased and honored
to see you."

The shadow of a grin passed across Shelk's face. He
was now aware that he was dealing with an unmitigated
rascal, and the idea amused him. Most of the people he
met he regarded as utter simpletons. This one might
turn out to be a simpleton too, but at any rate one of a
different breed. The man's brazenness took his fancy.

Shelk felt bored, as he always did after making an
elaborate plan and reaping success without even having
to test it. Fighting Whites was too easy. It had been different planning and executing the strike against those
mammoth-hunters last summer. The brilliant result had
been a reward in itself. Now there were no enemies left
worthy of his steel. But the very outlandishness of
Goshawk's appearance intrigued Shelk. Let him go on.

"Where have you been hiding?" asked Shelk.

Goshawk, grateful for the opportunity to speak, em-
barked upon a long tale about having been ill and
spending days in his winter house fighting death. He
went on to remonstrate about the practice of pricking
sick men's backs with spears, at which Shelk made a
move with his hand and the pricking ceased. Shelk
listened gravely, with an occasional nod, and kept his
imperturbable look all through, a look which had given

Goshawk qualms at first, but now encouraged him.

Then Goshawk was seized by an inspiration. He rapidly passed on to his favorite topic, which was the singularity of the children of the Gods. It was a lucky move. Shelk was now listening to him with evident interest. Sweating with earnestness, Goshawk told him about his experience. "The children of the Gods are inviolable, sir," he finished.

Shelk remained silent and thoughtful for a while. The idea was new to him. "You say the Troll imps die and the children of the Gods survive," he said finally. "Show me!"

"If it please you, sir, so I will," said Goshawk, and proceeded to facts. They were fortunately at hand. Shelk had, of course, noticed the large number of brown children, and had made inquiries about their origin; but all the Whites could tell him was that their God had vanished, and they seemed to think this was the reason for their defeat.

For the first time in Goshawk's life, the facts of the world were in his favor. Shelk still thought of him as a rascal, but an interesting and potentially useful one. His original idea of having Goshawk executed was forgotten. Instead he asked for details of Tiger's visit and the islanders, topics on which the Whites feigned ignorance and stupidity. Goshawk was quite ready to talk. His recollections were somewhat dim, however; he described Tiger as a charming young man, polite and intelligent. It was Tiger's good luck that Goshawk had not noticed his limp; nor had the Whites volunteered this information.

His story told, Goshawk was sent to headquarters at Caribou Lake in the company of a messenger who had strict orders not to lose the prisoner. It was not a pleasant journey. Goshawk was out of shape, and in the beginning he felt he would probably drop dead soon. In addition he had to spend the nights bound hand and foot, which really was superfluous, as he would not have had the strength to flee. But he had a healthy constitution, and his strength returned gradually. When he arrived at the Caribou Lake camp, he had lost a great deal of weight, and was in better shape than he could remember being for a long time.

Here he was amazed to find himself in front of Shelk again, and it took him some time to realize that it was not the same man. They looked alike, dressed alike; even their ornaments were identical. Each man wore the same magnificent amber necklace. In spite of the similarity, though, Goshawk found that this was a very different man indeed. Their interview was long, and he left it with many things to think about. He told no one what had been said until much later, when he shared his story with Tiger.

After a day's rest, the messenger was dispatched back to Blue Lake; but he never got there, and no news came back to Caribou Lake. After a long wait, another messenger was sent. He, too, was never heard of again.

Then, at last, news came through. The runner had been attacked and wounded on his way. His story was that Shelk (Right Hand) had been making ready to set out for the island, when the camp at Blue Lake was suddenly attacked by a strong group of Blacks. It was thought that they were led by Wolf, the former chief of Big Lake, who had managed to escape with some of his men when their settlement was taken. The attack had been repulsed easily enough, because the enemy, though unquestionably brave, was badly organized. Still, the expedition had to be postponed for a while. Now it was to set out. Viper would be in charge at Blue Lake, while Right Hand went to the island with Lynx and his company.

The story gave Left Hand a clue to the fate of the other runners. They had probably been intercepted by Wolf and his gang. The route would have to be changed.

That was the last Left Hand had heard until Fox came with his bad news.

"Everything has gone wrong since Goshawk came here," Fox cried. "Enemies attacking, messengers intercepted in the woods, and now this disaster!"

"Tell me more about it, Fox."

"The last message—as you remember, Left Hand— was that Right Hand was taking Lynx and his company to the island, leaving Viper in charge. Since then— nothing. But now Viper is here!"

"Viper!" said Shelk startled.

"He is here with all his men and the village people, too. After hearing Lynx's tale, he thought it necessary. Blue Lake has been abandoned."

"Temporarily," interposed Shelk sternly.

"As you say, Left Hand. But Lynx was the only man who came back from the island; and he is dead, too, these five days. He was found by Viper's scouts near the shore. They had to carry him back to Blue Lake, for he could not walk. He cried for water all the time, and his thirst could never be quenched. He pointed right and left in his terror, and said that there were mammoths and tigers coming at him, and that the moon was pursuing him in the daytime, and that the light was that of the northern lights—red, green, blue—not the light of our father the Sun—"

"Yes," murmured Shelk, "I saw it, too. I should have taken heed."

"Lynx told his story to Viper, but sometimes he had to stop and cover his eyes, for the ghosts were crowding in on him all the time—so terrible is the magic of Tiger! He said that the Trolls had taken refuge on a hill with their leader. Lynx actually saw him. He threw a javelin at Tiger, but the magic was working already, dimming his sight, and he failed to strike his target. He felt himself going blind, and he crawled away and hid in the thicket. There his sight came back, and he could see the Black sorcerer standing over Right Hand's prostrate body, his spear raised. That was all he could remember. After that he must have escaped in a coracle, which the scouts found by the shore.

"He told us this. Then he could speak no more, and died at sunrise. After hearing Lynx's tale, Viper decided to abandon the camp at Blue Lake and come back to Caribou Lake, for he did not feel safe so close to that terrible shaman."

There was a long silence while Shelk gazed into the dying fire. Then he rose and said, "It must be done now."

Fox burst into tears. "Please, Left Hand," he begged, "let me do it. You said just now that I have been as a brother to you both."

Shelk smiled at him sadly. "You know better," he said. "This belongs to me, and to me only. And I have no sons, Fox. I absolve your sons."

"If you would only let me—"

"No, Fox. I must do what has to be done, and I must do it alone." Shelk threw a handful of sticks on the fire and watched it blaze up merrily. "Your place is down with the men."

Fox sighed, then got up and went out. Shelk watched him go down the path and vanish out of sight.

When he was gone, Shelk started to work. He did it

methodically, but with an abstracted air; his thoughts were far afield. He searched the ground for some time, until he found a boulder that suited him. It was easy enough for a man of his strength to lift it, and it had one sharp edge, which he studied carefully. Then he nodded, almost as if performing to an audience. But there was no one to see him, not even the sun, for the sky was still grey with heavy clouds. He looked up as if waiting for a sign, but no sign came, and Shelk, with a powerful heave, lifted the rock and carried it to the door of the hut.

Inside, he placed it with the sharp edge facing upward, and moved it several times before he was satisfied. With a stick he raked some of the embers from the fire and left them glowing on the floor. Then he went out again, to start on a new search. This took longer, and he hesitated often. At last he held a big, smooth stone in his hand. He lifted it and swung it easily. Again, he nodded.

Shelk went back to the hut with the stone in his left hand. In the open doorway he stopped and stood for a while, looking down at both his hands: the left, with the big, smooth stone; the right, empty. Somehow the empty hand seemed to be no longer a part of him. He moved his fingers. They obeyed his will. He looked at the fingers, one by one, stretching and flexing them.

"Right Hand," he said aloud, marveling at it. It was supple and firm. It looked just like the other. He dropped the stone from his left hand and held both hands out in front of him. So similar. Yet his left hand was his work hand. But the right! It was the hand of pleasure, the hand that knew the softness of a woman's body, the luxuriance of a sable's skin, the roughness of the pine's bark, the smoothness of a stag-antler's velvet.

For a long time, he collected himself. He had decided,

but his hands were unwilling. Yet they would obey. He flexed his fingers once more, then bent down to retrieve the stone.

He stepped firmly into the hut, dropped on his knees before the boulder, and carefully positioned his right index finger across the sharp edge. His left hand rose with the stone and came down in a gigantic blow. Reeling with the shock, he pushed the finger-stump against the glowing embers on the floor, and the reek of burned flesh filled the hut. Then his strong body jerked back, and he fell on the floor.

Outside, there was a black flutter in the wind. A raven alighted, took a few steps toward the door, turned its great beak to the side, and cocked an eye into the hut.

"Son of the Sun, Guardian of birds," said the raven chattily.

GREYLAG

Each day they walk the sky
And measure time for man.

Vaftrudnesmál

Once more he was looking into the eyes of the old man. The intensity of their gaze was heightened by the halo of white hair around the thin, wrinkled face.

"Uncle Greylag! Uncle Greylag!" he said. As always in his hour of need, the apparition had come to comfort him. There were no further words, and the apparition faded away, but a sense of rightness, of an ordeal passed, slowly filled him, as if everything was fitting into place. That shadow from the past had been with him before.

The man who called himself Shelk had grown up nameless. His mother, who had lost her husband, returned to her father's house with her two newborn children. There she renounced her old name.

"Under that name I was married to the hateful man you chose as my husband," she said. "Now I am free, and I am the mother of two sons. I choose my own name, and so shall they when they become men. From now on you shall call me Skylark, for I feel as if I have wings and could rise straight into the sky, singing." But she never told anyone the real reason for her new name.

Her parents were astonished at the change in her. From a submissive girl, she had turned into a proud, self-willed woman. She soon took command of the house, for her mother was ailing; and four years passed by in this way. She refused to give names to the two boys, but they came to be called Left Hand and Right Hand, because they were mirror images of each other, and the firstborn was left-handed. The boys grew up with the marks of their father's race in their faces, and Skylark knew well what was said about them behind her back; but no one dared say anything to her face, for her anger was quick. She chose her lovers now among the young men, who stood in awe of her because of her beauty and strength of will. Only one of the young men she spurned, and he hated her for that, for the ridicule it brought on him; his name was Stag.

In the boys' fifth year, the Great Illness swept through the little community on the coast of the Salt Sea and killed more than half of its members. No one knew whence it came or why, but some of the older people muttered that it was the doing of Trolls, and that nothing good ever came of bringing up Troll imps among men. Whatever the cause, the twin boys never caught the disease, but their mother and grandparents died from it.

The two orphans were then taken care of by their great-uncle, old Greylag the Shaman, a brother of Skylark's mother. He lived well away from the village with his wife, Hobby, and a small adopted boy called Fox. The parentage of little Fox was unknown, but it was said that he was a foundling.

The Shaman was a learned man, who had spent many years of his youth wandering and picking up the secrets of his trade. It was said that he had lived with the Trolls and spoke thier language. He taught the boys a strange and secret tongue, which he later told them was indeed that of the White people. His powers were great: he could stare down an aggressive stranger and bend him to his will; he knew all about healing herbs and berries; he could cast a spell and send sickness or death to his enemies. As he noticed the quick intelligence of his two wards, he was pleased, and they soon became his disciples. Fox, one winter younger, was only able to learn the simpler tricks of the shaman's trade, but Left Hand made great progress and became old Greylag's favorite. Right Hand, though full of promise, was too often torn away by his passion for hunting and trapping.

Shelk's earliest memories were of the Shaman's wife. Her own children had long ago grown up and left their home, and the loss of them had affected Hobby's reason. She spent most of her waking life talking, as if every impression she received through her senses must immediately pass out again between her lips. Sometimes it was a monotonous mumbling, sometimes a series of interjections. She kept up a tireless commentary on every aspect of her daily life; every moment, every detail, duly registered.

"Oh! Oh! Oh! the firewood's gone, now I have to get some more, and the boys are away, skylarking like their mother, would they had been squirrels instead, bringing things home, and Oh! but was that a thunderclap, and Oh! Oh! Oh! the good old sun is coming out, yes he comes out, our good old Father the Sun, and just feel now how he warms me up, good and warm all into my bones, and look there, the tree pipit, he soars upward, there will be a song right away, yes there he is singing and coming down just like a falling leaf, and perches in the top of that pine, just think of sitting up there and seeing everything, bless his little heart, he sees all but he tells nothing, he just goes on singing, and Oh! that tern, she took her fish, what a splash she made, and now she flies back to her rock, what a swift! swift! thing she is, and Oh! the cloud is before the sun again, and the chill comes into my bones, but no matter, our Father the Sun will be out again soon, he comes back every day, and blessed are we to have him, Ouch! that was a sharp rock, should look where I am going, and now I must have a pee, seems I do nothing else all day long these days, *sssss:* many ants flooded I'm sure, and yes that was thunder that was, we'll have a storm soon, it's that way these hot summer days, our Father Sun knows we all need the water before the chives go all woody, here's a bunch and now let me try it, mmmm . . . yes I can still feel the taste, there's life in this old body still, good thing I keep spry, that's needed with these wild young things having to be looked after, and old Father Greylag just as bad as they with his spells and sorcery, but Oh! Oh! Oh! look at the buzzard and all the small birds mobbing it, you'd think they'd be afraid but no, plucky little things they are Oh! you startled me taking off like that, don't fret, little eider duck, I'm not out for your eggs today, and there's the redshank whistling and whistling, round and round he goes, legs trailing, I'm not out for your eggs either so calm yourself, now here is a good piece of driftwood: my, my, that will burn merrily, I wonder how it gets so smooth and beautiful, maybe the fish nibble off the bark, and Yes! here is old Father Sun again, welcome to you, and here are some good sticks, yes lovely sticks they are, Oh! there goes the tree pipit again, bless his little heart for that song, and keep him safe from the hawk, funny thing he's been back every summer and always sits in that tree, but Oh! I wonder if young Falcon will bring us some game soon, you'd think Father Greylag might do some trapping but he leaves that to Right Hand and Fox, well they are good at it bless them, and that capercaillie yesterday was wonderful, fowl and fish and oysters are the best for me with my poor teeth, here's another good piece of wood, I think I have all I can carry now, so back home it is, Oh! how fine the house looks from here, I have to hand it to Greylag he keeps it up, and that Sun Pillar is a noble thing, well I remember him carving away at it, yes we were younger then, Oh! that was a flash of lightning, we'll have rain soon, better get home while the wood is dry, now they'll be back soon and want a dry shelter . . .'' And so the old woman would hobble back toward the house, words pouring from her mouth.

All was well as long as she talked; she was then in a sunny mood, open to the world and reflecting its every facet, like a tranquil sheet of water. Sometimes she grew silent, and then nothing could reach her. She would sit cross-legged on the floor, an unusual position among the Blacks, rocking slowly from side to side and crying quietly. At these times, the household chores fell to Greylag. He would handle the necessities, such as tending the fire and cooking the food. Passing her by, he often stopped to stroke her tear-stained cheek. When he was unable to stand the dreadful silence, he would retreat out of doors, for a lesson with the boys perhaps, while Hobby wrestled with her demons in solitude.

In a somber mood, Greylag would sit down beside the great Sun Pillar, one of the wonders of the boys' world. It rose to the height of two men, its top crowned with the ochre-red Sun Globe, and its sides carved into animal designs.

"Those who have little wisdom follow the Moon," he explained, "but the wise man follows the Sun, who is our father, and takes little heed of the Moon, who is only his woman. This was known to the sages of the old times, but their teachings were forgotten until I called them back to life. For I have divined the ways of the Sun.''

Greylag had devoted much effort toward understanding the sun. The crude astronomy of the moon-stick was for him a thing of the past. Based on observations throughout his long life, he could predict the days of summer and winter solstice. When he and his tribe moved to their new village, more than five winters before the orphans came into his care, he had carefully chosen the site of his house according to the sun's decrees.

As befitted the secrecy and power of his calling, he settled well outside the village. There he erected his first sundial, a long stick that he drove into the ground, using a plumb line to make sure it was perpendicular. The length and direction of its shadow told him where true north was and the day of the solstice.

On that midsummer evening, he looked forward to the setting of the sun in the northwest. Days before he had worked up to the right position, so that he could watch the sun set right behind the small island he called Summer Island, on the horizon. This gave him one of his sightings. For the other, he had to wait till midwinter, when the sun set behind Winter Island. Where the two lines crossed, he erected the mighty pillar on which he had worked so long.

''The animals come and go as the Sun bids them, and the flowers bloom as he decrees. But the Sun's own cattle are the mammoth, the caribou, and the shelk. In the summer, the Sun goes north; you can see his glow up there at midnight, when he is beneath the land, and that is where the mammoth and the caribou are. You may see the majesty and power of the Sun in the mammoth, but do not forget that you see his gentleness and love in the caribou. In the winter, when the Sun comes south and the north is cold and dark, they follow him into our lands. Thus you see them at the base of the pillar, holding it up. Carried by them you see the hunters of mammoth and caribou with their gear: the mammoth-hunter with his fire and heavy spear; the caribou-hunter with his disguise and antlers.

"Above them you see the shelk, for he is still closer to the Sun, and he shares the majesty of the mammoth and the gentleness of the caribou. He is the summer animal here, the mightiest and proudest of the antlered tribe. But in the winter he draws south like the Sun. Above him, you see the shelk-hunter with his atlatl."

Many other animals climbed the pillar in an intricate pattern, and near the top a snake wound around it; because snakes are only abroad in the summer, when the sun is closest to the earth. Higher still was the flaming globe of the sun itself, red as the blood of life, red with the true color of the sun when it enters and leaves the world. The boys looked up in awe at the magnificent structure.

Greylag and his family lived in temporary dwellings for a whole year, until the second Midsummer Day gave him his final directions. He marked the spot where the Sun Globe's shadow fell: that would be the entrance to his house. By the time he built it, his youngest son, Falcon, the only one of his children who had accompanied him and Hobby to the new village, had already left them to make his own home with the tribe.

"By rights we ought to move with the Sun's cattle," Greylag said. "I did in my young days, but now I'm too old."

"Did you follow the caribou, Uncle Greylag?" asked Right Hand.

"I went north with the caribou one spring, when the

snow melted. It was a long trek, and I saw how the small groups of animals united into ever greater herds, until there was a sea of animals streaming north and the click of their hoofs grew into thunder. Then I lost them! It was in the land of the Whites, whom foolish people call Trolls. Instead of tracking the caribou, I stayed with the Whites for a summer and a winter, learning their ways and language."

Left Hand interrupted him eagerly: "Is it true that our father was White?"

Greylag smiled. "Your father was White, and a better man than those who drove him away. He was just a boy when he came to us, but when he grew to man's estate, he struck down the wrongdoer who abused your mother. Then he left us as mysteriously as he had come. Truly he was a denizen of the northlands, and he came and went like the caribou."

"When I grow to man's estate," said Left Hand, fiercely, "I shall seek him out and honor him. I wish to see my father before I die."

"That is right," said Greylag. "You should honor your father above all others except our Father the Sun."

Left Hand was silent. In his mind he saw his unknown father, a strange and wondrous figure, silvery white like the foam-topped waves in a westerly gale. He was faceless and radiant, a moving light in the night, or great and shining like the sun itself! He sighed. "I wish—" he began, but he was interrupted by Right Hand.

"Have you been in the south too, Uncle Greylag?"

"Yes. I have seen the world. I have followed the shelk, the noblest of the Sun's cattle, to the Land of Flints, which is their winter abode."

"What sort of people live there, Uncle Greylag?"

"The people are like us, and speak our tongue, but

there was an old shaman who knew the High Language and the wisdom of the old times. I learned much from him.

"They also have an animal that is unknown here. It is called the boar, and its meat is sweeter than that of any other four-footed beast, sweet as the white meat of the wood pigeon, sweet as the red meat of the salmon in the sea. Ah!" He smiled, reminiscing.

As he regaled the boys with such stories, Greylag's good humor returned. With a twinkle in his eye, he leaned forward. "You will turn into a goosefoot bush if you sit rooted to the ground like that," he told Left Hand. "Look!" and he pulled on orache stalk out of Left Hand's hair and held it at arm's length. The orache immediately sprang into life and shrilled at him in angry tones, "Not so! Not so! Give a poor fellow a chance, will you?"

The boys grinned. They knew these tricks almost as well as Greylag himself, but this was his signal for them to get up and leave him to his thoughts.

The great Shaman's fame had spread far. Many journeymen sought him out and stayed as his apprentices for a moon, a winter, or even longer. They were always welcome, for Greylag loved to teach, and the strangers brought news and stories as well as a humble trick or two of their own.

Skua was one of them, a young man with a pair of shrewd eyes in an ugly face, which he could contort into incredible grimaces; but his voice was more beautiful than that of anybody else. He stayed longer than any other, made friends in the village, and settled down as a member of the tribe. He attached himself to one of the most respected hunters, Stag, and divided his time between Stag's retinue and old Greylag's classes. His songs brought tears to every eye, and his stories of great hunts, of ghosts and Trolls, and of the mysteries of the Sun and Moon moving in majesty across the skies were made doubly thrilling by the measured swell and surge of his delivery. Skua's shows were rare events. He performed only seldom, knowing that this heightened the demand, and so he came to be the highlight of the festivals, especially the greatest festival of them all, the Midsummer Feast.

Colorful and gay as a wreath of midsummer flowers, the celebration focused on a moment of stillness and high solemnity. This was when the Chief of the tribe took the oath of leadership and devotion for the year to come. Year after year, old Lion the Chief had stood up, flanked by two immense shelk antlers forming a grandiose triumphal arch, to repeat the ancient formula administered by the Shaman one step behind him, while the sun dropped behind Summer Island.

The sign for the revelry to start again was given when Greylag fitted the lion-skin robe over the Chief's shoulders. With a shout of joy the people thronged around their chosen leader, and great bonfires blazed up. Now the merrymaking would go on through the brief, twilit night and peter out slowly in the morning. For once, Skua did not stint. He performed over and over again, greeted with roars of applause, until finally, exhausted but still cheerful, he had no strength to continue.

For all his majestic presence at the Midsummer Feast, Lion was now an old man who had survived his own sons. For a long time it had been tacitly assumed that Stag would eventually succeed him as Chief. Stag was a big man, in his mid-thirties by the time the twins approached the age of initiation. Taciturn and unsmiling, he had an angular, clamp-jawed face that seemed somehow larger than life; his gaze was steady and cold.

The boys feared him without knowing why. He never spoke to them for good or ill, but it was whispered that he had been an enemy of their mother's, and they did not relish the thought of his coming chiefdom.

In recent times, though, another man with the makings of a chief had come to the fore. This was Falcon, Greylag's son and a great friend of the boys. He lacked the impressive stature of Stag, being short and spare, but he was keen and sharp-witted, and more than once had shown such superior prowess as a hunter that many a provider wanted to be led by him.

Now the time had come. In the fifteenth summer of the boys' life a great change came over Sun Village. The old Chief died. It was said that he suddenly sank to the ground, and when the tribesmen tried to raise him, half of his face was dead, while the other half remained alive. He did not speak a word, and next morning his breath was gone, despite all Greylag's administrations. The Chief's people buried him in state on a high ridge overlooking the Salt Sea, and turned to look for a successor.

What deliberations were held in the Council of the Men, the boys never knew, but they saw Stag stomp off to his house with jaws clamped tight and a smoldering anger in his eyes; and they knew the outcome of the election even before Falcon came to them, smiling, the next morning. He carried two javelins.

"You are now coming of age," he said and embraced them both. "So I thought you could use these. As the future Chief of Sun Village, it behooves me to see that you have the best, for I look upon you as my young brothers."

The spears were of beautiful workmanship, with thin, deadly flint tips. "See to it that you make a straight throw. Their place is between the ribs of the caribou, or you will break the point."

Right Hand laughed happily, weighing the spear in his hand. "This is a great gift, Falcon. Its place will be between the ribs of the caribou, as you say. But if ever an enemy rises up against Falcon, it will find its way between his ribs, too."

"There are no enemies in Sun Village," said Falcon.

Right Hand looked thoughtfully at him. "Don't be too sure, Falcon. There is one who is not happy about your chiefdom."

"You mean Stag? I knew he wanted to be Chief. But he held his peace and bowed to the decision of the Council."

"That is what makes me suspicious," murmured Right Hand. But Falcon, in his happiness, took little heed of the boy's words.

Everybody now turned to the preparations for the Midsummer Feast. Hunters brought in two bison carcasses, to say nothing of smaller game. Additional fare was provided by the women, who also gathered salt and herbs to spice the meat. The salt was scraped from the drying rockpools and rubbed into the meat, together with sweet gale and tansy. Stocks of angelica, sorrel, chives, chickweed, and silverweed roots were laid up, and perhaps most important of all, hoards of berries and wine were brought out from secret hiding places. The berries were lingonberries and cranberries, their taste now sweetened by the frost of winter. There was still a skin or two of the autumn's black wine, which was now judiciously blended with the birch-syrup wine of the spring.

Evening after evening, the thrilled boys watched the sun set ever closer to Summer Island. Greylag smiled in-

dulgently. His reckoning would not fail him. He knew
the day.

On Midsummer Eve, the two shelk antlers were painted
with ochre and planted beside the Sun Pillar in front of
Greylag's house. The house was decorated with gar-
lands of green leaves and the small, tinted wild flowers
of early summer: red campion, speedwell, and heart-
sease. In the evening, the people of Sun Village gathered
on the beach, smiling with anticipation and admiring
the decorations. In the warm light of the evening sun,
the red-painted, many-tined shelk antlers seemed incan-
descent, like two great tongues of fire rising out of the
ground. There were appetizing smells too, infused with
the aroma of the sea. Beside a blazing fire the bisons
were being butchered, and some pieces were already on
the roast.

Nobody could say how much Hobby understood of
what was going on, but she was clearly in a happy
mood, moving about in the expectant throng and talking deliriously about the beauty of it all. The children
whistled through blades of grass, making sounds that
were interspersed with the sonorous tapping of tomtoms, as the drummers tried out their instruments. One
of them had his drum upside down and was using it for
a wine-barrel. All were amused by this new trick, and
fortifying sips were quickly distributed from the somewhat leaky vessel.

Right Hand stole into the lean-to to gloat once more
over Falcon's marvelous gift. On Midsummer Day no
weapons were allowed on the beach, and the boys had
reluctantly stowed away their new javelins. A moment
later Right Hand ran out, consternation in his face. He
wriggled through the milling crowd and caught up with
Left Hand.

"Left Hand," he asked softly, "did you take the javelins?"

"Of course not. Are they gone?"

"Come and see," said Right Hand, and tugged him along.

Inside, the boys rummaged around. Then they looked at one another, dismayed. The javelins were indeed gone, and as far as they could see, nothing else was missing.

"Someone's taken them," said Left Hand.

"A thief! But who would steal them? Everyone in the village knows them. Why, we've been showing them to lots of people."

"And there are no strangers here," said Left Hand. "Everybody says the people in Moon Village are thieves, but I haven't seen—"

Right Hand gripped his arm. "Wait! I'm beginning to understand," he said slowly. "Yes. Let's go out and look."

As soon as they were outside, Right Hand ran up to the edge of the forest, where he could survey the mass of people. "Almost everybody seems to be here . . . Uncle Greylag and Falcon, of course, are not . . ."

They knew that these two, the principal characters of the festivities, would not make their appearance before sundown, when Falcon was to take his oath and be proclaimed Chief. Until then, they would be secreted somewhere in preparation for the great moment. "They're either in Falcon's house or in the cave. That's my guess," said Right Hand. "But do you see Stag anywhere?"

"No," said Left Hand. "No, I can't see him, can you?"

"Just as I thought," said Right Hand grimly. "And if

I'm not mistaken, one or two of his henchmen are missing also; and so is our moon-prophet, Skua. There is deviltry afoot, Left Hand. We must find Falcon and Greylag and warn them. I see now what's being planned.''

"You mean—with our javelins?" asked Left Hand, suddenly alarmed.

"Yes. The javelins of the Troll imps, brother mine. You know what they call us."

Left Hand nodded. "I'll run to the cave, and you go to Falcon's house. There isn't a moment to lose."

No more words were needed; they separated and ran, telling nobody of their suspicions. And that was their first mistake.

Left Hand made his second mistake almost immediately. The cave was in the wood. It was not a real cave but a wide crack between two great rocks, covered by an immense boulder. Here, Greylag and his family had spent their first year with the tribe. Now Left Hand sped headlong down the narrow path, too filled by the urgency of his mission to take precautions. Suddenly somebody tackled him, and Left Hand went down, all but stunned by the fall. Lying on his face, he was pinned by several men, and one of them clamped a hand over his mouth to keep him from screaming out.

"Keep him down," somebody hissed. "Here, give me a rope. Stuff something into his mouth. Ough! He's biting me!"

The boy's hands and feet were tied. He tried to cry out, but the sound was muffled by the gag. "We'd better kill him," said a low voice he could not mistake: it was Skua.

The next speaker was Stag: "Good thing we heard him coming. That was quick work."

"Better kill him right away," said Skua again.

"No. Not now. That's bad luck. The others first."

"Oh, Stag," pleaded Skua. "It's dangerous to leave him alive. If it's all right to kill Greylag and Falcon, why not the Troll imp? Nobody will suspect us. They'll think he's fled—after murdering his benefactors."

"You don't understand, Skua." Stag was still holding Left Hand's arm in an iron grip, and Left Hand could feel the man shake with anger. "I'll kill Falcon myself. To put that undersized squirt before me is an insult. I'm more of a man than he'll ever be. And you shall be a shaman if you kill Greylag. But they come first. It's bad luck to start by killing someone else."

"In that case"—and there was an undertone of laughter in Skua's beautiful voice—"in that case we'll let him kill himself."

"How do you mean?"

Skua did not answer, but Left Hand felt a noose being slipped around his neck. His legs were forced backward, and he could feel the rope tied about his feet. Suddenly the men let go of him, but as he stretched out, he felt a terrible pressure around his neck. He labored desperately for breath. All his veins seemed to swell up, and his manhood rose in a futile erection. He dimly heard the mocking laughter of the men. Then they were gone. All he knew now was an incredible agony. He tried to force his legs and feet back to ease the pressure around his neck, yet every muscle in his protesting body was trying to straighten him out. He was blind, his mind filled by a single unceasing scream in a raging blackness.

That was how Right Hand found him, half strangled but not dead. He cut the bonds and, sobbing with fury, carried his unconscious brother into the wood to safety.

STAG

Mine eye hath seen his desire upon mine enemies.

Psalms 54:7

I have no sons.

The words brought another image, of a tall young woman, laughing, standing broad-legged in a landscape of silver-stemmed birches. Her chestnut-brown hair hung down to her hips. Her arms were stretched out to a caribou cow and her calf, who advanced shyly toward her. She was talking softly to them. He himself was standing behind her, hardly daring to breathe. The sweetness of the image hurt him inexpressibly more deeply than the memory of the agony he had suffered in Skua's noose. That agony had been avenged.

I have no sons, I have no father.

I have a brother.

He had come to life in his brother's arms, but it was not until the next evening that they heard the full story of what had happened on that fateful Midsummer Eve. It was Fox who told them, at their old hiding-place by Watersmeet. His story confirmed all their suspicions.

At the moment when old Greylag was to have robed his son Falcon with the Chief's mantle, both their dead bodies were carried in. It was Skua who stood up and told the people how he and Stag had found them murdered. Never had Skua been more eloquent; never had he swayed his audience as he did with this tale. There was terror in every heart, and all those who heard the story dissolved in sobs. At the climax of his speech, Skua pulled the murder weapons out of the two bodies and held them high for all to see in the last slanting rays of the setting sun. They were the javelins of the two Troll imps.

"Thus the Troll folk repay all the kindnesses that our dear Shaman and Chief-elect have heaped upon them for so many summers and winters," said Skua in his vibrating voice, while tears started into his eyes.

After recounting these events, Fox paused. Then he said simply, "Both points were broken. That's how I knew you couldn't have done it. So forgive me, but that man Skua could talk water out of a rock. I'm ashamed I ever doubted you, but when I saw those points, I knew."

Fox had no opportunity to protest his friends' innocence at the gathering of the tribes. A motherly woman took him in her arms, crying over the poor orphaned youth—orphaned for the second time—and practically smothered him at her ample breast. Fox saw Stag stand up. He spoke briefly, but to the point. If the tribe elected him Chief, he swore to hunt down the treacherous Troll imps and bring them to justice. If it was the people's wish, he would lead Sun Village, faithfully and devotedly, ever after.

At this a cry went up: "Stag for Chief! Stag for Chief! Death to the Troll imps!"

Then there was a hush. Hobby had worked her way through the crowd up to the bodies, and now stood silent, looking down at them. Then she raised her head, and her once-vacant eyes were bright and intelligent.

She turned toward Stag, and he backed away from the burning contempt in her gaze.

"You fool and coward!" she said.

Stag smiled, not a very convincing smile, and shrugged his shoulders. "The poor old woman is raving," he said.

"Very natural," interposed Skua sympathetically. "The poor bereaved one. She has been deprived of her reason by this terrible loss."

Hobby took no notice of him. "Carry the dead into the house," she commanded.

It was done in silence. The sun set behind Summer Island, but nobody paid any heed.

"Take down the Sun Pillar!" Hobby said. "Yes, you!" She looked at Stag. He glanced at his followers, then shrugged his shoulders once more. They all helped to tip down the pillar, and Hobby ordered that too to be put into the house. It was so long that the base stuck out of the doorway.

"And now," she said, when all was done, "my last words to you. You are all either fools or scoundrels, but I forgive the fools. You will never catch the boys. And you, Stag, will live to rue this day. Now go away, all of you! All but Fox."

Silently, and somewhat sheepishly, the people withdrew in the gathering dusk. At last only Fox remained, and Hobby stroked his cheek.

"You and the twins are all I have left now. I shan't stay with you; there is only one thing for me to do now, and you must help me. Then you must go and seek out the twins. You know where to find them, but beware that nobody tracks you there. You are big enough to fend for yourselves now, the three of you, and I think I know what you are going to do. My blessing will be with you. Embrace me, Fox!"

In the twilight of Midsummer Night, Fox helped Hobby carry out her final preparations. When all was ready, she told him too to go. Once on the beach, he turned his head. The house was dark and silent, and the beach looked strangely empty with the Sun Pillar gone. Later, from afar, he saw the blaze of the pyre, rising higher and more resplendent even than the Sun Pillar itself. For a long time he looked at it, towering in the still air of the night, until it spread in a burst as the roof fell in, and dwindled to a flickering glow. Then he turned away for the last time.

"And I mean to stay with you two, if you will have me," he finished.

"We will, but not yet," said Right Hand, who was now on his feet, striding impatiently back and forth on the river bank. "You must go back to the village. We need you there, as a spy. There is much to be avenged. I have grieved, but I'm finished with that. The murderers will pay dearly for their deed."

Left Hand nodded. "The murderers were four," he said. "Skua, Stag, and two of Stag's henchmen. You must be our eyes and ears in the village, Fox. Stag will boast of what he's going to do, and you must come here to Watersmeet to tell us."

So Fox made his home with the motherly woman who had taken pity on him, and nobody suspected that he was in league with the fugitives, for he renounced them, as they had told him to do, and made everybody believe that he trusted Stag and Skua's story. "Besides"—he grinned—"nobody bothers about what I think. I haven't reached man's estate yet, as you have done this Midsummer, and they don't think twice about a boy like me."

Stag made no secret of his plans. He meant to make a good show of his efforts to bring the murderers to justice, although he was secretly convinced that they had fled for good and that he would not be bothered by them in future. Skua thought so too, and Fox overheard him saying as much in a secret confabulation with his Chief.

"All you have to do is to spread your net wide for a few days," he said. "Send the men out in twos to track the Troll imps. A moon from now, everybody will have forgotten the whole thing, and we'll be quite safe."

Fox brought this piece of news to his foster-brothers at Watersmeet, and they smiled grimly.

"He has no idea what he's up against," commented Right Hand. "Yes, it's more or less what I thought he'd do, and it suits us perfectly."

"The Sun will lend us his light to strike down Stag," said Left Hand. "You're going to help us, Fox. Here's what you have to do." And he started to detail their plan.

That night Fox returned to Sun Village in an exalted mood. He had always admired his foster-brothers. Now his feelings were those of hero-worship, and the part they entrusted to him filled him with pride.

Right Hand felt that a rehearsal was necessary, and when Fox came to them next morning with the news that Stag had issued orders for a general search, the three boys went through the motions. Then Left Hand disappeared into the woods.

So it happened that Stag, together with one of his men, ran straight upon a trail that seemed almost too good to be true. Crossing a small stream, hardly more than a ditch, he was thrilled to see a series of freshly made footprints along its muddy bank. Both men examined the prints carefully and nodded to each other. It could only be one of the Troll imps.

"What a dunderheaded fool," said Stag contemptuously. "He's still hanging about here, and on top of it all he leaves a clear track."

"Well, it's the best way to get through there," remarked the other man, nodding toward the dense wood.

"Yes, but to leave footprints like a mammoth! Come along. He'll lead us straight to their hiding-place, and we can take care of both of them."

They hurried along the little stream, which wound through dense forest where it did indeed serve as a useful lane. The track was amusingly easy to follow. It was clear that the Troll imp had been striding along at a leisurely pace, apparently without a care in the world. The two pursuers kept shooting sharp glances right and left, but there was no sign of human life apart from the footprints.

Presently they came to a place where the wood receded on both sides of the stream. They stepped into a clearing with moss-covered bedrock and stopped for a moment to look around warily. There might be danger here. But what did happen to them was utterly unexpected and so frightening and amazing that they stood still as if rooted to the ground.

A blinding light stabbed them in the eyes. It was as if the sun had suddenly winked at them from straight ahead. But that was impossible, for the sun was shining all the time to their right. Once more that powerful beam of light flashed into their eyes. It seemed to come from the tree-tops in front of them. Then suddenly the man at Stag's side sank to the ground, a javelin between his ribs. He died without a sound.

Stag snapped into action. Roaring like a wounded bull, he charged into the wood in the direction from which the missile had come. But before he had time to go very far, a voice called out from behind him, "The Sun is striking you down, Stag!"

He recognized the voice of one of his quarries, and spun around to run back to the glade. But as he did so, the same words, in the same voice, echoed from behind him. Realizing his dangerous position, Stag was now shouting at the top of his voice, and finally he was answered by another party from the village. They found him beside the body of his companion. Rattled and incoherent, Stag tried to tell his story, pointing excitedly in the direction from which he thought the sun had winked at him. The hunters listened with amazement. One of them, kneeling by the body, cast a curious glance at Stag. "It's your own javelin," he said. "Look, here's your mark on it."

"But it was the Troll imp who killed him!" roared Stag.

"Are you quite sure you didn't—" began one of the newcomers. But he fell silent when he read the fury in Stag's face. "We'd better carry him home," he said. "It will be a sad day at Sun Village."

"But the Troll! The murderer!" cried Stag.

"Well, he seems to be gone," said the man almost apologetically. "We'd better go back. Don't you think so?"

Still arguing in a loud voice, Stag followed the men who carried their slain comrade into the forest.

Shortly afterward, Left Hand, Right Hand, and Fox met at Watersmeet. Right Hand was exultant.

"Good work, Fox," he said. "You handled the sun-pool perfectly. I knew it would stop them. That thug by Stag's side was like a sitting bird."

Fox handed over the great mica crystal with which he had dazzled Stag, and smiled a little wanly. "You know,

I was shaky all over," he admitted. "I wasn't sure I had it right, even after we tried it out and you signaled to me."

Fox had indeed had some difficulty learning to handle the cat's-gold mirror. When they first told him to throw a beam of light at a target, he had made as if to throw a javelin with the atlatl. They had to spend the better part of the day coaching him.

The twins had kept the mica crystal as a secret and sacred thing ever since Left Hand found it the summer before and took it out of the rock. He had always been fascinated by the pinpoint flashes of light given out by crystals in the veins that coursed across the rock surfaces like frozen streams. He used to think that the sun was hidden in the living rock, peeping out at him. Then the discovery of a loose feldspar crystal taught him that he could hold this miraculous light-generator in his hands and direct the beam of light where he wanted it to go. The twins soon had a hoard of such crystals at one of their hiding-places. They called them sun-pools, for they gave back the sunlight just like a rockpool.

The great piece of mica, as large as Left Hand's palm, was vastly superior to anything he had found before. From painful experience he knew the brittleness of the stuff. It took him days of patient work to prise it out, undamaged, from its place in the rock. Pointing the beam at the shadow side of a cliff where the spot of light was clearly visible, he learned to handle the crystal with precision. It was an object to be revered; somehow, it was related in his mind not only with the Sun but with his unknown White father. The two sometimes mingled in his dreams. He shared his treasure with no one but his twin brother.

Now it was different. For their plan to work, the crystal had to be entrusted to Fox. Fortunately, practice made him ready. Then Left Hand, the decoy, located Stag and left the trail which led the ill-starred Chief straight into Right Hand's ambush.

"We're indebted to you, Fox," said Right Hand. "You did a good job sneaking that javelin out of Stag's store. He's going to find that very hard to explain to the tribe, even though he gave us the idea when he took our javelins."

"I don't think he ever thought that out himself," said Left Hand. "That was Skua."

"Yes, it does have the Skua smell," agreed Right Hand. "Well, we'll deal with him too, all in its own time."

"What beats me is why you didn't kill Stag," said Fox.

"We have other plans for him," answered Right Hand. "The man I killed was one of the murderers. Now, for the next strike, we really ought to have another of Stag's javelins."

"I can get one for you," offered Fox promptly.

"Impossible, I'm afraid. Stag's going to check his spears every day. He's not a complete fool"

"Not far from it, though," remarked Left Hand, gingerly touching his neck. "To let me get away was a thundering mistake."

"Even so, we mustn't underestimate him, nor that moon-prophet of his. We'll just have to make another javelin ourselves, and put his mark on it. What are you doing, Fox?"

Fox, looking slightly uncomfortable, handed over the piece of bark with which he had been occupied. "We killed a man," he said hesitantly. "Don't you think we ought to—?"

Right Hand raised his eyebrows. On the smooth piece of pine-bark, Fox had engraved the crude likeness of a man. "That's for giving him an afterlife, Fox," he said, "but the man was a murderer, evil, and it was right to kill him. It isn't like killing an innocent animal."

"Still," Fox persisted, "I'd feel better."

With a kind glance at Fox, Left Hand took the piece of bark, and with his finger traced the outlines of the picture. "You're right, Fox," he said, while Right Hand looked on and frowned. "But you're not much of a draftsman, are you?"

At this, Right Hand laughed. "Neither are we. Well, I suppose the fellow only did what he was told to do. Give me the picture."

Before they parted, Fox was given new instructions. No doubt the story of Stag's hapless manhunt was already being told all over Sun Village, and the trust of the people in their new Chief would be seriously shaken. Fox could help by starting a rumor or two. Above all, he must try to listen again to Stag's talks with Skua.

These talks were held in the night, when Sun Village was asleep, which was a great help to Fox. He found it easy to hide by the wall of Stag's house and overhear the discussion. Skua was obviously puzzled by Stag's story. The mystery of the javelin was simple, he said. One of the Troll imps must have stolen into the village at night and taken it. "There's no danger of that now, with Badger sleeping in the store." Skua pointed out.

The sun shining from two places, though, was something Skua could not explain, and it made him uneasy. "Whatever happens, you've got to catch the Trolls as soon as possible," he said. "Otherwise we'll have no peace."

"I'd like to lay my hands on them," said Stag reluctantly, "but I don't want to fall foul of the Sun, if that's the consequence."

Skua drew an exasperated breath. "Never mind the

Sun. I'll take care of that. I'm your shaman, see? It wasn't the Sun you saw, it was a trick. I just can't think how it was played. You go out tomorrow, and don't walk into a trap again."

"Hm," mumbled Stag. "I don't much like that."

"And you call yourself a chief!" Skua chided. "Take four or five men with you. That should be enough to handle those Troll imps. You're not afraid of them, are you?"

"Of the imps? Never!" Stag fumed. "But the Sun sorcery . . . If they have some kind of power . . ."

"The man was killed by a javelin, not by the Sun," stormed Skua. "You have to put a stop to all this nonsense, Stag."

The rumors started by Fox soon took effect. Many people were reminding each other of Hobby's words to Stag, and the mystery of the javelin remained a matter of curiosity and suspicion in spite of Skua's explanations. Above all, the story of the flame of the Sun, which foreboded the death of Stag's companion, loomed ever larger in everybody's mind. What had they done to incur the wrath of the Sun? Was it possible that there had been a different kind of foul play from what they had been told, when Greylag, their beloved Shaman, and Falcon, their Chief-elect, had died?

These developments were faithfully reported by Fox. Right Hand listened. Then he said, "The thing works so well I think we'd better go on in the same way. As long as the weather stays fair, the Sun is on our side." So they laid their plans.

The weather held, and the next morning Fox was perched in a tree high up on a hillside, eagerly scanning the landscape in front of him. He knew that the twins were tracking Stag's party, but he did not know where. Then, somewhere in the land of forest and glades in front of him, he saw the minute spark of reflected sunlight from Left Hand's crystal. He knew now where they were, and from time to time another flash told him of their progress. At last he saw a group of men step out into an open field, where a forest fire had raged two summers ago. He carefully aimed the powerful beam of his sunpool straight at them.

They were too far away for him to see their faces, but he saw them stop for a moment; then a ripple seemed to pass through the line. He gave them another flash, and to his amazement he saw them throw down their weapons and run, vanishing into the wood. Fox looked respectfully at the miraculous object in his hand. Then he climbed down and set out for Watersmeet.

Later, in the village, he heard of the party's un-dignified return. The hubbub brought Skua out of Stag's house. "What's happened?" he asked.

"We're doomed," panted one of the men. "We're doomed! The Sun struck at us, just as Stag described it!"

Scornfully, Skua said, "So? You're hale and hearty as far as I can see. What do you mean, doomed?"

The men looked sheepish, and Skua went on, elaborating his point: "you're like a woman, frightened by your own shadow. Where's your atlatl? Here you are, scared out of your wits by a couple of impudent Troll imps, and the only scratches on you are from the rose-bushes you tore through in your panic."

In his anger, Skua had forgotten that this description applied equally to Stag. The people of Sun Village, gathering around, observed their Chief's confusion and started whispering among themselves.

"Then where is Badger?" someone asked.

It was true Badger was missing. He had been standing at Stag's side when the light struck. For a moment Skua was speechless. Then he collected himself. "He probably fell and hurt himself trying to run away," he said. "Is no one man enough to go back and find him?"

Stag's men looked at their Chief and at one another. "Why don't you go yourself, Skua?" asked one of them.

"Me?" Skua was shocked. "I'm your Shaman. I have better things to do than look for a panic-stricken coward. Watch your tongue!"

A young hunter stepped forth. He had been one of Falcon's men, and his level gaze swept the agitated crowd. "I'll go," he said. "I have no reason to fear the Sun, as some others seem to do. I'll go alone and unarmed."

Fox was back in the village by the time the hunter returned, carrying Badger. He was dead, and the javelin between his ribs bore Stag's mark.

After this, events developed quickly. At midnight Fox was back at Watersmeet with his report. "Badger's dead," he began. "He was brought back by Stoat."

"I know," said Right Hand. "I got him with a slingshot. I had my eye on him the whole time. He was one of the murderers."

"But he had Stag's javelin between his ribs," said Fox, perplexed.

Right Hand grinned. "I put it there. Stag dropped his arms, like the others, when the light struck him. I bet that javelin made a sensation."

"And how!" said Fox. "A council was called immediately. Everybody was there—men, women, and children—everybody but Stag and Skua. They started by deposing Stag from chiefdom and electing Stoat in his place."

"They did well," said Left Hand. "Stoat's a good man. He was a friend of Falcon's."

"Then they decided to call in Stag and Skua. Stag was hauled from his house and charged with killing both of the hunters who were found with his javelins in their bodies. He swore by the Sun he had nothing to do with it. He said the javelins had been stolen. I'm sure he'd been coached by Skua. Then they asked him about Greylag and Falcon, and he swore he had nothing to do with that either. He kept asking that Skua be brought in to testify. So they started a search for him, but he's disappeared."

"He probably ran away as soon as they found Badger's body," said Right Hand. "Most likely he'll go back south where he came from. No matter, I'll find him."

"When he knew Skua was gone, Stag broke down and blamed him for everything. He said Skua wanted to be Shaman and had enticed the others to help him. Stag himself had nothing to do with it. He swore again by the Sun and everything sacred that he was innocent. They took him back to his house and put two men on guard. Then they decided what to do with him."

"And what was that?"

"Send him away," said Fox. "They're just kicking him out. They don't want him in Sun Village any more. Everybody is against him, even his own woman. She says she hates him. The whole tribe is talking of leaving and starting afresh somewhere else. They say there's a curse on the place."

It was Left Hand who found Stag the next day. He was unarmed, and seemed to have been wandering aimlessly all night. He looked shrunken, with red-rimmed, unseeing eyes. When Left Hand appeared before him, he stopped. Left Hand's eyes bored into him, and although the Troll's lips did not move, Stag heard voices. They seemed to come from a bush here, a rock there. They accused him of murdering Greylag, murdering Falcon.

"I didn't do it!" screamed Stag, suddenly defiant. "I didn't! I didn't! I swear by the Sun . . ."

At that, there was a tremendous flash of light.

Left Hand watched as Stag raised a hand to his lips, then fell to the ground. He could hardly believe what he had seen. A murderer and blasphemer had been struck down by the Sun, and lay dead without a wound on his body. He felt his own body shake like a tree in a storm. "I'm glad, I'm glad," he whispered to himself, trying to overcome the terrible emptiness and fatigue that suddenly overwhelmed him.

The words died on his lips, and the great crystal fell from his hand. His heart was telling him a truth as blinding as the flash of light he had wielded.

He was at the point of confession and repentance. If you had given him the time, he would not have died. You had no right.

Left Hand closed his eyes. His lips formed new words: "Father, great White father . . ."

The piece of mica lay in the moss at his feet. There was a rustle in the wood, and Right Hand appeared.

"Thought I heard someone call out," he said. Then his eye fell on the dead man. "So you got him?" he said, with cold satisfaction. "Serves him right. Now we'll settle with Skua."

BLACK CLOUD

—à l'horreur, qui m'obsède
quelle tranquillité succède—
Oui, le calme rentre dans mon coeur—

Nicolas-François Guillard, Iphigénie en Tauride

After Stag's death the brothers separated. Right Hand was grimly determined to take vengeance on Skua. Until that had been done, he would know no rest, and he swore to hunt the murderer down before next summer. But Left Hand was still overwhelmed by the emotions that filled him when he witnessed Stag's death, and he wanted, above all, to find his White father. So they agreed to meet next midsummer at Watersmeet. Yet more than ten summers were to pass before the brothers saw each other again.

The first stop on Left Hand's northward journey was the last outpost of the advancing Blacks on the Salt Sea coast. The place was called Moon Village. To him it came as a great surprise, for that name had always figured in his people's traditions in a most unflattering way. Perhaps that was a different Moon Village, somewhere else and in some other time.

Like Greylag, many of the Sun Villagers believed that the Moon was an inferior deity. Its connection with woman was evident from its phases, which governed her bleeding time. The Moon Village of their fancy was populated by blunderheads and simpletons who had a woman for chief and a new-born babe for shaman. Everything foolish and crooked could be found in that imaginary Moon Village. In the first place, everybody knew that the Moon Villagers were inveterate thieves. In Sun Village you could leave your gear anywhere and find it undisturbed when you returned the next day, even the next summer. In Moon Village you hardly had time to belch before somebody had sneaked it away. A Moon Villager could do nothing right. If he went to hunt the mammoth, the mammoth invariably ended up hunting him. Nor did he know how to impregnate a woman. He chose the wrong orifice, so the children were born with feet in place of hands, or with heads between their legs, and had to be left out for the hyenas. Here, a sensible and helpful man could come to their aid and have his own pleasure out of it, as long as he took care to hide his things out of reach of the villagers' sticky fingers. When a Moon Villager came to a stream, he would stop and wait for the water to flow by so he could cross. He would die of starvation unless somebody happened to come by and help him. He hunted the caribou in the summer, and went fishing for trout in the frozen rapids of midwinter. Building a house, he started with the roof and ended up with the cellar. He used the throwing-stick as a javelin, and the javelin as a throwing-stick. In early summer every Moon Villager went out to pick cranberries.

The foolishness and incompetence of the Moon Villagers was due to their descent from the Moon rather than the Sun. To them, day was night and night was day. One had to pity them, and when an ordinary person did something silly, he had to swallow his vexation at being called a Moon Villager.

Probably no one really took all this very seriously,

and Left Hand in fact found that the people of this Moon Village were no different from his own. The children were perfectly normal, the Chief a skillful hunter, the houses well built. As for thieving, he had to admit that the only time anything had been stolen from him was in Sun Village when Skua and Stag took his javelin.

Left Hand told people he was an itinerant shaman, and he was welcomed warmly. Moon Village had lost its Shaman a winter ago, and they wanted him to stay. He found himself in possession of a house, a woman, and also a name. The name came to him unexpectedly when he was asked about it. He was reluctant to let them know his true identity. There might be stories abroad, false stories about the Troll twins, arising from Stag and Skua's brief reign in Sun Village. At the time he was standing at the center of the village. In front of him was its noblest ornament, two great shelk antlers painted with ochre. They reminded him of the triumphal arch at Sun Village, and without hesitation, he told them his name was Shelk. The name stuck.

So it happened that young Left Hand, now Shelk, became the Shaman of Moon Village for two winters and a summer. He got on well at first. He had been old Greylag's most brilliant pupil, and was really good at his work. The people of Moon Village congratulated themselves on having found such an excellent shaman. He had a profound knowledge of medicinal herbs and was a great healer. Sometimes the masterful gaze of his eyes, beneath their brooding brows, was enough to scare away the evil spirits. To see him speak to the spirits of the rocks and trees and receive their answers was a new and unforgettable experience for the villagers.

The woman they gave him was the widow of the former Shaman, a few years older than he, yet healthy and able. There was one thing wrong with her, though: she did not give him a son, and this began to prey on his mind. As time passed, he got the feeling that people looked at him with pity and tactfully avoided the subject. He told himself that he was imagining things, but the woman, too, was unhappy at being barren. In the end Shelk decided to leave Moon Village.

The Chief accepted his decision with sorrow. They could not wish for a better shaman, he said. If Shelk wished, they would give him another woman. Yet Shelk had made his resolve. Perhaps, secretly, he feared that another Moon Village woman would be no better. When his plans became known, many Moon Villagers whom he had nursed to health came to him, weeping and bringing small farewell gifts. Shelk was moved and grateful, but nothing could shake his resolve. In the time of the melting snow he started out, going north.

Again he felt that he was hunting for his White father. Once he found him, perhaps everything would be all right. He was no man unless he had a son. Satisfying a woman was not enough. Any blackcock in the woods was more of a man than he, but the White One far away would surely know what to do.

Shelk now came to the land of the Trolls, the world of the Whites. He already knew their language, so ponderous and circumstantial, so slow-spoken and ritualistic compared with that of the Blacks. His first encounter was disappointing. Could these short, clumsy people with their pink skins and strange, large faces have anything to do with the white shape in his dream? He towered over them, and they regarded him with awe as one of the children of the Gods. Did they know anything about his father? They told him long stories of their ancestors, but he could get no clues from them. Could one of the White women give him a son? He stayed with the Trolls in their winter village and found that the women desired nothing more than to be embraced by a child of the Gods. He learned the art of love White fashion, the woman astride her man. Hope revived, but once more it was killed by time.

When the sun rose high in the sky, the Whites broke camp. They migrated with the seasons, pitching their summer tents in distant lands to the north. He traveled with them, and when they stopped, he pressed on alone. Everything White came from the north: ice, snow, and in his mind now his father became a luminous, icy figure beneath the polestar.

After years of travel, Left Hand found himself in the Land of Birches. Here, for the first time, he heard of the woman who was to change his life. Many stories were told about her among the Whites. She came and went like a cloud, so she was named for neither plant nor bird, but was called Black Cloud. The Whites looked at Shelk and nodded at each other.

"Is she your sister?" they asked.

Sister? Yes, they explained, she, too, was a child of the Gods, and she had wondrous power over all living things. She had been seen traveling with the caribou, her hands on their antlers. She had been seen playing with wolf cubs like children in the snow. When she raised her hand, the birds of the sky alighted on it, and she spoke to them in their own language. She was a Guardian of birds and beasts.

Where to find her? No, they could not say.

Thus Black Cloud became the object of Left Hand's search, the destination of his journey. He moved from village to village, always asking for her. She was known everywhere. Yes, she had walked by, it might have been last winter; she was moving north—no, east, or perhaps south. No one could be sure. She came and went, like a cloud.

Winters and summers alternated in the Land of
Birches just as they did in the Land of Pines and on the
coast of the Salt Sea. Here, though, the winter was
longer and the snow was heavier. Living among the
Whites in this country, Shelk learned more words for
snow than he thought possible. There was a word for
the kind of snow that formed a hard crust; another for
the soft kind that took faithful foot impressions; yet
another for the light powdery snow of the cold weather
and for the big sticky flakes of the warm. There was one
for snow with alternating layers of soft and hard. For
the large-grained snow at the bottom of such a deposit,
which was melted for drinking-water. The snow that
blew into fine-grained and tightly packed drifts. The
treacherous snow that fell on your neck from the branch
of a tree or hid a pothole under your feet. The snow that
filled the air, like a white darkness, in a snowstorm. The
snow that swept thin veils across the open country under
a clear light-blue sky. The snow that rolled down a slope
in a growing ball, and the snow that slid down in a single
massive sheet. All had their own names and their own
spirits, as did the black and grey clouds, heavy with un-
shed snow. The Guardian of the snow was powerful,
and you had better keep on good terms with him, just as
you did with the Guardians of beasts and birds.

Mammoths paraded across the snowbound plains on
their migrations between the northlands and the forest
in the south. There were solitary rhinos, short-sighted
and surly in their woolly brown coats. The musk oxen
formed a living wall at the sight of men; they would
snort and stamp and refuse to break; no spear could
penetrate their bony foreheads, but a skillful throw at
the body might bring one of them to its knees.

Roving lion prides came from the plains to the north.
One grey autumn morning Shelk, almost dumbstruck,

heard for the first time in his life the roar of a male lion. He watched the great predators hunt down a young rhino; they moved in tactical concert, and the confused woolly pachyderm was finally brought down by the onslaught of two lissom lionesses. The first to fall, though, was the great grey, black-maned lion whose deep voice he had heard that morning.

There were creatures even stranger and more foreboding than lion or wolf, bear or hyena. Two black tigers crossed Left Hand's path. They pattered on, tall and silent, without a look at him. Carrying their heads proudly, they spied as from a tower for bigger, worthier prey; and they vanished in the snow and the twilight like incarnations of the powers of the night.

Once more spring came, and the birches, which had been standing bare and dead for so long, lit up with the tenderest of green. Still Left Hand asked for Black Cloud.

By then word had reached her, too, of the stranger who had been looking for her so intently. The winds are generated by the clouds, the Whites used to say; now Black Cloud asked her wind to carry her to him. The leaves of the birches had just come out when they met.

Left Hand saw a woman tall and brown like himself. Her hair was plaited and artfully coiled around her head, with a raven feather in it. She was younger than he had expected. Under her heavy brows so like his own, her eyes were merry and brown. Her broad nose bore witness to her ancestry, as did her full face, but her mouth had the sensitive lines of a Black woman's, and her body, scarcely concealed by the short caribou-skin frock, was longer and more slender-waisted than the bodies of White women. Her feet were bare; her long legs, like those of the Blacks, were straight. Yet her skin was a light brown. He raised his own arm and saw the same color. Captivated, he looked at her.

Black Cloud saw a man unlike all the Whites: taller, darker, broader-shouldered and narrower-hipped, with more masterful eyes than any White man. He too was dressed in caribou skin. He stood with his arms stretched out to her. His bundle and weapons had fallen to the ground. Every lineament of his face was familiar to her, incredibly and incomprehensibly. In all her life she had been the only one of her kind. Her eyes filled with tears.

She went up to him, laid her arm around his shoulders, and said, "Come!" She pulled him to the nearby tarn. Together they leaned over its surface. There, side by side, were both their faces, each with the same incredulous smile.

"You are me," she said. She spoke in the tongue of the Whites.

"I am you," he agreed.

Their eyes were reflected radiantly in the water.

"Are you my sister? Am I your brother?" asked Shelk.

"No, it is more than that," said Black Cloud. "We were destined for each other when time began. There are none of us except you and me."

They looked at their reflections in silence. Then she said, dreamily, "Only now I know that she down there is I."

"She is you. Why should she not be?"

"To me, she was always the water spirit. How could she be I? There are no humans like that. People are White or Black, but she who looked at me out of the tarn was neither. Yes, she did all the things that I did: plaited her hair, put the feather in it, laughed and wept; never did she make a mistake. Yet if she really was I, then I could not be one of our people. So I went away, leaving my human name behind. Now you are here, and you are just like me. Now I know that I exist.''

She pushed her nose flat with one finger, and the girl in the tarn did the same. Black Cloud laughed.

''There you are: she is I. Up to now I have not even dared believe that it is my real face. Perhaps I had no face at all. Perhaps my hand deceived me when it felt it, perhaps I saw without eyes, ate without a mouth, heard without ears. Perhaps I and all the world existed only in my dream, or in the dream of the water spirit. But you,'' and her fingers moved over his face, ''you have eyebrows like mine, cheeks like mine.''

''A beard, too,'' said Shelk, smiling.

She hardly heard him. Her hand caressed his forehead, nose, and mouth; then her own.

''Who are you?'' he asked. ''They say you are Guardian of birds and beasts.''

''What does it matter what they say? To us they do not exist any more. We are the Different Ones. And now there is no one else but you and me.''

So it was, and so they wanted it to be, this summer and every summer to come.

''My mother was White and my father Black,'' said Black Cloud, ''but I only saw him as a child, or in my dream, I do not know which. I have always been Different, and always wanted to be Similar. They called me a child of the Gods, but I did not want to be a child of the Gods. I wanted to be an ordinary human child, and I wanted to grow up into an ordinary human woman. That could not be, so I left it all: my tribe, my mother, my name. I told the water spirit, 'Go!' and I could see that she told me the same.''

''And where did you go?''

''I went to the animals. If I was not human, then

perhaps I was one of them. I hunted with the wolves and traveled with the caribou. Wait!"

She brought a skin and gave it to him. "Drink!" she said. He put it to his mouth and drank while she watched him, smiling. A strange, sweet liquid flowed into his mouth, and he looked with wonder at the white drops that fell on his hand.

"This is a magic potion and you are the greatest of shamans," he said. "How did you brew it?"

She looked at the sun. "It is time," she said. "Come with me, but take care and move silently."

He followed her through the wood to a rocky hill where the moss had been scraped from a shallow crevice. Here Black Cloud stopped, raised her arms, and began to talk. This was no longer the talk of the Whites. New sounds came from her lips, sounds like the calls of birds and beasts, tender and irresistible; and out of the wood came a caribou cow with her calf.

The cow had only one antler, but the one she had shed was in her mouth, and her jaws were slowly grinding away at it. Black Cloud, who had let down her hair, lifted her short frock. Standing broad-legged like a man, she made water on the rock, and the frothing liquid collected in the crevice. Slowly the cow came closer, until it was right in front of her. Then it spat out the antler, dipped its muzzle, and started to drink. Black Cloud's fingers closed softly on the antler.

Shelk dared not move. In truth, this woman must be the Guardian of the caribou. Now she was at the animal's side, her hand on its back. In the next moment she was on her knees and had started to milk it.

Black Cloud used the excretion of her own body to win the affection of the caribou. This was the same need that made the animals chew their own antlers to stumps, in a saltless and chalkless land. Sometimes three or more caribou would compete for the delicacy. In exchange they gave her their milk, and meat when necessary. Occasionally Black Cloud chose a bull to be butchered.

"But never a cow or a calf," she said. "They are too close to me."

The cows and calves were quite tame, and showed evident delight at being caressed by the children of the Gods. "Now you know why I follow the caribou," said Black Cloud. "Had you done the same, we could have found each other much earlier. Alas, we have lost many summers."

"I could see myself in my brother," Shelk told her, "while you had no one but the water spirit. Perhaps that is why I never doubted like you."

He told her his story, and how he had started out to find his father. He described the shape he had seen in his dreams, and Black Cloud said, "Then perhaps he really is the Sun, whom you revere as the Supreme Being. Perhaps you are the son of the Sun."

"If that is so, I shall never find him here on earth."

"And what did you want with him?"

"I have no son. Perhaps he could have helped me. But now I have you, Black Cloud, and you shall give me a son."

"You shall give me a daughter," she added. "We are the chosen ones. From us the Different Ones will come. They will guard the cattle of the Sun and the birds."

Shelk nodded. Half-forgotten stories emerged from his mind. "We, 'the children of the Gods,' as the Whites call us, have brought forth much of what is wise and good in the world of men. Old Greylag once told me it was one of us who built the first coracle, and one of us who used the first atlatl. Here you stand, and you have made yourself the Guardian of the caribou."

"I shall make you the Guardian of birds," said Black Cloud, laughing.

She kept her word. One day she put a newly hatched raven in his lap.

"It is yours," she said. "Feed it, care for it like your own child, and it will become a true friend. I had a raven once; he died. This one you must attach to yourself."

He did so, and the raven became his.

Once, to amuse Black Cloud, he made one of the caribou cows answer her call. In the language of the Whites, the caribou said, "May you fly high, Guardian of the caribou!"

Black Cloud laughed. "I must remember this."

She bided her time, and took her opportunity when he was out of the way. One day, when the raven alighted on Shelk's raised hand, it uttered in the language of the Whites:

"Son of the Sun! Guardian of birds!"

THE EAGLE FEATHER

The black flints, which are common here, give the strongest fire.

Linnaeus, Scanian Voyage

One summer day, many years later, Shelk returned to Watersmeet, his dreams and hopes far behind him. Black Cloud had given him no son; he had given her no daughter. He trudged along, numbed by his long, solitary journey. Now his steps led him, without any conscious effort, toward his and his brother's old hideout. The raven was his only companion.

Back in the country of his childhood, something rekindled his spirits. He began to think of those he had left behind so long ago, and to wonder what had become of them. He met a stranger, and was going to pass him with only a brief greeting. Yet something in the man's face made him stop. The stranger bowed respectfully.

"You are early, Shelk," he said.

"You know my name, but I don't know yours. To me it is late," said Shelk.

"You are joking, Master," said the man, smiling.

Shelk took a closer look at him. He was a fine figure of a young man, very tall and slim, but broad-shoul-

dered and athletic. His face seemed to radiate hardness
and resolution. A very tough-looking fellow indeed,
thought Shelk. He wore a headband with a single eagle
feather; his hair was thin.

"As if you don't know Viper, who's been at your side
in so many fights," he said. "Are you going back to the
camp?"

Shelk was filled with a sudden suspicion. Once more
he was Left Hand. "Come with me, Viper," he said,
keeping a wooden face. "Take me to the camp. I have
been thinking deeply and have forgotten everything else
for my thoughts."

"That's good," said Viper, looking pleased. "We are
all waiting for your decision."

The raven swooped down to settle on Shelk's
shoulder, uttering its usual greeting, "Son of the Sun!
Guardian of birds!" in the White tongue. Shelk smiled
at Viper's surprise. "Is that your guiding spirit, O
Master?" asked Viper in the same language. Shelk only
smiled ambiguously and hastened his steps. The young
giant, silent and respectful, walked by his side.

They arrived at Watersmeet, and Shelk found it
changed beyond recognition. There was now a big camp
there, with many tents and large numbers of men,
women, and children. He was met by awed glances. The
women bowed low; the men let go of whatever they had
in hand and came smartly to attention. He found it all
very strange, but his face gave away nothing.

"You will find your woman in your tent, Master,"
said Viper politely. Shelk, following his gaze, noted a
tent that was larger than the others and stood by itself.
Without hesitation, he went over and walked in.

The tent was indeed a chief's dwelling-place, richly
furnished and with a comfortable bed, from which a girl
flew up at his entrance. She went down on her knees,

saying, "You're back sooner than expected, Master. Do you wish for anything?"

He searched her face. She was beautiful, according to the standards of the Blacks, but for him no woman could compare with Black Cloud, who had left him and returned to her own people. He said curtly, "Nothing just now. You may go."

The girl went out obediently, and Shelk threw himself on the bed, so tired that even his curiosity was forgotten for the moment. No doubt everything was most strange, but he knew now that Right Hand was alive and would probably be there soon. Somebody touched the door-flap, and into the tent came Fox, older and more lined than the boy Left Hand remembered, yet still the same.

"Is there anything wrong, Right Hand?" asked Fox. "You came back sooner than we thought."

Shelk rose. They looked at each other, and Fox's eyes widened. Then his face lit up in an expression of incredulous surprise and happiness.

"Left Hand! You're back!"

They embraced, laughing and weeping, both talking at the same time. Then they were silent, gazing fondly at each other.

"You're just as like Right Hand as you used to be," said Fox. "But I recognized you."

"And you're the same, just as you were the day you used the sun-pool."

"I've got it still," said Fox, rummaging in his pouch. "You left it behind when you went away."

He pulled out the great mica crystal, and Shelk looked at it thoughtfully. Once the sight of it had filled him with triumph, then with horror. Now he saw it without emotion. It was a thing of the past. He gave it back to Fox. "Keep it. I don't need it. But where is Right Hand?"

"He went to Sun Village," Fox told him. "He wanted to see if anybody lives there now. We came here only yesterday."

"Then you'd better go and tell him," said Left Hand. "Everybody thinks I am he. If he should come back openly, they will be confused."

So Right Hand, notified by Fox of his brother's return, crept into the camp in the dark, and the three of them were reunited in the Chief's tent, under the pale light of the oil lamp. At first Left Hand did not say much about his travels to the north, but Right Hand and Fox had much to relate of their adventures in the southern lands. They had tracked Skua all the way to the Land of Flints. When they found him, he had established himself as a powerful and feared shaman. So great had his power waxed that it took Right Hand two winters to outwit him. He collected around him a group of warriors who swore him blind allegiance, but the one who finally helped him bring Skua to his doom was a boy whose voice had barely started to break. It was Skua's partiality to beautiful young boys that became his undoing. He died the death that he had designed for Left Hand and that he had meted out to many others in the days of his power. He suffered many deaths, for they called him back to life as many times as they could. When all was finished, they gave him to the hyenas.

Right Hand's task was done. He wanted to disperse his band immediately and return to Sun Village, but his warriors protested. They had become used to being led by an invincible hero and to taking what they wanted from peaceful villagers—food, weapons, ornaments, and women—rather than toiling themselves. Thus Right Hand settled down as a robber baron in the Land of Flints. By then he was already known under the name of

Shelk. Like his brother, he had taken that name in memory of the triumphal arch of Sun Village; also because he had now followed the shelk to its winter country just as old Greylag had done long ago.

Right Hand's decision was due in part to the youth who had helped him break Skua's power. The boy, called Viper, was the son of the shaman whom Skua had succeeded after cleverly bringing about his death. Right Hand himself had no son, although there was no dearth of women. He came to think of Viper as his own son, finding in him a willing and ambitious disciple, and teaching him the secret White language as well as the principles and practice of war. For Right Hand's intelligence and imagination were now firmly turned toward this new concern, the art of war; herein he became a great creator of new ideas. Soon he was renowned and feared far and wide. Men found him utterly invincible. From the start he realized that war required the same sort of organization as a mammoth hunt, only more highly developed. His men were now a well-drilled army. He demanded absolute obedience, but also boldness and initiative. No slackness or insubordination was tolerated; the punishment was flogging and expulsion, and the punishment for cowardice in the face of the enemy was death. Yet more and more warriors flocked to him, for the rewards of good conduct were great. All the good things of life were within the grasp of a brave warrior. Those who wore the eagle feather in their headband thought themselves the betters of all other men.

The peaceful villagers complained bitterly, but nobody took heed of them. As time passed, however, Right Hand found that there was less and less to be got from them. The years of plundering had taken their toll, and the once opulent people in the Land of Flints were now poor and devastated. So Right Hand broke camp and marched off to the north with his warriors and their women and children, looking for a new country to ravage. In the course of the years they moved ever farther north, and now they were in the old territory of Sun Village. But the village was gone; the people had moved away long ago.

"These days, we're not enjoying the same success as we used to," said Right Hand. "The people here are poorer than the villagers in the Land of Flints. Too often we have to hunt and work like ordinary villagers. This does not suit my warriors, who are used to taking what they want by force."

Left Hand stood deep in thought.

"I may be able to give you what you need," he said finally. "I now have power over the cattle of the Sun, like that of nobody else in this land, and this power can give us all a good life."

Left Hand described Black Cloud, how she had tamed the caribou so that they gave her milk and meat. Right Hand listened with interest and growing enthusiasm. Then they laid their plans as in the old days, with Fox as an admiring witness.

It was Right Hand's idea to keep his twin brother's identity a secret.

"The men will fear and revere us the more if they think we're the same man, who can be in two places at the same time," he pointed out. "They must never see us together. No one knows but Fox; no one else must be told. From now on, I'll pitch my tent well away from the others. Then we can get together without anybody knowing."

"But your woman?" asked Left Hand.

Right Hand shrugged his shoulders. "She's of no account," he said. "She is one among many; you're welcome to see if your luck with her is better than mine. We must share all things: the leadership, the tent, the woman. From now on we're Shelk, the one and only.''

He hung an amber necklace, the double of the one he wore himself, around his brother's neck. ''I've kept it for you ever since I took the two of them from a chief in the Land of Flints. He'd made some funny remark about my having no sons, and that was the end of him. His private parts were taken off and stuffed down his throat. Now, with our dress, our headband, and the eagle feather, you will look exactly like me.

''But now I'll go,'' he went on. ''Rest from your journeys, speak with Fox, call in the woman. Tomorrow we start for the Land of the Caribou; there's nothing here for us. Truly you came at the right moment, my brother.''

PART THREE

TIGER

THE REDS

Demuth des Menschen gegen den Menschen, sie schmerzt mich.

Beethoven's conversations

"I don't like the look of the weather," said Baywillow.

He and Tiger were alone on an immense expanse of ice. Baywillow had stopped to look around. The sun was low in the sky, right ahead of them, and the reflections of its slanting rays from the rippled surface were dazzling. A thin line, far away at the horizon, showed them the land. Behind them, clouds rose rapidly. They could no longer see the distant speck of Morningland, but the dead seals they had in tow were evidence enough of where they had been.

Morningland, where the grey seals gathered in late winter to bear their young, was a skerry far out in the sea. It could barely be glimpsed on the northeastern horizon on a clear summer day, but in winter, when the sea froze over, it became accessible, and the tribe of Veyde's Island had known it as a sealing place for many generations. The grey seals were shy, but at pupping time they were easy enough to club. The hunters did their business swiftly and competently, killed as many seals as they could pull back to the camp, and tried not to disturb the others. Now Tiger and Baywillow pulled three seals each in a single line behind them. One walked in the other's tracks to take advantage of the trail broken in the snow, and they took turns in the lead.

"No, it doesn't look good," Baywillow went on. "I smell snow in the air."

"Do you think we'll get a snowstorm?" asked Tiger.

"I wouldn't be surprised. The weather is unusual. You can feel the wind coming from the northeast." Baywillow was speaking from experience, as a native islander and seal-hunter. "We'll get a strong northerly with dry snow; then it's going to veer to the west with lots of wet snow. Question is, how soon? What we have to do now is to strike straight toward land. That way," and he pointed to the distant dark line in the northwest. "There's Deadman Island, where Mister Buckthorn son of Clover was found dead many winters ago. It reaches farther out than the other skerries. I don't trust the ice on a day like this."

He stood listening for a moment. "Yes, you can hear it," he added, pointing to the open sea. There had been a great silence all around them ever since they traveled out of earshot of the noisy seals of Morningland. The soft snow muffled their footfalls, and the only sound was the rustling of the seal bodies sliding along. Now they heard a new noise.

"It's the swell of a storm at sea," observed Baywillow. "It probably started as an easterly, then ripped up a heavy sea where the water's open. That's how it goes. We'd better start moving, Tiger." He turned and started pulling.

Distant cracks reverberated through the ice under their feet. Tiger hitched his towline over his shoulder and followed in Baywillow's steps. Only a thin layer of

snow covered the ice, and the path made by Baywillow's
seals made pulling easy.

Suddenly the air was full of snow, and everything
around them vanished. Baywillow, hardly visible
through the driving snow, called out, "Just follow me,
Tiger. We'll keep the wind on our right." The wind suddenly increased, almost blowing them over, and the
snow stung Tiger's cheek. He pulled at his hood. There
was a louder crack in the ice. He steadied himself and
caught up with the last of the seal bodies trailing behind
Baywillow. He caught an occasional glimpse of his
brother in the thick snow. He felt his heart warming
with trust and love.

His brother! Pulling through the snow, he fell to
musing once more on this incredible fact. He, who had
lost all of his family, had found a brother on Veyde's
Island, and an older brother at that! Miss Angelica had
told him how she had met the Chief, Tiger's father,
many winters ago. Realizing her opportunity to become
the mother of a child of the Gods, she had followed him
into the wood. Why had she not told him this before?
At the question, even the masterful Miss Angelica had
been silent for a moment, arranging her thoughts. Then
she said:

"I did not know how you were going to take it, Mister
Tiger. What I regarded as an honor and a privilege
might perhaps, in your eyes, be a disgrace. I did not
wish for your memory of your father to be stained. We
Whites do not know how the Gods think about these
things. But," she added, with a smile, "I did not know
you then as well as I do now."

"I can only thank you, Miss Angelica," said Tiger.
"I have regained a brother, in place of the one I lost."

"And I," said Miss Angelica, "am now not only the

mother, but also the grandmother, of a child of the Gods.''

Veyde's child was born the day after the Battle of Platform Hill, as they called it. Contrary to her expectations, it was a boy. He was well-shaped and strong, and came into the world with a lusty yell. Old Mister Silverbirch, who assisted at the birth, had never seen a stronger and healthier baby. His skin was brown. Veyde looked into his dark eyes, and proudly counted his fingers and toes. Her happiness was complete. She now was the mother of a child of the Gods.

Contrary to the custom of the Whites, Veyde asked Tiger to name the boy. A child of the Gods was special, and old customs were overruled. Tiger, who was now a man in the most important respect—he was the father of a son—called the child Marten, in memory of his brother. On the wall of their winter house he engraved the symbols of man and woman, and beneath them the likeness of a marten. Veyde also wanted the boy to have a White name signifying the bird guise in which he would enjoy his afterlife. She called him Dock, and his bird was the crossbill.

Afterwards, Tiger was approached by Baywillow and Silverweed, who had a proposal to make. They were still childless. Among the Whites, it was the duty of a brother to step in, so with Veyde and Baywillow as witnesses, Tiger impregnated Miss Silverweed. Next summer, the happy result was a daughter born to the proud parents.

It had been a happy and untroubled year. The shadow of Shelk and his Devils had been lifted from the island. At first Tiger was uneasy because the coracle was gone, which suggested that one of the attackers had escaped. As time passed, though, the menace faded from their memory, and the present filled their life with its unceasing demands on their thought and energy. And Tiger, together with Silverbirch, built a new and bigger boat.

They lived from season to season, often wandering far from their island base. Early summer always found a strong party on the mainland, where salmon was taken in great numbers in the river winding down from Blue Lake. Later on came the time of the great berry harvest; then the mushroom season. Elk was an important game throughout the year, but especially in winter when tracking was easy. Winter meant the coming of the caribou, and when the sea froze over, the seal skerries could also be visited. Ringed seal could be had close to Veyde's Island. To hunt the large grey seal, they had to journey all the way out to Morningland. It was worthwhile, though. Tiger and Baywillow's present trip, two moons after midwinter, was in the nature of a reconnaissance. They were returning with the good news that the seals were there.

Moving numbly in Baywillow's wake, Tiger almost stumbled over the seal that had been dragging along in front of him. Baywillow had stopped, and Tiger ran up to his side. It was getting dark.

"Listen," said Baywillow anxiously. "The ice is breaking up."

The ominous cracking was repeated.

"The snow is wet now," he said. "I think the wind has been veering. We have to keep it more in our faces, Tiger."

"Do you want me to lead, Baywillow?"

"No, I'd better go first. I've been out in this kind of weather before. Just keep close behind us."

They moved slowly against the wind, which hurtled masses of wet snow in their faces. Breastplates of snow formed constantly on their bodies, then fell off. Again and again came the cracking sound, and Tiger felt the shocks in the sea-ice under his feet. As if from a great distance, he could hear Baywillow call out encouragingly, "Not far now . . . Soon there . . . Deadman . . . right in front . . ."

Suddenly there was a cry and a splash. Tiger left his seals and started to run.

"Stop! Don't come closer!"

"But I can help you up!" cried Tiger.

"No! I can get up! You'll just fall in too!"

Tiger peered into the snow. "Can I throw you a rope?"

"No, I'm getting up," said Baywillow. Tiger could hear him splashing around, and knew he was using his javelin as an ice-prod to pull himself out of the water. He heard the ice breaking, then renewed splashing, then a breathless shout:

"Tiger! I'm up on the ice! Don't come this way. Try to the left!"

"I will," shouted Tiger. He caught up his rope and started pulling, the snow plastering his side. A distant voice reached him: "Remember . . . prod . . . ice . . ."

Tiger took his javelin and struck it into the ice ahead of him. Aghast, he felt the point go through. He turned left again and walked a few steps, trying the ice each time. It seemed thicker here. Again he faced the wind and snow. After two steps the javelin went through once more.

He stopped, called out, and listened. He thought he heard a shout, but was not sure. Again he turned his back to the wind, walked ten steps, and turned right. The ice was good here, but whenever he faced the wind, a few paces took him back to thin ice.

"Baywillow!" he shouted. There was a splintering sound in front of him, and he could feel the tremor in the ice, stronger than before. Then the wind carried faint words to him, Baywillow calling out at the top of his voice: "South . . . Go south . . ."

Which way was south? There was nothing to guide Tiger except the raging wind. The snowfall was turning into torrents of rain. The darkness was complete. For the last time, the voice came to him through the darkness, a world of love and anxiety in it: "Careful . . . Careful . . ." From his left came a curious grinding noise, and a series of new shocks passed through the ice. He realized that he was standing on an ice-floe and that it had collided with something. South! Could he reach the fast ice that way? He started walking with the wind on his right cheek. He must be going south now, if the wind had veered to the west as Baywillow thought. Careful! He made himself thrust the javelin into the ice at every step, but it always rebounded on hard ice.

The grinding had ceased and there was nothing now except the sound of rain and wind. He stopped suddenly. There was a different note in the rain: it was splashing. Yes, there was open water in front of him. He stumbled forward, trying to see in the darkness. It seemed blacker in the distance; there was no way to safety here. A tremendous gust of wind and rain made him stagger. He could not go on.

Tiger stood motionless, almost overwhelmed by panic. For a moment he considered running forward, jumping into the water, swimming to safety. But he knew that only death awaited him in that cold black water. Slowly his reason returned. He was still holding the rope attached to the seals. It felt vaguely reassuring. What would Baywillow have done? Probably he would go away from the open water. Tiger went back to the first seal, then walked slowly away from the wind. Better not go very far. There was nothing to do now. He would have to wait, wait for daybreak, wait for the rain to stop, wait until he could see. And all the time his ice-floe would be drifting out to sea.

The thoughts were milling in his head as he stood with his back to the wind and rain. He stared into the darkness. Time passed, and passed, and passed. Much later—or just a moment later?—he was sitting on the body of a seal. The rain poured down. The wind was on his cheek. Had it changed direction, or was it his ice-floe that was turning around?

More time passed. He had forgotten where he was. No, he is back on the island. It is summer and little Marten-Dock-Crossbill is at Veyde's breast. Tiger is smiling and joking about all the names of his son. There is sun and wind, and the eider and tufted ducks are out with their young in the bay. A few goldeneyes fly overhead. The smooth rocks feel warm to the touch. The drying rockpools are bordered by yellow pollen, but one of them has red water in it and Veyde avoids it. There is an evil spirit in it, she says. A small patch of earth in a sheltered spot by the shore is a wilderness of flowering mayweed and stands of orpine, their stiff meaty leaves turning red in the dry weather. Behind them, as they sit on the beach, the pines stand gnarled and defiant, their new shoots a golden brown or light green. A couple of oystercatchers fly by swiftly, their calls ringing out. In a grassy cove to the right, buttercup and silverweed flower in bright yellow patches. A cuckoo calls, and a tree pipit sinks down with stiff wings, the last languishing note of its song drawing out into infinite, caressing sweetness.

Still later, the sun is low and the wind is gone. The reflections from the water weave a billowing network of light over the pines. Marten is sleeping in his arms. Old Mister Silverbirch rakes a few goosander eggs out of the dying fire. Someone tells a story, and everybody laughs.

With a start, Tiger remembered where he was, still on
the ice-floe, sitting on the seal. The rain had stopped,
and suddenly two stars shone out overhead. It was
clearing up. Again he looked around. He seemed to be
on a gigantic ice-floe. No water was in sight before him,
but from the other side he could hear the lapping of
small waves. The wind had died down, and through the
stillness came a sound as of distant voices, repeated time
and again. He strained to hear the words, but they were
unintelligible: *hah-iyeh, hah, ho.* Suddenly he understood: it was the barking of seals. He must be near
Morningland.

He tried to recapture his dream, but it was gone. He
felt weak and suddenly hungry, and he cursed himself
for finishing his provisions before starting back from
Morningland.

More stars came out, and he could now see the
polestar, though it wasn't much use; there was nowhere
to go. But wait—he had heard the seals in the east. That
meant he was still to landward of Morningland. Maybe
he would drift ashore. Then at least he would have solid
ground under his feet, and he could hunt the seals for
food.

Seals! Fool that he was! Here he was sitting on his
food! He came to life and carefully penetrated the neck
of the dead seal with his javelin. Soon he was sucking
the blood, still lukewarm. A new glow filled him. He
stretched his numbed body, hopped up and down,
waved his arms. Yes, he was still alive.

The seals had fallen silent, but now there was a slight
breath of wind in his face. Where did it come from? He
looked to the stars: southeast. He jumped a few more
times, and his hopes rose. With the wind from that
direction he would drift back toward land. Again the
wind picked up, and a blackness in the east blotted out

the stars. He could hear the surge of the sea against the outer border of the ice, and suddenly he felt a tremor under his feet.

Panic gripped him. The waves were beginning to break up his ice-floe, the stars were gone, and once more blackness engulfed him. Yet a picture was forming in Tiger's mind, the bird's-eye view he had seen two winters ago from the coracle. He saw it now as clearly as he had then, and his mind's eye traced the outlines of the skerries, identifying them all: Deadman Island, Morningland, and the others. Now he knew where he was, and he could tell, approximately, where he was going—if only the wind would hold.

The long night finally coming to an end, Tiger realized that he could see again. Eagerly he looked to landward, and saw the contours of an island, not far away, outlined in the murky light. Then he looked back to the sea and saw that a large part of his floating island had been lost: the waves were breaking only a few fathoms away.

Suddenly there was a terrific snorting, and a huge white head rose out of the water. Two gigantic paws with long claws gripped the edge of the ice. An enormous bear turned its wedge-shaped head toward Tiger, staring at him with small, piercing eyes. The animal looked as if he were about to clamber up on the ice.

"No!" Tiger cried out, terrified. The ice-floe cracked straight across, and Tiger got himself onto the bigger piece with a desperate jump. Two of the seals' bodies slid into the water. The bear, diving and surfacing in a single fluid movement, caught one of them in his jaws and made off with it. Before Tiger had time to catch on to the rope, the last seal was pulled down, and the bear swam toward land, one seal gripped between his teeth, two trailing behind him.

Utterly shaken by this encounter, Tiger sat down gingerly in the middle of his ice-floe, and watched the waves lapping at its borders, constantly threatening to swamp it. In front of him there was open water, but closer to the island he could see ice.

The island was wooded, with a high, sloping, rocky beach on which he recognized the immense, polished excavation of a giant's kettle just by the shore. The steep slope of the beach probably meant deep water outside. There was a lot of floating ice. Nearer the shore he could make out a dark shape, lying motionless on the fast ice. A seal? Could the bear have left one of the dead seals on the ice?

Tiger's ice-floe ground against the floating ice near the shore and gently came to a stop. There was nothing to do now but jump, and probably swim. His first jumps were lucky. The small floes sank under his weight, but not before he had time to jump to the next. He was closing in to land rapidly, lurching this way and that, his arms flailing. Then he made a false step and fell through. He surfaced and struck the point of his javelin into the ice, trying desperately to pull himself out and to work his way landward. The ice gave way; he tried, and finally wriggled himself out of the water.

Shivering all over from cold and exhaustion, Tiger got up and ran toward the shore, nearly tripping over the dark shape he had seen at a distance. Now he realized that it was a man. For a moment he thought it was Baywillow, but this man was differently dressed, wearing sealskins from head to foot. Tiger turned him over, and looked into a foreign face. The man was a White, but different from all the Whites Tiger had met. He was deathly pale, and his face was peppered with reddish spots which stood out against the pallor. Tiger had never seen a freckled face before; his first impression was that the man was touched by some strange disease. His eyebrows were a russet color, and a wisp of red hair showed under his hood.

Tiger longed above all to get to drier land and to make a fire, but he could not leave the stranger here. Two years before he might have regarded this creature as a Troll ox; he might have turned his back. Now he knew better. Tiger lifted the man in his arms and staggered up the steep beach until he reached a large rock, partly covered by the crown of a pine. There he put the man down and ran off to get fuel. Everything was sopping wet, but he found some small dead pines that were easy to snap off, and dry and powdery within.

Tiger now took out the possession he prized almost as much as his father's tiger tooth. It was a lump of pyrite and a piece of flint which he had received from the Chief at his initiation, and which he carried in a pouch in his belt. After a few tries the fire blazed up, and he tossed more wood on it. Now he would have to make a shelter. Mumbling apologies to the spirits of the trees, Tiger broke one branch after another and built a hut, which he made waterproof with moss and juniper twigs. When this was done, he put the stranger, still unconscious, in the hut, and stayed by the fire for a while, warming himself.

Now only one thing was missing: food. Warmed and greatly cheered, Tiger walked to the place where he had seen the bear go ashore. The steep, rocky slope was bare of snow, but the bear's footprints on the ice led him to the right place. He found tracks in the wood and followed them cautiously. He had reckoned right: the bear had eaten one of the seals but left the others untouched. Even the rope was still there. Tiger hitched it over his shoulder and pulled off his booty. Suddenly he laughed, for a strange thought occurred to him: the seals had saved his life. There could be no doubt that the polar bear had originally intended to attack him, not the seals. And now the bear had saved his life by pulling the seals ashore. Tiger would never have been able to handle them while jumping across the ice-floes.

The smell of food aroused the stranger. He stared vacantly, then focused on Tiger. To his surprise, Tiger saw fear and dismay in the man's face.

"May you soar high, Mister," said Tiger, using the traditional greeting of the Whites and smiling reassuringly. The man uttered a few words in a strange language, and Tiger repeated his greeting. The stranger seemed stunned, but finally spoke a few words in the White tongue, brokenly and with difficulty:

"You Black. I Red. You speak White. Why?"

"I live with the Whites," explained Tiger. He gestured invitingly with the spit. "Do have some food."

"Black—Red," said the man and drew his finger across his throat. "No good. Dead Black—good." He grimaced hideously. His face had flushed a dull red which obliterated the freckles, and he was crouching, as if to attack.

By the Great Mammoth, Tiger thought, that's a funny way to show your gratitude. Out loud he said, "I am a friend. I found you on the ice. I carried you here." He wondered how much the man understood, but the sight of the grilled meat seemed to help. The Red man accepted it after some hesitation, and started to eat. While chewing, he pulled together his mighty eyebrows, as if struggling for words. He patted his chest and said, "Red—beautiful—good." He paused. "Black—no beautiful—no good." Then he raised his eyes to Tiger, and his features softened: "You Black. You good."

Tiger stifled an impulse to laugh. Maybe I'll be beautiful too, in a little while, he thought. But he nodded kindly and started to eat. They ate in silence, and Tiger put more wood on the fire. The short day was coming to an end; he suddenly felt very tired.

In the morning, Tiger woke up, warm and dry, and looked out at a world with traveling skies, rosy from the rising sun. The Red man made it clear to him that he lived near by, and they set out together, Tiger supporting his companion, who had an injured foot. They worked their way slowly across the fast ice to the inner skerries, and entered the Red village when the sun was in the south. The village lay in a sheltered harbor on the south side of an island and differed from the settlements of the Whites in that it had simple huts made out of branches and lined with moss. The beach was littered with butchering refuse and animal bodies, and a great bonfire was blazing. Many people were at work, but at the sight of the ill-matched pair they left everything and ran to meet them.

Tiger's comrade now poured forth a torrent of words. When he was through, a young woman stepped up and greeted Tiger with a hug. She was pale-faced, freckled, and red-haired like the others. Otherwise she resembled the Whites, though Tiger noted that her eyebrows did not meet above her nose, but were curved, giving her face an expression of permanent surprise. Her eyes were flashing green and had the same air of quiet assurance as those of Miss Angelica.

"May you soar high, dear Mister," she said, revealing to Tiger's relief that she spoke the White language fluently. "Thank you for rescuing poor Goosander. I have to apologize to you on his behalf. He is not very bright, as you may have noticed, but he is a good seal-hunter. My own name is Swallow. The Whites call me Buttercup, for among them a human receives his bird-name only after death. We have different name-traditions: we are the Reds. I bid you welcome to our village. I hope you will stay for many days, so that we can thank you.''

Tiger was impressed. ''My name is Tiger,'' he said, ''and I come from Trout Lake, far inland. I have lost my family and my tribe, and for two winters I have lived with the Whites on Veyde's Island.''

''Then you have much to tell,'' said Miss Swallow, ''and you must stay with us long enough to share your story. Now, though, we must look after poor Goosander.''

Goosander had suffered nothing worse than a bad sprain, but he had endured a lot. He had been seal-hunting on a group of islets northeast of Morningland and had fallen on the slippery rocks. Crawling back, he got caught in the storm, which utterly confused him. Tiger described how he had found Goosander on the ice.

That day Tiger also told Miss Swallow the story of his life, and she translated it to her people, who listened with great interest. The first stars were coming out in the east before he finished. ''But now, Miss Swallow, I want to hear about you. I never heard about the Reds: you must be strangers from far away.''

''It is getting cold,'' said Miss Swallow. ''Let us go into my hut, and I will tell you about my people.''

Tiger followed her into the hut, where a seal-fat lamp was burning. He recoiled slightly at the sight of two death's-heads, piebald with ochre, on a stone slab. Miss Swallow bowed to them and passed her hand over her face. Tiger shuddered. He certainly would not care for a couple of dead people in his house.

''My parents,'' announced Miss Swallow. ''This is Tiger, an honored guest.''

Tiger imitated Miss Swallow's bow and passed his hand over his face. She smiled and sat down, cross-legged.

"I can understand that you are curious about us, and I want to tell you our story as frankly as you have told yours. But before I start, there is one thing I must say to you. You yourself, your behavior, and yes, your story too, have taught me a lot. You have turned my thoughts and emotions in a new direction, as if a river were changing its bed. But you shall judge for yourself.

"We come from the east. We have walked across the ice, winter after winter, to get as far away as possible from the Blacks who took our country. You heard what Goosander said, 'The only good Black is a dead Black.' I was the first to say that, and it was I, too, who first said, 'Red is beautiful!' Without the pride and will to endure which these words have given us, we should have perished many winters ago.

"But alas, not all of the Reds realized it. Many of our people just stood open-mouthed from wonder and admiration when the Blacks came. The Blacks, they speak a tongue which seems to sparkle and sing like that of the birds, and when we hear it we feel that we bleat and bellow like the ox and the ibex. The Black men are tall and proud, and they regard us as the soil under their feet. They loom up like visions, with their dark eyes and long beards, and our women lie down on their backs for them. But the Blacks only use them for pleasure; they laugh at the foolish Troll bitches.

"Our customs are nothing to them. When we show our courtesy in our own way, with our hands before our eyes, they make fun of us, flinging their hands about and laughing. If a Red or a White is in a Black man's path, he pushes them aside, for he regards himself, with his throwing-stick and his elegant weapons, as our better. We have only our simple handiwork, which we have learned from our ancestors since the beginning of time. The Black men kill our holy birds—the white swan, from whom everything emanates, and the gaudy long-tailed duck, who brings us the lovely summer—and take the eggs.

"To our village came two of these Black men, tall and bearded. We fell down and worshipped them like gods. They spoke in their fluid tongue, laughing at us as soon as we opened our mouths. They took our food and drink; we waited on them and obeyed their orders. From our berries they created magic potions which made them laugh still more and whetted their appetite for our women.

"I was hardly more than a child. I was afraid of their loud voices and laughter, so I kept away. But one of them tricked me into drinking the magic potion, which made me sleepy and confused. They took me, first one, then the other. That night I, who had never known a man, became a woman, and when they slept I killed them both.

"All the people in our village were bewildered and afraid. What was going to happen to us? They talked of a neighboring village in which the people had risen against the Blacks—killed one and chased the others away. These people thought themselves rid of the Blacks, but one night they returned with many men and killed everybody they could find—women, men, and children. They razed the huts to the ground, made a bonfire of them, and threw on the living and dead. Would this happen to us, too?

"Then I spoke to them, inspiring them with courage and defiance. I pointed to the dead Blacks and said, 'The only good Black is a dead Black.' Most of them agreed to come with me, and I led them away from the

village. The only things we took with us were our
weapons and our dead, whom you see here. That was
the beginning of our long march west across the sea, for
the Blacks in our country came from the east.''

"I always thought the world came to an end at the
sea," said Tiger. "Now you tell me there is another
country on the other side; that there are Blacks and
Reds in it, just as there are Blacks and Whites in this
country. How strange!''

"Yes, but it is very far away. We have journeyed
many winters. Once we stopped, after going from island
to island. We had reached an ice-field that seemed to
have no end, but a clear day showed us land far away,
and we went there. Then we crossed more land, arriving
at a sea that looked endless; no land could be seen on
the other side. That autumn we saw long-tailed ducks
and swans flying west, and when the ice came we
followed them. After a long, long march across endless
ice-fields we saw land in the distance and knew that the
birds had not led us astray. Here, we thought, is our
new country; here we can live in peace from the Blacks.

"I am not saying this to accuse you, Tiger. On the
contrary: you have taught me that there are also good
Blacks, Blacks who give their hand to help, Blacks who
do not despise our language and customs. From your
story I realize that there are good and bad people among
you, just as there are among ourselves. Still, I have to
tell you what we have gone through, so that you can understand why Goosander feared you.

"On this side of the sea we met the Whites for the
first time. They received us kindly, and we lived with
them for two winters. Many of us learned a little of their
language, but I had to learn it fully, for I am the leader
of my people and I had to lead them farther. We could
not stay and abuse the hospitality of the Whites. Each

autumn we saw the birds fly southwest, and we were full of unrest. I had to speak with the Whites, to find a place where we could stay without encroaching on anybody's hunting grounds. So I lived with a White family, and spoke their language every day.

"This winter we started out once more, and from what you tell me, we can go no farther. The Blacks are now in front of us. So I ask you, Tiger: Do you think we can stay here, on this island, and live in peace? To us it is good. There are plenty of fish, seals, and other game, and the berries ripen every summer. The nearest White village, in the direction we came from, is three days away. We do not wish to intrude on your territory either, Tiger, so I ask you for advice."

Miss Swallow fell silent and looked expectantly at her guest. She had been sitting quite still while she told her story; now she unconsciously raised her hands to her red hair. Behind her the two dead gazed with empty eye-sockets into the dim light, as if echoing her question. Tiger, too, was silent for a moment.

"Miss Swallow," he said, "the sea is great and the islands are many. Of seals and other game there is enough for all of us, and the bilberries rot away each autumn for the lack of women and children to pick them. Nothing could make me happier than to have you as our neighbors, and nothing is better than a good neighbor. Thus I say, and thus my people will say: Stay here."

He stretched out his hands, and Miss Swallow took them in hers.

THE BIRDS OF THE SOUL

Here comes a candle to light you to bed,
And here comes a chopper to chop off your head.

Nursery rhyme

Tiger stayed with the Reds for a few days, resting after his terrible experience on the ice. In company with Miss Swallow he visited the injured seal-hunter, Goosander. He was lying in his hut, his foot watched over by two skulls, one human, the other a bird's.

"He will be all right," said Miss Swallow. "I have sucked the evil from his foot, and now his departed ones are watching over it. For such a slight illness there was no need for me to send out the bird of my soul. Twice I have sent her all the way to the Land of the Dead. It is a long and terrible journey, and once I did not get there in time. After such an ordeal my poor body lies as if dead for a day and a night."

"But that one," remarked Tiger, nodding toward the bird skull, "is not human."

"You have seen that we do not bury our dead the way the Whites do, or cover our graves with flowers. We move from place to place, and we need the aid of our dead. We also strive to be united with those whom we cherish. When one of our people leaves us to go into the Land of the Birds, he gives us that which is most precious—his brain, with its living thoughts, emotions, and knowledge. This becomes our holy communion; with it, part of his soul enters us.

"Sometimes, though, one of our people gets lost and is never found again. That is what happened to Goosander's father. Then we seek the bird whose name the departed bears. We treat it as we would a human skull, for we have been taught that in the moment that the sacrament touches our lips, it is changed into the flesh and blood of the departed."

Tiger was thoughtful. He realized that Miss Swallow was a powerful shaman, and though his father, the Chief, had been no friend of shamans, the composed and kindly Miss Swallow was certainly very different from the shamans the Chief had spoken about. Perhaps the Red and White shamans were better than the Black.

Well-fed, with a supply of meat for his journey, Tiger set out across the fast ice, following the chain of islands. There had been a light snowfall a few days before, but now the sun was out, and by midday it felt distinctly warm. Toward evening, when the glare diminished and the sun was red on the horizon, he passed familiar landmarks, and finally arrived at the two skerries closest to Veyde's Island: the Old Man, long and meager, and the Old Woman, who turned her round buttocks to the sky. There they rested forever, in company, and seemed to agree. Perhaps their spirits sought each other in the night. They were good-natured and friendly, two silent but nice neighbors.

Dusk was falling when Tiger reached Veyde's Island and went up on the long moraine spit pointing south. In the summer, terns and turnstones would nest here; now it was icy and barren. he ran along the path through the wood to the winter village.

"Veyde! Veyde!" he called out.

There was no answer. There was no fire. Nobody was in sight.

He called out again, and ran to the house he shared with Veyde. It was empty and cold. The small lamp, which always burned day and night, had gone out.

With mounting terror Tiger stepped outside again. Suddenly he was running about in a panic, shouting, listening, shouting again. Now he was in the wood, stumbling over stumps and fallen trees, now on the ice, now on the bluffs where the summer tents used to stand.

Much later he was back in the house. He had filled the lamp and lighted it with shaking hands. He looked around in a daze. There was nothing to show what had happened to Veyde and Marten. It was as if they had gone out for a moment, planning to come back directly. On the floor he saw a half-made fur blouse and some sticks that Marten used to play with, squeezing them in his small hands, striking them together and listening intently to the sound. Now Marten was gone, but the sticks were here.

Tiger went from house to house, carrying the lamp. All were empty like his own.

He stood outdoors. The air was still and cold. The whole island was frozen in an immense silence, and above him were the stars. Everything had passed away as in a dream. The world was empty, and he alone was left in it.

Tiger looked up at the silvery star-dust bridge that arched above him. The stars hung in still clusters. Only the Star-Hunters, the roving ones, moved each night. The Wolf Star was red in the west: was there a message for Tiger in its hot gaze? To the south he saw the calm eye of the Slow One. But the Hunter of the Evening, the sun's fierce warrior with his changeable moods, could not be seen. He had gone to rest for the night. Tiger knew that the Whites thought of the great bridge as the path of the birds, along which they would make their last journey. In the icy stillness a falling star crossed the sky, and Tiger flinched as if he had been struck. Was that a soul-bird flying away?

Finally quieted after his panic, Tiger spent the night between sleep and waking, dozing, then starting up. He heard a voice; somebody called his name: hope returned, time and again. But no one came; nobody was there; all was silent.

At dawn he was outside again, looking at the white sheet of snow. The only signs of life were his own footprints, a confused pattern, recalling to his mind the awful night and the hopeless search.

The sun rose higher, its rays falling on the snow and the tracks between the tree-trunks. Now Tiger saw what he should have seen from the start. His footprints were red, as if his own blood had been pouring out of him at every step. He scratched the snow away with his foot. Underneath, the rock was covered with frozen blood.

The certainty hit him like a fierce blow in the stomach, and he sank down on his knees. Shelk had returned. He had promised to do so, and he had kept his promise.

Yet Tiger had seen him die; he had buried him. It was true, then: Shelk was immortal. He had risen from his grave and returned, bringing vengeance with him. So it must be. Shelk was mightier than anyone else; mightier than the shamans, mightier than the Guardians. He had traveled to the Land of the Dead and he had come back. What was it he had said? "I am the Son of the Sun; I am

the Guardian of birds.'' To such a man even the spirits
who keep watch over the gate to the Land of Dead Men
must defer.

In these moments Tiger experienced the most extreme
terror of his life. Alone in front of his and Veyde's
house, in the clear sunshine of the winter morning, he
stood stupefied, blindly accepting his fate, balancing on
the verge of an abyss of witlessness and self-destruction.

Finally he became aware of movements somewhere in
the distance, and he looked up. It was a bevy of cross-
bills fluttering eagerly among the pines. At the unexpected sight of the small birds, which brought Marten
and Veyde back to him, it seemed that a cool and fresh
wind blew through his mind. "No!" he cried out. He
felt a surge of defiance. Yes, he was alone; but he was
still alive. Shelk had not killed him yet, so he was not
omnipotent after all.

"Shelk, you shall die for the second time," he said.

Why not? What was it they had said about him? That
he could be in two places at the same time? Then he had
two lives. Baywillow had taken one; Tiger would take
the other. He stood up decisively. "O Black Tiger, make
me cunning and deathly like yourself," he prayed. In his
mind's eye he saw the shape of the great Guardian rise
out of Trout Lake. "You must teach me," he whispered. He was going to the Land of the Osprey, to challenge the Great Devil!

But first there was another truth to find out.

Tiger found them without difficulty. A mound of
branches had been thrown together in the wood, and
later covered by the new-fallen snow. With loving care
he removed the branches, and the first thing he saw was
the pale face of Miss Angelica. For a long time Tiger
looked at her. Even in death she retained her proud,

authoritative mien, but somebody had closed her eyes, had laid her to rest.

Beside her was Mister Marestail, wounded by many spears. In his icy face there was wrath but also triumph. You avenged her, thought Tiger. More corpses came to sight. There were Mister Alder, young Campion, Miss Silverweed—at the sight of her Tiger was filled with an even greater bitterness. She who had lived so often in her own mysterious world; she whose body he had penetrated while it was still living and warm; she whom he had given a child for Baywillow. They were all cold and their faces stony under his caress. Carefully he covered them up again.

Now he knew that Veyde was alive, that Marten was alive, that many of the others were alive. He also knew that somebody had been here after Shelk. Loving hands had laid the dead to rest. Yet Tiger felt that it had to be done better. For two days he carried rocks to make a great cairn to cover them all and keep them safe from wolves and hyenas. "The others I shall see in the Land of the Osprey," he told himself. "I am going to kill Shelk; but in the summer we'll come back here to scatter flowers over the grave."

Once again he was traveling.

THE DANCE OF THE TIGER

If, as claimed, the large sabers made it very difficult to eat, the animals took 40 million years to starve to death.

G. G. Simpson, Major Features of Evolution

The sun rose in a high arc, and a noonday thaw filled the air with the moist fragrance of melting snow and the scent of the pines. Freezing and thawing built strangely inclined fences of brittle ice, which glittered in the sunlight, along the edges of the glades. In the open spaces, a carrying crust had formed upon the snow, so Tiger avoided the dense woods and walked along the eskers. Because they led consistently aslant of his course, he had to shift now and then from one ridge to the next, always moving in a zigzag trail.

One evening a light snowfall covered the crust, and in the morning the surface carried innumerable footprints of the forest's wildlife. Tiger passed along quickly, but noted with rapid glances what animals had been afield. He was beginning to feel hungry, and his pack of food was growing light. He marked the trackways of hare and fox, horse and hyena. He lingered for a while over the footprints of an elk, but finally went on; the trail was cold.

Suddenly he stopped and bent down, a puzzled frown on his face. Here was something new. Never before had he seen any footprints like these; fresh, too. They looked a bit like lynx tracks, but much bigger. And there was something else, something eerie about that pawmark. There were too many toes. Tiger shook his head, grunted, and looked around. There was nothing in sight. Too many toes! That was the mark of a hind foot. He whistled. Here was another hind foot, this one just a bit smaller, with four clearly outlined toes; like the lynx, but still too large. So there were two animals.

"Here are the front feet," Tiger murmured. Again like the lynx, again impossibly large. Yet the lynx was a big-footed beast. And what was this? It must be a front foot of the other one, of the one who had six toes on his hind foot. Tiger could not make it out. There were four toes and then something which looked like a blurred bunch instead of the inner toe. He stared incredulously, trying to recollect all the footprint lore his long experience had taught him, but never before had he seen these prints. What strange beasts were loose in the forest?

Then, in a flash, he realized the truth. Two great cats hunting together, male and female, could mean only one thing. With shining eyes he turned away from his route and started tracking. The footprints were fresh. The animals must have passed through just a short while before. And he had always thought that the black tigers were gone forever! Wild plans and schemes thronged in his brain; foremost was his yearning to see the tigers. In the grip of a wild exhilaration, he ran on, his hunger forgotten.

Tiger crested another ridge and skidded to a stop. Look! Coming in from the west, not just a trackway, but a great furrow in the snow, with big cakes of crust thrown aside; and within the furrow, the immense circular imprints of mammoth feet. Tiger read the story

easily. It was a small family: a bull, a cow, and a calf.
The bull had walked in front, plowing his way through
the snow, the calf behind him, the cow in the rear. They
would be tired soon, walking at that pace, breaking
through the crust. The tigers had followed the mammoths. He could guess how eagerly they were bounding
from the longer spaces between their tracks. He ran on
after the mammoths.

It was a long run. He was puffing and winded when
he suddenly saw that the tigers had left the mammoth
trackway and drawn off to the right. He sensed the importance of this; the mammoths had moved downwind
and the tigers, closing in, were making a detour to
prevent their scent from betraying them. He had better
do the same. For a moment he considered following the
tigers, but prudence won, and he took off to the left.
Flushed, tired, and cautious he made his way up the little ridge ahead. There were the mammoths, clearly
visible in the glade on the other side, where they had
stopped. There was no sign of the tigers.

Tiger froze in his tracks and studied the mammoths
intently. Apparently they had not noticed him, or were
not concerned. They were at the southern edge of the
glade where the shade had protected the snow from the
glare of the noonday sun and no crust had formed. The
big bull was using his great curved tusks to sweep off the
snow. In the patch he had cleared, the cow and calf were
at work pulling up big bunches of grass and chewing
voraciously.

Tiger moved back behind a big pine tree. He hoisted
himself up to the lowermost branch and scaled the tree,
still staying behind it. Halfway up, he found a good
place to sit. Here he could survey the scene without
being noticed. The wind was bearing crosswise between
him and the mammoths. He admired their great, shaggy

black shapes, and marveled at the power and speed with which the bull had cleared away the snow.

Now the bull fell to, and all three animals ate, moving their trunks dexterously and rapidly from the ground to their mouths.

Suddenly the mammoths stopped foraging and simultaneously lifted the tips of their trunks. They had smelled something. It could not be his scent, for the wind was steady from his right. Both the bull and the cow stared upwind. Tiger craned his neck and saw his living totem.

The tiger was a big animal, yet it looked ridiculously small compared with these mighty mammoths. It had emerged from the wood on Tiger's right, directly in the mammoths' line of wind. The mammoths now stood stock still, facing the tiger. Trying to control his excitement, Tiger devoured the great cat with his eyes. The tiger—it must be a male, he was so big—also stood still, facing the mammoths. He had an air of the utmost innocence. He seemed to be surveying the mammoths with a look of benevolent apology, as if he had appeared on the scene by sheer accident and would bow out presently.

This animal was the most remarkable and unforgettable Tiger had ever seen. He stood very high in front, on long forelegs, his back sloping to low hindquarters, his head erect. It was the stance of a playful puppy, and the tiger's eyes seemed to radiate innocent wonder. A small V-shaped white throat patch on the black skin enhanced the clownish appearance of the creature. The only feature marring his amiable expression was the white glint of the left scimitar-tooth, clearly visible against the black chin. The tiger stretched his neck, as if measuring his height against the mammoths. Then he rose for a moment on his hind legs, lifting his forelegs with hanging paws, more like a playful puppy than ever. The mammoths, on whom these antics made no impression, continued to stare.

The tiger, still a picture of faultless good will, sank down on all fours and sauntered forward at a leisurely pace. On this side of the glade the crust was firm underfoot. There came a warning rumble from the mammoth bull. His trunk moved restlessly and his ears flapped out. The cow and calf closed in beside him, the calf sheltered between its parents. The tiger, whose high stance and proudly carried head gave him an air of superiority despite his smaller size, continued to amble forward.

This was too much for the bull mammoth. His trunk flew high, and with a scream of rage he rushed at the tiger.

With a single pained glance, which seemed to deplore such a misconstruction of his intentions, the tiger veered around and gracefully evaded the onslaught. The bull, after driving him away, turned around to rejoin his family.

The tiger sat down and yawned, baring his great curved scimitars, and closed his jaws with an audible click. Tiger could not help grinning. His heart was going out to that fearless, cunning, clown of an animal, a midget fighting a giant.

Then in one quick, flowing movement, the tiger rushed the mammoths.

He never reached them. The great bull whirled around to counterattack, and the tiger dashed away. He moved without effort on the snow crust, which the mammoth broke through at every step. The bull returned to his mate.

Ears cocked, the tiger sat down and meditatively watched the mammoths. He had lost nothing of his look of innocence. Then came another rush, another response, and the tiger sprang back, only to make a dash toward the cow while the bull was retreating.

The snow was flying; the dance continued. The tiger made his rushes from a new angle every time, forcing the mammoth to plow unbroken crust in his defense. As the tiger circled the mammoths, the cow became more and more flustered and was occasionally drawn to try an attack. Another dash; another onslaught by both mammoths, and suddenly there was a flash of black in the dense alders at the other edge of the glade.

The calf, unprotected for a moment, had eyes for nothing but its parents and their fight. The tigress, meanwhile, had been lying in ambush in the woods behind him. Now she was out in the open, unnoticed by anybody but Tiger, who saw her swollen belly and knew that she was pregnant. In her desperate rush, she rose very high up on the side of the calf. There was a momentary embrace; her scimitars flicked as she thrust them into the calf's neck. Then, with a jerk, she broke away and dashed back to cover.

The calf gave a squeal of pain as blood gushed from its neck where the tiger's scimitars had ripped two great wounds. The bull, trumpeting with rage, crashed into the wood after the she-tiger, but was hopelessly impeded by the alder thicket. The cow tried to keep between the calf and the male tiger, who was still maneuvering in a half-circle, making a sally from time to time. The baffled bull emerged from the wood and immediately charged at the tiger, who evaded him as easily as before. Now the bull was implacable. He continued to pursue the tiger, who led him a long dance over the glade. The mammoth sank into the snow and became more and more winded. Traces of blood showed that even his tough skin was getting frayed by the ice.

At last he could do no more. He stopped in his tracks just below Tiger, and looked at his tormentor with smoldering eyes. The tiger sat down and started gravely to lick his paw.

After its first fright the mammoth calf went into a state of complete shock. The single attack of the tigress had severed the artery in the animal's neck, at the same time mercifully robbing it of its senses. The blood spurting from the wounds made great red patches in the snow. The calf sank down to its knees, then fell over, its life flowing out in a final burst of blood. The male tiger stopped licking himself and looked on tranquilly as the bull mammoth slowly walked back to his calf.

The mammoths stayed with the dead, and when Tiger looked back, the male tiger had vanished. Rejoining his mate, thought Tiger. There was nothing to do now but wait. Tiger climbed down and found a place where he could make himself a den. There he slept, after finishing the last of his food.

When Tiger returned in the morning, the mammoth parents were gone, and the tigers were feasting. They had already eaten the trunk and much of the meat; the entrails lay in the snow. The enormous meal had already satisfied the female tiger, who was now lying at rest, while the male continued to eat half-heartedly. He appeared to be sated too, and finally joined his mate. Rolling over on his back, his four paws in the air, he started to lick himself, all over his magnificent black breast with the shining white patch.

Tiger was drawn irresistibly to the great cats. Slowly he moved toward them, talking softly to them all the time; afterwards he could not remember a word of what he had said. The sated tigers looked at him briefly but without interest, until he was only a few feet away. Now the male tiger looked at him attentively, craning his neck to do so while lying on his back. He did not stir. Brimming with awe and love, Tiger studied the great beast. His big paws were remarkable, and the hind feet did indeed have six toes. The front paws were peculiar; instead of the normal inner toe, which he could see in the female, there was a bunching of three vestigial toes which hung limply and flapped about as the tiger moved his paws. He understood now why the tracks were so queer; yet the tiger did not seem to be bothered by his abnormal condition.

The male rolled softly to his side, and Tiger admired his silky black fur and brilliant throat patch. His head was long and narrow; his eyes had greenish irises. The tiger yawned, displaying his fearsome teeth; then his eyes closed. His whiskers bunched forward. Most were black, but a few hairs were totally white.

Following an impulse, Tiger drew his hand-axe and cut a few strips of meat from the dead mammoth. The tigress opened her eyes, big and round, to look at him, but she did not move. Tiger stuffed the meat into his pack and bid the animals a ceremonious farewell. Then he slowly retraced his steps, under the gaze of both tigers.

The tigers spent the next few days by their kill, and Tiger rejoined them several times. Hyenas and wolves showed up; Tiger chased them away. Then one morning the tigers were gone. Their tracks showed that they were heading north. Tiger was tempted to follow them, but he kept his head. He knew that he had things to do, and now he thought he knew how to do them. He would appear gentle and innocent, but behind that mask he would be as swift and deadly as the tigress.

There was one thing he had to do before he went on. Not far away, he found what he was looking for: a great granite hogback with a smooth, ice-polished surface, where the wind had swept away much of the snow and the sun had melted the rest. Tiger built a great fire and, armed with charcoal and mammoth fat, went to work.

He sketched out a great picture of the scene he had witnessed. The immense black mammoths took shape under his hand. Then came the tigers. He worked in ecstasy to reproduce in sensitive lines the flow of power, the clownish insolence, the mastery of the male tiger; to catch the urgency and precision of the female, her single, high-rising attack, the one unerring stroke of violence in the whole combat. There was no hate or anger in her, only the rapture of fulfillment. He too knew that sudden flood of peace from a task well done. He worked as in a trance.

Still he was not finished; there was one area of the rock-face that he had not filled with pictures. There he drew a different image, which came from another secret place in his mind. There were only two figures here: one, a majestic shelk; the other, a black tiger moving in to attack. The shelk, for all its glory, was touched by the premonition of death, while every line in the tiger was alive with implacable anger.

After days of toil, all was finished. Exhausted, yet with a consciousness of purpose and resolution that was new to him, Tiger contemplated his work.

"That is the way it will be done," he said. The pictures sealed his compact with the great Guardian. He slung his pack over his shoulder and walked away. The sun felt warm. His eye fell on a nosegay of hepaticas, deep blue against a background of melting snow. He smiled. He was hungry. There were great things to be done.

THE WASP

And you could be stung by a wasp. There are those who have
died of that, too.

Lars Huldén, Heim

Soon Tiger came to a well-trodden path. It was
covered by new snow but formed a well-defined furrow,
and he was glad to see that it would lead him in the right
direction. He was now well provided for, and since he
did not have to stop and hunt for food, his progress was
rapid. There was still light in the evening sky when he
stopped to spend the night under the branches of a
fallen tree.

Tiger had been thinking of his plans all day. This
time he was going to be prepared. Like his father he
tried to look forward, to gauge the enemy's moves and
to choose his own. The Chief had pitted his cunning
against that of the mammoths; Tiger had a far more terrible adversary. It was Shelk, once killed, yet still alive,
unique in power, with a hundred warriors to obey his
call. Surely, then, Shelk could use another warrior, and
he, Tiger, would apply to become one of Shelk's gang.
He would probably have to pass a test, but he was a
good atlatl shot, and a good artist besides.

A new idea struck Tiger. He spoke the language of the
Whites, which very few others did, apart from Shelk

himself. There must be many White prisoners. Whatever Shelk's purpose with them, he would find a good linguist useful. Once a member of the band, he would bide his time as cunningly as the black tigress. Sooner or later the moment would come, when he was alone with Shelk. Then he would strike.

But wait! He must have a story to tell. Shelk would certainly ask him about his past. It would not do to say he came from Trout Lake. No, he knew what to say: he was an itinerant artist. They were not uncommon. Sometimes they were apprentice shamans who traveled from village to village. His home was—by the Salt Sea? No, he did not speak like the Salt Sea people. You knew them from their speech, as he himself had known Goshawk. He would say he came from Falcon Hill. His father had told him about the place. It was far to the south. Where had he learned the language of the Whites? That was easy. He had been in the north, in the land of the Whites.

He lay awake that evening, perfecting his plan. At last he went to sleep, but he was rudely awakened in the grey dawn by somebody pinning him to the ground. Sleepy and terrified, he saw a man bending over him, and felt a spearpoint at his neck.

"One move and you're dead," the stranger tittered.

Tiger tried to break loose, but the spearpoint pressed into his neck. A second man brutally turned Tiger over and bound his hands behind his back. Then he kicked him and said in a deep, mournful voice, "Get up!"

Both men were Blacks. "Who are you? Are you Shelk's men? I—" started Tiger, but the man with the tittering voice cried fiercely, "Shut up! Time enough to talk when you meet our Chief—talk, or hang."

He was a heavy, squat fellow. He stood broad-legged and kept his spearpoint at Tiger's neck.

"Get up," commanded the other man, who was tall and thin. Tiger shrugged and rose, and the men immediately stepped to his sides, gripping both his arms. "Come along, and mind you, no funny business," said the tall man.

"But—" Tiger began, and got a smart blow over his face with the shaft of a spear. "Shut up," ordered the short man. "Not a word before you stand before the Chief."

During the walk, the men talked to each other, paying no heed to the prisoner. "He'll hang like the others, Glutton, old man," said the merry one. "The Witch'll be pleased to cut out his liver."

"Take it easy," murmured the gloomy Glutton. "Maybe the Chief will let him live. You shouldn't be such an alarmist, Beaver. If you cut out his tongue and take off his left hand, he can still be useful. You see everything in black."

"Yes," said Beaver, laughing, "that's what I'm like. It's too bad that such a nice-looking man will have his guts running out of him while he hangs in the tree with the other one, but that's how you have to deal with his sort, my dear Glutton."

"I wouldn't lose hope in his place," said Glutton lugubriously. "If he speaks fast and plenty when the Chief interrogates him . . ."

"You always try to put false hopes into the poor things' heads," said Beaver reproachfully.

"While there's life, there's hope," mumbled Glutton.

Tiger listened to the talk in silence. He thought he could manage that chief of theirs. But who was it? Shelk? If so, he was close to his goal. In his mind he started to review his plan. Meanwhile the conversation about his probable fate continued. Soon, though, Beaver hit upon a new topic.

"I told you he was limping," he said contentedly. "Now you see, I was right. They must be sorely pressed to send a lame fellow on such a trip."

Glutton did not condescend to answer, and Beaver put his face in front of Tiger's. "I saw it from his footprints, that he was lame, but you didn't believe me. You said he was carrying a heavy pack. Ha ha!"

Glutton looked displeased. "So what? You don't have to kill a man because he's lame. Enough to break both his legs. Then he can limp evenly in future. I don't like all this hanging."

"The Witch likes it," said Beaver with an attack of laughter which almost made him lose grip of Tiger's arm. "In the night she sneaks out and cuts the tongue off the hanged. Then she serves it as caribou tongue. You've eaten many of those without knowing it, Glutton."

"It's the Chief who gives the orders, not the Witch," grumbled Glutton. "And speaking of tongues, you have borrowed yours from the hyena."

Beaver was amused by this scandalous charge, but before he had time to answer, Glutton said, "We're there."

"Yes!" cried Beaver happily, and for the first time he turned to Tiger: "Look, there's your comrade! We're going to hoist you beside him. Then you'll both be ripe and good when your friends find you."

With a shudder Tiger looked up at the hanged man. Then he heard a fierce scream, and a very small, old, and wrinkled White woman came rushing toward him. She wielded a sharp stone and babbled excitedly through toothless gums. Beaver raised his hand and checked her. "Chief!" he said.

"Chief!" said Glutton as a distant echo.

"Chief!" roared Beaver.

There was a rustle in the bushes, and out stepped
Wolf, the man who once was the Chief of Big Lake, the
man who had promised Tiger his beautiful daughter
Hind. Tiger recognized Wolf at once, though his hair
and beard were now white.

"Wolf!" he cried. "Don't you know me?"

The former Chief of Big Lake walked toward Tiger
with a puzzled frown. His left arm swung energetically,
but his right dangled.

"The voice sounds familiar," he said. "Familiar, it
sounds. "Almost it is as if Ferret of Trout Lake were
talking to me. Yet he is dead these two winters. By the
Great Mammoth, what's this? Isn't that you, Tiger,
Ferret's son? Bound? Cut the ropes at once, Beaver!
I'd embrace you if I could, Tiger, so happy am I to see
you; yes, happy to see you. My right arm doesn't obey
me any more—a scratch from the fight against that
monster Shelk, a trifle . . . But this is incredible! Tiger!
Tiger, Ferret's son! I've mourned you as dead."

Before long, Tiger, now an honored guest, was sitting
by the fire with Wolf, the chief who was to have been his
father-in-law. His gaze took in the simple camp, only a
few hastily made huts.

"Not like Big Lake, you're thinking?" said Wolf.
"No, you're right. But we never stay long. We've
learned a thing or two these winters, a thing or two. And
we're on our way, Tiger, we're on our way. I haven't
said my last word to Shelk. My spear-arm is no good,
but I have many brave men. With you I have one
more."

"Beaver and Glutton thought I was one of Shelk's
warriors, didn't they?" asked Tiger.

"So they did. They didn't know you; they come from
the west, from Swidden Moor where that big fire was,
many winters ago. Shelk took their village, but they

escaped. They took you for one of his messengers. We got another a few days ago; he's hanging in the tree over there."

"Have you been here long?" asked Tiger, and Wolf chuckled.

"Does it look like it?" and he described the situation. Shelk had put in garrisons at Big Lake, Blue Lake, Swidden Moor, and doubtless other places too. Wolf had escaped from the fight at Big Lake with a handful of his men, and spent some time as a fugitive. Other fugitives flocked to him, until finally he felt strong enough to attack Shelk's garrison at Blue Lake.

"That was a mistake," Wolf admitted. "We were repulsed, and my spear-arm destroyed. We use another tactic now. We have divided into three groups, and we harass Shelk's lines of communication. We don't stay more than a few days in any one place, so we keep him on the run. He's sent many troops against us, but we always avoid them. Meanwhile, we're gathering strength to assault his headquarters at Caribou Lake. This is the road from Big Lake to Caribou Lake, and it's time for us to decamp. There will be an enemy patrol before long."

"How many men have you got?"

Wolf had some thirty warriors all told. "And the Witch, of course," he added with a grin. "She comes from one of the Troll villages, and she hates Shelk's gang worse than anyone else does. Nobody can make out what she says, but she's learned to understand a few words of our language, and now she's our cook."

To her surprise and pleasure, Tiger greeted her in the White language and exchanged a few words with her while Wolf listened, intrigued.

"Well, well, well," he said. "He speaks the tongue of

the Trolls, too. You have much to tell us, Tiger. All we knew was what one of Shelk's messengers told us before we hanged him, that you and every other male from Trout Lake had been killed. Ferret and Ferret's son Tiger, he said. But you seem to have more lives than Shelk himself, since you are sitting here by my fire. I couldn't wish for a better man.''

So Shelk knew his name, Tiger mused, while Wolf went on talking and outlining his plans, which were simple enough. He intended to continue his war of attrition, to sting and escape. "I'm a wasp, Tiger," he said. "I fight like the wasp. I collect a swarm. One day there will be enough of us to sting Shelk to death. Look here!''

From under his neckband he pulled out a piece of amber. It was as long as his finger, flat, and polished by wear. Inside it was a wasp, motionless in a golden prison, as if time had stopped. Tiger admired the powerful talisman, in which the sunshine seemed to gather. For a moment, he wavered in his decision. Maybe with such a protector Wolf could win. When the little troup set out, Tiger went with them.

The calls of migrating cranes filled the air. Tiger walked for a while with the old White woman whom the Blacks called the Witch, and she told him her story. She came from the Land of the Osprey, from a White village at Caribou Lake. That was where the Devils had struck their first blow, four winters ago. Some of the Whites had been killed, her daughter among them. The others were taken to the vicinity of the Gorge, where they lived with the roar of the rapids in their ears, day and night. All the people had prostrated themselves to the Supreme Devil, for they saw that he was the Guardian of the birds. His guiding spirit, in the body of a raven, alighted on his outstretched hand and spoke to him in the words of men. Later, the Blacks brought the caribou and taught the prisoners how to tend them. The Great One must be the Guardian of the caribou, too. He made them so fond of human piss that they became quite tame. But this woman had wanted her freedom, and in the end she managed to get away. No one took any heed of what an old woman did. Now she lived for the day when the Devils would be chased away, when everything would be as it was in the old days.

Tiger also talked to the two men who had taken him prisoner, and found that they quarreled about the future just as they did about any other topic. The solemn Glutton was fanatically convinced that Wolf would lead them to eventual victory, while Beaver scoffed at his hopes. "You're dreaming, Glutton," he said. "For every one of our men, Shelk can raise a hundred. What can we do but make a snap at his back and run? It's fun while it lasts, but it won't last long."

"The Shelk can't live forever," Glutton muttered.

"I know what I would do in his place," said Beaver. "I'd send a hundred women against us instead of all these fighters. Then we'd give in at once. By the Great Mammoth, sometimes I get so keen on a woman I almost want to try it with the Witch." And he doubled up with laughter.

Tiger saw that Beaver was right, and when they stopped for the night, he told Wolf about his decision and his plan. Wolf tried to talk Tiger into staying, but gradually he came around, admitting that it might be useful to have a friend in the enemy's headquarters. Next morning, when Tiger bade him farewell, Wolf embraced the younger man.

"I wish you luck," he said. "You're following a more

dangerous road than we are and you need all the help you can get. Take my wasp; it'll help you to sting the Shelk to death. Send it back as a token when you have carried out your plan. I'm lending it to you, mind, but it was to have been your own when you married Hind. Perhaps that too will happen, one day.''

THE OVERSEER

Our county sheriff is really a brute;
Broad as a bull, and shameless to boot.
Join him for ale and a few hands of poker,
But don't call his bluff, or you'll be the joker.

Swedish lampoon

       The calls of the cranes followed Tiger on his journey as the birds came in endless arrays. Watching their slow, purposeful wingbeats, Tiger felt uplifted. If Shelk had power over caribou and ravens, as the Witch had said, the cranes at any rate were flying as they did in the old days.

Then Tiger became conscious of a new sound in the forest. It was a strange, deep murmur that seemed to roll at him from a great distance. He stopped and listened. In front of him was a clay slope, bare of snow but full of meltwater puddles forming a pattern which reminded him of the islands he had seen in that strange vision long ago. When he put his heel into the rim of the biggest puddle, the water broke through, and started to run down the slope in a widening stream. Then he realized what he was hearing. It was the roar of the Gorge. He must be almost there.

A bit farther on, beside a birch, he saw a Black woman. She was cutting into the trunk of the tree with a stone knife, and on the ground there were several vessels made out of birchbark. Tiger approached her and greeted her courteously. She spun around, frightened and wide-eyed. She was a young girl.

"Oh, you scared me!" she cried. Then she looked closer at him, and her fright gave way to a coquettish smile. She saw a tall young hunter, and the great tooth on his breast was more impressive than any trophy she had seen before.

"Isn't it lovely," she said, fingering it. "You must be a great hunter. What's your name?"

"Wildcat," said Tiger, who had decided on that name because it was close enough to his real one. "And yours?"

"I'm Tern," she said, looking up at him with her big eyes, which were beautiful in spite of a slight squint. Actually that only enhanced the piquancy of her appearance. Then her expression changed, and she took a step back.

"You haven't got a feather," she said accusingly and pointed to his head.

"Feather?"

"Yes, the eagle feather. All the warriors have them."

"Of course." Tiger smiled. "I'm a stranger. But I've come here to become a warrior. Whom should I talk to?"

"Oh," she said, "is that so? I suppose you'd better talk to the Overseer. He's coming here today, so you can stay awhile with me."

"Who's the Overseer? What's his name?"

"Ooh, I've forgotten. He's new, but he's nice. Much nicer than the old one. Not as good looking as you, though, Wildcat."

"What's wrong with the old one?" inquired Tiger, amused.

"Oh, he was terrible. Old Crow. Crowshit, we called him. You wouldn't believe it, but he promised to make an extra cut in my work-stick if I slept with him! But nothing doing,'' said Tern primly, whereupon she spoiled the effect by continuing chattily, ''He was no good anyway. He'd just pant and paw at me, and I didn't get a rise out of him, though I tried to help.''

''So the new one is better?''

''Well, I mean he seems to be nice. I've just met him once.'' By now, she had moved so close that her body touched Tiger's, and he observed, ''But I'm keeping you from your work.''

''Ooh!'' cried Tern. ''I must hurry.''

''I can help you.''

''You can't do that. You're a warrior.''

''Where I come from warriors can do anything,'' said Tiger. ''Here's your knife.''

They worked side by side, cutting the bark, thrusting sticks into the wood to lead the trickle of the sap, and fastening the birch-bark vessels. Tern had made them herself, she said, and caulked them with resin.

''You really are nice to me, Wildcat,'' said Tern, wiggling her hips. ''A great warrior and hunter like you has never cared to help me.''

When all was done, Tern sat down on the ground. ''I have to wait for the Overseer before I go to camp,'' she informed him. ''He's going to check what I've done. Ooh, I'm hungry!''

Tiger brought his bundle. He had a great deal of meat left, and Tern accepted the food gratefully. They had barely finished their meal when she looked up. ''The Overseer,'' she said.

Tiger rose in surprise. The man who approached them, with an eagle feather stuck jauntily into his headband, was none other than Goshawk, the fat God from Blue Lake, somewhat less obese than Tiger remembered, but still exceptionally fullbodied. Goshawk smiled radiantly and embraced Tiger as if he had been a boyhood friend.

"Tiger, my dear fellow, what a surprise! What brings you here?"

"Ooh," said Tern, "is he called Tiger, too? You told me your name was Wildcat."

Goshawk paid no attention to her. He was busy patting Tiger's shoulder.

"I've come here to join Shelk's warriors."

"Ah," said Goshawk, "you're well advised to do so. It's a good life. Our Master is lucky in everything; and we, his men, are the bravest warriors in the world."

Then he struck his forehead.

"But by the Mammoth, Tiger, you can't!" he cried.

"Listen, Tigercat, what's your real name?" asked Tern. "Not that it matters. You're nice, and good-looking too."

"Why can't I?" asked Tiger.

"Why, don't you know, Tiger . . . Ahem, you aren't exactly . . . I mean . . . Well, to put it briefly, I'm afraid the Master will have you hanged in the tallest pine tree at Caribou Lake, if you show up there."

"He can't do that," cried Tern agitatedly. "Such a nice man. Say something, Wildcat!"

"Why should he do that?"

"Why? Well, you are . . . I mean, everybody knows you're a tremendous shaman, the enemy of the Sun, the man who killed Shelk or at least his shade, or the other Shelk . . . Forgive me, I'm a bit confused."

"Ooh!" cried Tern. "Are you a great shaman, Tiger-cat? Please show me what you can do. Look here, I've got such a funny spot on my breast, couldn't you . . ."

"By the Great Mammoth," Goshawk exclaimed, annoyed, "who are you?"

"I'm Tern, don't you remember? You said I was

pretty, too," said the girl reproachfully.

"But Shelk never met me," said Tiger.

"No, that's true, but he's heard about Tiger, the great shaman . . ."

Tern, who had now uncovered her chest, jumped up and down in her excitement. "Look here, Wildcat, look here, Tiger! I'm sure it is an evil spirit, and you can blow him away. I always wanted to meet a great shaman. Old Crowshit said he could . . ."

"My name isn't Tiger now," Tiger explained, "it's Wildcat." Goshawk held his forehead with one hand and pointed at the tiger tooth with the other.

"Your name may be Wildcat or Mole, but if you appear at Caribou Lake with that thing on your chest, I swear you'll hang before sundown."

Tiger slipped the tooth inside his neckband. "You're right, Goshawk, I didn't think of that. Many thanks. Do you think I can have this one instead?"

He pulled out the golden wasp. Tern's eyes widened more than ever, and forgetful of everything else she began to finger it, sighing ecstatically. Goshawk seemed to become aware of her presence for the first time.

"By the Guardian of all hyenas," he said, "why are you standing there half-naked like a Troll bitch? Tiger—Wildcat, I mean—you're lost! She knows who you are! She can't hold her tongue any longer than you can belch!"

"Don't think I don't understand what you're talking about," said Tern angrily. "I'm not such a fool as you think. He's my shaman and he's nice to me. He's promised to blow away the evil spirit. And you're mean, mean, to call me a Troll bitch. I'm much prettier than any Troll bitch. They're pale-skinned and have crooked legs and no waist at all, and their tits are like flaps of skin, and they have big jaws like a bear—but I—I—I was the Master's woman for two moons—and you promised last time that you'd cut the marks without caring too much about what I had done if I only—just like Crowshit—''

Groaning, Goshawk sat down on a tree-trunk, waving his hands in an attempt to stop her. ''There you are, Tiger,'' he said. ''She's the worst talker this side of the Salt Sea. She'll bring us both to ruin.''

Tern looked at him critically. ''You look poorly, Overseer,'' she said. ''Do you feel ill? Please give me my daily marks before you drop dead.''

She pulled a small wooden stick out of her bundle. It was scored with a row of notches. She waved it in front of Goshawk's nose.

''You'd better give her what she wants, Goshawk,'' said Tiger.

''Goshawk, why, that's his name,'' said Tern delightedly. ''I knew there was something funny about it.''

Tiger patted her cheek. ''Tern, you're a clever girl, aren't you? As clever as you're pretty. And you want to help me, don't you?''

''Of course I want to help you, Ti—Wildcat. Your name is Wildcat. May the Guardian of the caribou strike me dead if I forget it. I don't want you hanged in a pine tree, no, I don't.''

Goshawk rummaged feebly in his bundle and brought out a sheaf of sticks, which he looked at in a forlorn way. ''Which is your mark? What did you say your name was?''

''Tern, I've told you. That one's mine.''

Goshawk placed the two sticks side by side. The notches matched. Each notch signified one day's work, and beside one of them the mark of the full moon was carved. Sighing, he got out a flint knife and started to cut new marks across the sticks.

"And you haven't even looked at my work," said Tern approvingly. "That shows you trust me, Gos—ha-ha—Goshawk. You're nice after all. Three marks, thank you! Now I have three days off. I'll come with you to Caribou Lake."

While they walked, Tiger asked about Caribou Lake and what was going on there. Goshawk was eager to tell him, but as usual he was filled with his own importance and spent some time pointing out the great responsibility of his position and how the Overseers were a very select group.

"I was entrusted with the post of Overseer because I know the language of the Whites. Now I'm responsible for the girls' camp in the Forest, Blacks and Whites alike. Perhaps you too could become an overseer, Tiger—"

"His name is Wildcat," Tern corrected.

"Wildcat, I mean. I know you speak the Troll language too. Before this, I used to be Overseer in Sunwood—"

"Sunwood, what's that?"

"Oh, that's where the caribou are—the cattle of the Sun. It's the big wood in the bend of the Gorge. It's surrounded on three sides by the Gorge and by Caribou Lake. The War Camp is on the fourth side. So the caribou are safe there, and their keepers too. Most of the keepers are Trolls, both oxen and bitches, but there is a Black women's camp too, and nobody can get out of there. Every spring and autumn, when the caribou pass by, we drive new animals into Sunwood to replace those that are killed for meat."

"I've been there too," said Tern, "but then I became the Master's woman—"

"I was Overseer in Sunwood for two winters," interrupted Goshawk, "but it gets tedious after a while, what with the noise from the Gorge; and the Troll oxen make a lot of trouble. Recently a new warrior came to Caribou Lake who speaks the Troll language. He's a bastard, by the way. In fact, sometimes I feel there's something familiar about him."

Tiger felt suddenly excited. "Do you know his name, Goshawk?"

"His name? Let me see, I think it's Buzzard. Anyway he took over my old job in Sunwood, and I moved here to succeed old Crow . . ."

"Crowshit," corrected Tern.

"Crowshit, I mean," repeated Goshawk mechanically, but checked himself: "Shut up, girl! Crow, I mean."

Tiger kept his eyes down so as not to give away his excitement. The buzzard was Baywillow's bird. Could it really be . . . ?

"Crow is getting old and he can't see very well any more," Goshawk explained. "But the Master takes care of the old, showing his benevolence to those who have served him well. Crow doesn't have to work any more. For myself, I was pleased to move here. It's calm and peaceful, and there are no bothersome Troll oxen. The girls are good, Black or White. Only the safe ones are put to work here."

"What do you do with the sticks?"

"The Master thought that out. Everyone, except the warriors, of course, has to work six days. I see to it that they really do their work . . ."

"I know what you see to," said Tern in such a low voice that Goshawk did not hear her.

"Everybody has her work-stick, and I have its double in my pack. After six working days each girl gets three days off and can do what she likes. You'll understand in a moment. As you see, I have to keep track of a lot of things, but I know my responsibility. Nothing escapes me. Now we're coming to the gate.''

The gate was formed by two big pines. On each side stretched a stockade, so dense that there was hardly room for a hand between the logs. Two sentries, armed with spears, were guarding the gate. Like Goshawk, each had an eagle feather in his headband.

"You see the gate is very wide," said Goshawk. "This is where we take in the caribou for Sunwood. They usually pass by just outside, and we take out ten or twenty animals at a time, to bring them in here.''

Tern had gone to one of the sentries and had given him her stick. He looked at it, put it into his bag, which was beside him on the ground, and nodded at her to pass.

"Now she is off duty," said Goshawk. "After three days she's got to fetch her stick and go back to work. You saw the mark for the full moon. You can't fool the Master. I only hope," he added nervously, "that she won't talk too much. But come along, Ti—Wildcat, and leave the talking to me.''

The sentries raised their spears and looked suspiciously at Tiger. Goshawk said in his grandest manner, "A new warrior. I'm taking him to the Master.''

"Do you vouch for him?''

"Of course I do. Have I not brought him here myself?''

The sentries exchanged grins. "Well, in that case," said one of them with mock humility, and Goshawk strutted through the gate, followed by Tiger.

A succession of strange sights met Tiger's eyes as he entered the camp. To his left, in a valley where a small stream flowed, was a large village of solidly built houses. In front of him and to his right rose a forested slope. The Gorge was not in sight, but the din from the rapids filled the air, seeming to well out of the forest itself. Tiger was even more intrigued by what was going on down by the stream. At least thirty men, all with eagle feathers, were behaving in the oddest manner. They walked to and fro, always in a straight line. Beside them walked another warrior, who gave a shout. Suddenly they threw themselves on the ground with a collective thump, clearly audible through the noise of the rapids. Another shout, and they were up again, throwing their spears. With wild cries they rushed ahead, each with a knife in his raised hand. They seemed to attack an invisible enemy, sticking their knives into him and pounding him to death. Yet another shout, and everyone rose and stood at attention.

"By all the spirits of the forest," said Tiger, amazed, "have they gone utterly mad? What do they think they're doing?"

"Curb your tongue," said Goshawk. "It's war-practice. What do you think the warriors do all day—lie around in the sunshine? Soon you'll be there too, if all goes well. Come along with me."

He took Tiger up a winding path where a well-timbered house came into sight. If the war-practice had seemed nightmarish to Tiger, a more pleasant view presented itself here. Children were playing; a rotund and motherly woman was tending them; and a thin Black man watched and smiled. He turned expectantly to Goshawk.

"Fox, I've brought you a new recruit," said Goshawk ponderously. "Wildcat is his name."

The man looked searchingly at Tiger. "We'll put him to the test, if the Master pleases. What can you do, Wildcat?"

"I'm a hunter and an artist," said Tiger. "The renown of the Master has reached far and wide, and I should like to enroll with you, if you have any use for me."

"I vouch for him," said Goshawk.

Fox smiled, and Tiger noted with surprise that he found the man attractive. "Thank you, Goshawk. I'll take him to the Master. You can go."

Fox's smile grew more cynical when Goshawk had left. "The fat fool's recommendation isn't really worth much," he observed. "But we need an artist. Are you any good?"

"Put me to the test, Fox," said Tiger. "Also, I speak the White language."

Fox looked at him, his interest heightened. "The Master will put you to the test," he said in the White language. "Do you understand what I am saying?"

"I do, Mister Fox," answered Tiger in the same tongue, "and if you permit me to say so, you speak the language as well as a White."

Fox gave a delighted chuckle. "You'll do. Come."

A few moments later Tiger was standing in front of Shelk.

THE RECRUIT

CUNNING.—N. Cunning, craft, subtlety, maneuvering, temporization, circumvention, chicane, sharp practice, knavery, jugglery, concealment, guile, duplicity, foul play.

Roget's Thesaurus

Shelk's house was the biggest Tiger had ever seen. Like the stockade, it was built of standing logs, but here the chinks were carefully lined with earth and moss. In front of it was a great pillar, made from an enormous tree-trunk. It was crowned by a red globe, which Tiger thought must represent the Sun. From the house the ground sloped down to the valley and the village, but when they came closer the wide panorama of the ice-bound Caribou Lake came into view.

Fox asked Tiger to wait while he went in, and as Tiger stood there alone, still bewildered by all the strange things he had heard and seen, a new idea struck him with a flash of terror. What if Shelk recognized him? Then everything would have been in vain, and death was certain. Twice they had met. The first time, at the Summer Meet, Tiger was a beardless youngster and Shelk had hardly noticed him. But the second time! Then Shelk was dying. Baywillow had killed him, yet he had promised to come back. Was it the same man, or was the one who had died on Veyde's Island only his shade? How could he know?

Whatever happened, it was too late to get away. Tiger collected his wits, stopped trembling, and moved with firm steps when Fox gave him the sign to come in. He entered a room greater than any he had even dreamed of. It must have been the length of five men and the breadth of four. The ceiling was so high that even the tallest man could stand erect. Tiger remembered how the Chief his father had had to bend his head in his own house. The walls were decorated with skins of caribou, bear, elk, wolf, and other animals. Daylight streamed in through four windows. Never had Tiger seen anything so impressive. His eyes went to the far wall, on which a shelk antler was hung. The man sitting under it must be the Great One himself. Tiger had expected the lord of Caribou Lake to transfix him immediately with an all-seeing stare, but instead he was talking to another man whose back was turned to Tiger. Fox told Tiger to wait by the door while he joined the others.

Only then did Tiger notice that there was yet another person in the room. A young girl was sitting on a pile of skins by the side wall. She was sewing, her head bent over her work, her black hair hiding her face. The sunlight from the door fell across her bare knees. Tern's successor as the Master's woman, thought Tiger. He probably changed them often. For Tern, two moons had been enough, but maybe that was because she talked so much. In the next moment Tiger forgot his cynical thoughts, for the girl, suddenly aware of his gaze, looked up. He reeled as if struck blind, whether out of terror or despair he did not know. The girl who was sitting in Shelk's house was Hind, Wolf's daughter, the girl who was to have been his bride.

He imagined that he had cried out; in fact he was struck dumb. He was certain that she would cry his name, but she did not recognize him at first. She looked

at him listlessly. Then recognition dawned, and with it
dismay and fear in her eyes. She drew in her breath, and
the blood left her dark face, which became grey and
lifeless. Her lips opened. Tiger gave her a rapid wink,
and to his relief she closed her mouth. A deep flush
colored her face. Tiger cast a glance at the men. No one
appeared to have noticed anything. When he looked at
Hind again, she had returned to her sewing, but her
hands were shaking, and she bit her lip. She breathed
quickly.

Apparently the conversation had come to an end, for
the man who had been standing with his back to Tiger
turned around and went out. It was Baywillow. Tiger
registered this new shock dully. He had actually expected to see Baywillow ever since Goshawk mentioned
the name Buzzard. Still he felt grateful to Baywillow for
his habitual self-command, which was probably never
put to a harder test. His eyes met Tiger's without a show
of interest, but just as he passed, he let his eyelid flutter.

Fox beckoned to Tiger, and the man who was sitting
under the great antler raised his eyes. When Tiger met
Shelk's gaze he felt that the man was able to read every
thought and every plan in his brain, every feeling and
hope in his breast. As he walked those few steps, it
seemed that all he had felt and thought ran away like
meltwater, leaving him empty and helpless.

"You wish to join my warriors, Mister Wildcat?"
said Shelk in the language of the Whites. "Mister Fox
tells me you speak this language."

Tiger realized, with some surprise, that Shelk had
noted his confusion, that his kind words were designed
to help him over it. The courtesy, and the polite address
of the Whites, which seemed to raise him to the rank of
the Master, brought him to his senses again. This was
the beginning of a conversation that Tiger could never

look back on without a feeling of extreme terror. He felt he was balancing on the edge of the Gorge, in danger of falling. The rush of the water seemed to engulf him here in Shelk's room.

Was this the same man? The face, the figure, the amber necklace—all were the same as at the Summer Meet. Yet he was different, and while the talk proceeded, Tiger felt sure that he was not the same man. The other had been aloof, stern, forbidding. In the searching eyes of this man, he sensed a thoughtful sadness that was utterly unexpected.

Shelk went on asking questions with unwavering politeness. Tiger tried to keep his voice steady and to answer with apparent frankness. Once he thought, Now Hind will cry out and say that it's not true, what I'm saying. But she made no sound. Tiger heard himself describe journeys he had never made, adventures that had happened only in his imagination. It was all part of his carefully rehearsed story. No, he'd never seen the Salt Sea. Yes, his father, Badger, was dead, killed by a wounded wisent. Yes, he'd seen the Great Water and had lived there for a winter and a summer, with the Whites. Where? Far to the northeast, in a place called Outer Island. (That was in fact the place where Miss Swallow had learned the White language.) Shelk nodded thoughtfully. He had never been that far east himself, he said. Did they get plenty of caribou there? No, not particularly. The main winter game was seal.

The questioning seemed to go on forever, but finally the commanding gaze was lowered. Shelk rummaged in a pile of skins and turned up the inside of a caribou skin. Tiger noticed that his right hand lacked the index finger. "I have been told that you are an artist, Mister Wildcat. Let me see if you can draw a caribou here; a cow that has lost one of its antlers, and is chewing it."

Obediently, Tiger kneeled down, took the charcoal Fox gave him, and started to work. Soon he forgot everything else. His hand was steady: this was his proper work. A great pride and pleasure filled him. Never was his hand surer than when something big was at stake. Suddenly he noticed that Shelk and Fox, who had been talking, were now silent and attentive. Hind, too, had come forward to look.

There was the caribou cow, the antler in her mouth. Tiger heard Shelk's voice, almost choking: "Mister Wildcat, can you draw a calf beside it?"

Tiger went to work again. The calf emerged under his hand, as lifelike as the cow.

"There you are, Mister Shelk," he said at last, and put down the charcoal. "Anything more?"

Shelk did not seem to hear him. Unconsciously, he made the habitual gesture of the Whites, briefly covering his eyes with his hand. He looked steadily at the picture, his face inscrutable. His eyes shining, Fox looked from Shelk to Tiger, saying nothing. It was Hind who spoke at last.

"It's a very good picture, stranger," she said in a low voice. "What's your name? Mine's Hind."

"My name, Hind, is Wildcat."

"I see," she said tonelessly.

Shelk came out of his trance and spoke in the Black tongue, like Hind: "Thank you, Wildcat. This picture has penetrated my heart."

Only now Tiger realized that his fear of Hind had been unfounded. Of course she did not understand the White language; the entire conversation must have been unintelligible to her. Yet he felt that she would not have betrayed him anyway.

"Your pleasure is my reward," said Tiger.

"And you want to become a warrior here. Very well,

you shall take the oath. But warriors grow like grass out of the earth. An artist like you one finds only once in a lifetime. I may have other plans for you in future.''

Shelk administered the oath, and Tiger repeated the words. He swore allegiance to the Sun, to Shelk, and to his leaders. He swore to defend them with all his power and to reveal any plot of which he became aware. It all seemed unreal to him. Here he was taking oath to Shelk, the man he had sworn to kill.

They left, Fox with his hand on Tiger's shoulder in a friendly manner. ''I'm glad you're here, Wildcat,'' he said. ''Did you see how your picture pleased the Master? Never have I seen him so surprised and captivated. It touched something he hides deep within himself. There is magic in your hand, Wildcat.''

Tiger, exhausted, moved as if in a dream. ''What do you wish me to do now, Fox?'' he asked.

''You will join Diver's Company. He lost a man recently, a messenger who never came back. We think he was taken by Wolf, a bandit who operates in the forest east of here.''

Tiger nodded. He thought he knew the fate of the man.

''This Wolf, he may think himself a wasp, like the one you carry,'' and Fox pointed with a smile to Tiger's talisman. ''But in truth he's nothing but a mosquito, and we'll squash him like one.''

Tiger checked the words that rose to his lips, and said instead, ''But after that? The Master told me he had other plans for me.''

''That's true, and I think you have a great future here. But first you have to be broken in as a warrior.''

So Tiger became a recruit in Diver's Company, knowing that he replaced the man whom he had seen hanged in Wolf's camp. He lived with eight others in a house much smaller than Shelk's, and every day they were trained in the art of war. The actual handling of weapons was somewhat less important than he had expected. That was already second nature to every hunter. The most important thing was to obey orders. The commands were given orally at first, then by signs. He learned to keep his eyes always on the man next to him and on his commander. He learned how to attack and retreat. He learned to wait, silent and motionless, from midday to dusk if need be, without letting his attention wander. After a moon of this he understood only too well why Wolf's brave men had been defeated at Blue Lake. No personal bravery, no feats of arms, would avail against the murderous discipline and cooperation that Shelk's cold brain had instilled into the Men of the Eagle Feather, and which they retained under Viper's harsh rule.

For Viper, the commander of the army, was indeed a stern and demanding leader. He had a heart of stone, the men said. He had not always been like that. After his humiliating retreat from Blue Lake, every human feeling seemed to have frozen within him. His cold eye missed nothing, and woe to those who made a mistake. In comparison with Viper, Tiger's immediate superior, Diver, was a cheerful and easygoing person. Though he could flare up in anger, it always passed quickly. Viper never forgot anything.

Many of Tiger's fellows in the company were veterans from the times in the Land of Flints, and they had many stories to tell. Some of them talked nostalgically of the good old times.

"Then, you simply took what you wanted," said one of them, a man named Owl. "No fooling about with caribou and such things; rich chiefs to rob; pretty women to win. Ah well, that's life. We're becoming ordinary caribou-keepers in our old age."

"So we always have food," remarked another. "Many times you had to go hungry in the old days, don't you remember?"

"Food, yes; everything is so well-ordered and dull that you get bored to death. All our fighting is just play. Shelk doesn't lead us any more. Instead, that Viper is snapping at us with his fangs. Sometimes he takes us for a promenade in the woods—we're supposed to catch those bandits, Wolf and his gang, but they're too smart for Viper. Then, of course, we took the Troll island. That was meant to be a war, but it wasn't really."

Tiger pricked up his ears. "What happened?"

Owl, the veteran, told of their assault on Veyde's Island. It was a big operation. Everyone knew who was there! The great Black Shaman, the one who killed the Master's shade, said Owl in lowered tones. The Master himself came with them; and Viper, of course, as army commander. He was probably ashamed about the time when he came back from Blue Lake with his tail between his legs. But was the Shaman there? No! From what the Trolls said, he'd been lost on the ice! Hah! Not much of a shaman, hey? Everybody laughed.

No, Owl went on, it turned out to be as easy as anything, after all those preparations and all that practice. They had waited for the winter and the ice, to get a big troop across to the island. Ho! Ten warriors would have been plenty. Of course, you couldn't guess that beforehand, and it was true that everyone felt his ears tingle when he thought about that dreadful Shaman.

They crossed the ice in the dark of night and stole up to the village. At dawn they had it completely surrounded, before the Trolls were even awake. Then a Troll bitch came out of her house, carrying a spear. Behind her came a Troll ox, unarmed. He was the biggest Troll ox they had ever seen, like a great boulder, yes indeed! Some other Trolls came out too, but these two were the leaders.

Viper spoke to them. Now he, Owl, didn't understand a word of the Troll lingo—just bah-bah-bah—but he heard afterwards that Viper had ordered them to surrender the Shaman. The bitch told Viper that the Shaman was dead, that they had better get out of there. At that Viper started to laugh, and the bitch raised her spear.

"She shouldn't have done that," said Owl seriously. "Bunting, who was standing beside me, thought she was going to throw it at Viper. It didn't look like that to me, but he let fly with his spear, catching her right in the chest. And you know, that big Troll ox just sprang into life. He came straight at Bunting with his bare hands outstretched. Right away ten spears were launched at him. He had more spears in his body than a hedgehog has spines, but that didn't stop him. I never saw such a tough Troll ox. He put out a hand as big as a bear's, got Bunting around the neck, and pulled the head off him, just like that, like a child picking a flower! By the Mammoth, I never saw such a surprised-looking head as Bunting's.

"Then, of course, the ox died. We might have butchered all the Trolls—a few more got spears in them —if the Master had not intervened. He called a halt, raised his hand, and suddenly his guiding spirit was there, high above us, calling out his magic words. That did it; the Trolls fell to the ground. After that they came along without trouble, and now they are in there"—he pointed to Sunwood—"with the other caribou-keepers."

Owl shook his head. "No," he said, "it wasn't much of a war. There's nothing to tell about it; nothing, ex-

cept for one thing—that Troll ox. Such another Troll ox
I never saw."

Tiger nodded. It was not a bad obituary for Mister
Marestail, he thought. And he rejoiced at the con-
firmation of what he had read in the frozen face of his
dead friend.

After one moon in Diver's Company, Tiger looked
back at his earlier ideas of defeating Shelk with an
armed force and smiled pityingly. What kind of chance
would he, or even Wolf, stand of defeating the Men of
the Eagle Feather? Caribou Lake was an impregnable
fortress. It was guarded by the Gorge, by Caribou Lake,
by the palisades, and above all, by the invincible warriors who manned it. Fox was right: Wolf was but a
mosquito. He could do mischief for a time, but no real
harm. There was a new power in the land, one that had
never been seen before.

The defenses had a dual purpose. They kept human
enemies away; they also kept away the carnivores that
might be dangerous to the caribou. In the early days,
before all was ready, they had made a lot of trouble,
especially the hyenas. But being intelligent animals, they
had now learned their place and wisely kept away.

The only animals that made trouble these days were
the itinerants, those who did not have a permanent
territory like the hyenas. It might be a wolf pack coming
across the ice of Caribou Lake, in which case there was
a great hunt. The greylegs were driven into the bend of
the Gorge and killed off. Bears were another menace,
but they were abroad mostly in the summer, when the
lake was open. It sometimes happened that a drowsy
and hungry bear managed to get across the ice in the
spring, and he always ended up on the spit. As for the
occasional solitary hyenas, they were demoralized from

the beginning and easily dealt with. Few cared to eat their meat.

By far the most troublesome animal was the glutton, an elusive beast. Free from their greatest rivals, the wolves, the gluttons were having a good time in Sunwood. No matter how many were killed, new ones seemed always to crop up. Many times the warriors were sent into Sunwood to hunt out predators, but Tiger had to stay at home. He was not yet fully trained.

And the caribou, the cattle of the Sun? They were causing trouble too. The warm summers were hard on them, and many died, especially the calves. Fortunately, the losses could be made up when the migrating herds passed by. The warriors learned to cut off groups of animals from the main herd and drive them into Sunwood. They needed food, though. Caribou don't live on Troll piss alone, as Owl put it. Big as it was, Sunwood was getting short of caribou food. So were large areas of the land around Caribou Lake. Lichens were collected by women in camps like Goshawk's, and the burdens were carried to Sunwood by Troll oxen, long lines of them, toiling under the escort of warrior patrols. The other garrisons at Blue Lake, Big Lake, and Swidden Moor had to contribute by hunting. So the Men of the Eagle Feather were gradually turning into ordinary villagers again, who must hunt to keep alive, even though they now had slaves to do the more tiresome tasks.

There were always many women in the camp. Whether they worked in Sunwood or in the surrounding forest, they usually came to the camp for their days off. When a warrior had his woman in the camp, he worked half-time, unless he had had the misfortune to bring down Viper's ire upon his head. The half-time rule did not apply to Tiger, who was still a recruit, but he did have some time off, and Tern had appropriated him immediately, by the simple device of announcing to Diver that she was Wildcat's woman.

At such times they had the use of one of the family huts which had been built close to the place where the little stream joined the Great River. This was close to the Gap, where the river was transformed from a thundering cataract into a serene sheet of flowing water. The Gap itself was hidden by a spur of rock, but flying spray rose in the air, and at sunrise the foot of a rainbow could be seen. The roar of the rapids drowned most sounds except occasional piercing screams from the huts where men and women gave vent to the desire accumulated during their six days of abstinence. Above all, however, the family village was an idyll, separated from the War Camp and its harsh regime. Children played under the proud eyes of their parents, fathers coached their young sons in the skills of the hunter, and young lovers went around hugging each other tenderly. Most of the women who spent their free time in the family village were Black, but there were also a few White girls, and Tiger sometimes had to act as interpreter between a Black warrior and his White woman.

Tiger was grateful to have Tern's favor, and not only because she was pretty, cheerful, and affectionate. It was more than that. She was the only one for whom he permitted himself to entertain friendly feelings. True to the task he had taken upon himself, he refused to see the warriors as anything but cold-blooded murderers. Mentally he had armored himself against them, although he was careful to keep up a friendly appearance. To a young man of Tiger's frank and open nature, this situation would have become unbearable if he had not found an outlet for his emotions in the company and embraces of Tern.

There was another reason, too, which he admitted to himself. As long as he was "nice" to Tern, as she herself put it, he could at any rate be sure that she was not going to betray him. So it happened that he was loath to let her out of his sight. Tern attributed this to jealousy and was flattered. She had a flighty nature, and in the normal order of things would probably have turned her interest in other directions soon enough. But there was so much to keep her curiosity alive. Why had Goshawk called him a great shaman? Why did he have two names? Why did he hide his greatest treasure, the big tiger fang? To her he became a figure ranking almost with the Master. None of Tern's questions was answered, but Tiger's untold secret bound her to him as much as his obvious, passionate need of her presence.

And now, after one moon in Diver's Company, when Caribou Lake was ice-free at last, Tiger was called to Shelk once more.

THE ARTIST

Eagles and lions can never be so plentiful as pigeons and antelopes.

*A. R. Wallace, On the tendency of varieties to depart
indefinitely from the original type*

Tiger and Baywillow were together again.

Unknown to him, Shelk had arranged this when he
took Tiger out of Diver's Company, after one moon of
training, and made him the artist of Caribou Lake. The
decoration of the Sun Pillar was Tiger's first commission, and Shelk wanted it ready for the Midsummer
celebration.

Tiger's second interview with Shelk was less trying
than the first. No questions, no wandering in a nightmare of lies. The conversation was in the Black
language, and Hind sat listening in her usual place.
During the pauses, Tiger saw Shelk's eyes stray to the
picture of the caribou cow and calf, which now hung on
the wall beside him.

Shelk described the animals he wanted on the pillar.
Three were important, the Sun's cattle: the mammoth,
the caribou, and above them both the shelk. As for the
others, he gave Tiger free rein. The commission pleased
Tiger, because it meant that he was now freed from
Diver's Company; and the work was challenging. He
and Shelk spoke for a while about the composition and

232

the animals to be rendered. Already Tiger saw pictures in his mind, and he offered several suggestions, to which Shelk readily assented.

"Then we're agreed," said Shelk. "You will move away from the company today, Wildcat. You have learned enough to be a good warrior, should the need arise; but in peacetime you are now free of service. I want a pillar to delight the Sun and the Guardians of the animals. You must devote all of your time to it. A house has been built for you in the village of the Overseers, and I trust you'll find what you need in it. If there is anything you wish, speak to Buzzard, one of the Overseers of Sunwood; he'll arrange things for you. I must tell you in confidence that he's the best of all the Overseers and speaks both languages perfectly. I have instructed him to give you all the help you need."

Tiger's eyes were shining, and Shelk smiled. "I can see you're glad to get work that suits you better than the drudgery of the company," he observed.

So Tiger moved into his new house at the far end of the Overseer's village. In accordance with Shelk's wish, he went to see Baywillow as soon as the Overseer returned from his usual round in Sunwood. The brothers had much to tell each other of their adventures since they had been separated on the ice at Deadman Island, but Tiger's first question was: "Veyde? Marten?"

"Alive and well. Veyde's taking care of Marten and of Centaury, my daughter. She knows you're here, and she is ready to do anything to help you. She has talked with those of the Whites whom she can trust, but there are many who are awed by Shelk. They think he's the Guardian of birds, because he has a raven that goes everywhere with him and speaks to him in the language of man."

"He may be that," said Tiger, "but we'll find a way.

We are here now, and we must go on. Do you know anything about my family from Trout Lake?''

"Yes. Your mother, Oriole, died last summer, but your sister—our sister—Godwit, is alive. She lives with another woman from Trout Lake in the village of the Black women in Sunwood. There are many women and children from Trout Lake." Baywillow, who as Overseer had all the names in his head, reeled them off. Tiger listened, deeply moved. Once more he was in the country of his childhood, with his mother whom he had lost forever. But Godwit was alive. How had she fared?

"She is a grown woman now," said Baywillow, "intelligent and beautiful. I'm proud of my sister, but I haven't made myself known to her. I'll do it if you wish, Tiger, and I'll tell her about you."

"Do, Baywillow, if you can do so in secret. But don't tell anybody else; we don't know whom we can trust. Many of those women live with Shelk's warriors. We are in constant danger as it is; too many people know my secret." Tiger told him about Goshawk, Tern, and Hind. Baywillow shook his head. "From what you say, we can trust the girls. Goshawk may betray you from sheer foolishness. We'll have to keep an eye on him."

Then Baywillow told Tiger about the storm. He had managed to get ashore on Deadman Island, and had built a hut where he stayed until the weather cleared. After that, he spent a couple of days searching for Tiger. In the end he gave up and returned to Veyde's Island. Tiger already knew what Baywillow had found there. Like Tiger he had resolved to join Shelk's army in the hope of avenging himself.

"Tell me, Baywillow, how did you get to be an Overseer?''

Baywillow had been lucky. Close to Caribou Lake he met a warrior who turned out to be a messenger on his way home. They made the journey together, and the warrior recommended Baywillow to Fox. Baywillow was put in a company—Horned Owl's, not Diver's—but he had to stay for only half a moon. Crow, one of the Overseers, had fallen ill and was unable to do his job. Goshawk, who up to then had worked in Sunwood, was transferred to Crow's job; and Baywillow got Goshawk's vacant post in Sunwood.

"That nitwit Goshawk boasts that he knows our language," said Baywillow. "In reality he speaks such a queer lingo you don't understand half of it. He was having trouble in Sunwood, because that's where most of the Whites are, and Shelk was pleased to find a good linguist for the place. So that's how I got here, and now you're here too. If Shelk only knew!"

"He'll know one day," Tiger answered. "But if the Guardian of the tiger and mammoth wills, it's going to be on our terms. Have you got a plan?"

Baywillow shook his head. "I've seen one thing: no human power can break the power of Shelk. The only people on our side are Veyde and her Whites. What can they do?"

"We could arm them and take over Sunwood," suggested Tiger.

"Shelk's fighters would kill them like so many caribou. You've seen them yourself: do you think we could stand up against them? Even with the help of your friend Wolf? No, Tiger, it has to be done another way. But how?"

They had reached the beach at Caribou Lake, shelving at this place; to the east it rose steeply. Tiger looked out at the great sheet of water, now calm and like a mirror in the light of the setting sun. It was bigger than any other lake he had seen, bigger than Trout Lake. It reminded him of the sea. Its spirit must be the most powerful of them all. Perhaps it was he who roared in anger when his waters were compressed and forced through the Gorge.

Baywillow spoke of his original plan: to kill Shelk suddenly and unexpectedly when alone with him. Tiger had had the same idea; but afterwards? Viper and his men were sure to kill them.

"Besides, Baywillow," said Tiger, "I don't know if I could do it. When I'm alone with Shelk, my blood becomes cold and thin like the water in Caribou Lake. He frightens me."

"I, too, feel frightened by the presence of a man who is so powerful and evil."

"He doesn't frighten me because he's evil," said Tiger. "He frightens me because he's good."

Baywillow looked at him in wonder, and Tiger went on: "There's something wrong, Baywillow. I've heard a great deal about how it all started. The Men of the Eagle Feather are robbers and murderers. They have lived by killing their fellow men and taking their goods. Perhaps it was the other Shelk, the man you killed, who was their leader then. This Shelk is different. He talks about how the caribou can help us live a good life under the Sun. All the things he said when he spoke of the pictures on the Sun Pillar were true and good. I just don't understand it. But one thing I do know. With cold blood like this"—and he bent down and dipped his hand in Caribou Lake—"I can't kill him."

"Yet we must strike him down," said Baywillow.

"I know, but the only way we can do it is with the help of something greater and more powerful than ourselves."

Later still, Baywillow and Tiger stood on a hill. The setting sun and the edge of the distant forest were mirrored in the water. A buzzard flew overhead, mewing piteously; Baywillow looked up with a fleeting smile. To the west was Sunwood, high and dark; to the south, the little stream and the valley with the War Camp. Baywillow pointed to a higher hill in the east. "Up there is a place where Shelk sometimes goes to be alone. No one else is allowed there, except Fox."

Tiger hardly heard him. Once more the picture of the islands in the sea rose to his inner eye. Then it changed into the meltwater pools in the forest. Unconsciously he dug a furrow in the ground with his heel. The cataract growled in the distance, and he heard a note of eagerness in its voice, as if it had something to tell him. The scenery seemed to darken, and he felt the presence of the giant spirit who rose out of Trout Lake. The image of Miss Swallow came to him, with her eyebrows arched over green eyes. Again she raised her hands to her red hair, and he heard her voice. What was it she was saying? How she had felt about the Blacks, and how her emotions had changed when she met Tiger?

All these visions faded, and again Tiger was standing at Baywillow's side, conscious of his brother's searching glance.

"You have a plan, Tiger?" said Baywillow. Tiger shook his head in bewilderment.

"It is as if the spirit of the lake wants to tell me something," he said. "Yet I don't know what it is."

Tiger slept badly that night, alone in his new house. Tern was in the forest camp. Many times he woke from a strangely foreboding dream, feeling that he was close to a revelation. Somewhere in the vicinity, the Powers were active, but they were keeping their secret. In the morning, he went to work, chilled and thoughtful.

The Sun Pillar was a pine-trunk, the height of two men, stripped of its bark. Tiger walked around it, searching the white wood for patterns, leading lines, knots, and other things that might reveal to him what the Powers wanted him to do. Somewhere in the wood there were already the images that it was his task to call forth and make visible, with his engraving tool, with ochre, charcoal, and woad. He made a scaffold to climb up and scrutinize the upper part of the bole. Yes, it was speaking to him; here—here—and here! He caught a glimpse of an eye, a line that might be the hump of a mammoth, the arc of a horn. The wood was alive. He saw it and felt it. Now the Powers were on his side. He stood three fathoms from the pillar and walked around it several times. Already he saw it fill up with pictures.

Shelk stood at his door, tense and expectant. He kept still, so as not to disturb the artist.

There was the mammoth. Tiger studied the invisible picture from various angles. Yes, it was there. With complete assurance he seized his engraving tool and went up to the pillar. Silent and impressed, Shelk looked on as the young artist started his work.

The Powers were on his side! The days passed, and the Sun Pillar became covered with animal shapes. The inspiration never left him.

The southern face of the pillar was the place for the cattle of the Sun. At the base was the mammoth, tall and humped, a fusion of bold, interlacing curves; the tusks, the trunk, the lines of head and back, all massive and black, a vision of unbridled strength. This was the foundation of the composition, as if the great animal were carrying the pillar on its back.

Above the mammoth the caribou emerged, drawn with affecting mildness. The angular antlers, branching beautifully, spoke of the animal's fragility and vulnerability. In its eye there was an appeal, but the body revealed a tough will to live, to endure long migrations, snow and ice. Behind the caribou, an approaching herd was suggested, a forest of antlers on the march; you could almost hear the cracking of the hoofs.

The place for the shelk remained empty. Instead, Tiger worked on the other animals, which were grouped around the central figures in an intricate composition. Though they were smaller, all of them were as alive and expressive. The carnivores were there too, but not big enough to threaten the cattle of the Sun.

On the northern face was the bison, black and russet, a second center of power in the hierarchy. Its body pattern signaled far and wide across the plains: Here am I, the steppe wisent! Its weight was concentrated in the withers; the hindquarters were slim, almost delicate. The black double mane on neck and back; the long horns, their points deflected backward.

There were two horses, each with raised head, hanging belly, and straggling mane. Ears cocked: Where is the enemy? A play of muscles under the skin, the moment before exploding into a gallop.

The great bear with its rolling gait, heavy and ungainly, yet a great striding shape still, with toe-in feet and long black claws, clicking against the rocks. A wolf seemed to threaten the mammoth—vain hopes! Grey and angry, with a long muzzle and greedy eyes, but its tail crept down between its legs.

The figure on the base of the northern face was the woolly rhinoceros, alone and unconcerned, its head hanging almost to the ground, and its long horn pointing forward. Here I go and nothing scares me; step aside, please, I don't see you, I don't hear you; my world is mine and I am alone in it.

Hyenas, two; one hyena is nothing, but two are a pack, ready for anything. They smiled at each other; you could hear their twittering laughter. The lynx with its round face, pennants on its ears, legs like pillars, big soft paws, and its tail-stump raised: the spirit of the tree.

The Powers were on Tiger's side. He did not know how and when they had answered his questions, but one morning he woke at Tern's side, and everything was clear to him, everything that he had searched for; everything the Powers wanted to tell him through his visions and through Miss Swallow's voice. When he told his plan to Baywillow, and when Baywillow passed it on to Veyde, it was out of Tiger's hands. There was nothing he could do himself; Sunwood was out of bounds to him.

So he continued to bring forth the pictures that were already visible to him on the flanks of the pillar. The glutton, the seal, the polar bear, and the salmon found their places. A knothole became the eye of a squirrel; the line from a glancing axe, the plume of its tail. Here the elk waded as if in a tarn, long-legged, its muzzle hanging. A butterfly fluttered; it was the mourning-cloak. A grasshopper chirped its monotonous song. Even the wasp had found its place.

Then birds invaded the picture, connecting its many parts in a rhythmic whole. There was the eagle with its commanding eyes, the horned owl in rocklike stillness, swifts and terns, their wings clipping.

Still the place of the shelk was empty, and time was running out. A moon and a half had passed. Now it was in its last quarter and the shadow of the Sun Pillar almost reached the door of Shelk's house. Tiger could see where the Shelk was in the wood, and he knew it wanted to come alive. It frightened him, but there was nothing he could do. He fought against it, and tried starting anew, but the lines in the wood, the lines his own eye recognized, were too strong. At last the shelk was there, as magnificent and proud as the one he had drawn after his adventure with the black tigers. This was its twin in majesty, but it also had the same mark of death upon it.

Shelk saw it. He had followed Tiger's work with thrilled admiration. Faced with the new picture, he stood motionless, staring with a wooden expression. Then he passed his hand over his eyes and sighed.

"Yes, we're all mortal, Wildcat. Is that what you wanted to tell me? You are right."

Tiger came down from his scaffold, stood beside Shelk, and studied the picture. "My hand isn't as sure as it used to be," he said.

"To me it seems surer than ever. But I seem to miss some animals. Where is the black tiger?"

"I can only draw the animals I've seen," said Tiger returning to his jungle of lies. For him, the tiger was there already. He saw it clearly in the empty space beside the shelk, and he knew that it alone would be the consummation. It was the finishing link. With it the whole picture would spring to life. The tension built up by the other animals would culminate and be discharged through the shelk and the tiger. Yet here Tiger had to betray his inspiration. Shelk must never see that picture.

"I understand," said Shelk. "The musk ox, the lion—I have seen them and you not."

"That is so, Master."

In the empty place of the tiger, he drew a wildcat. It was ugly. The face, with its low-lying ears, seemed to sneer, and the animal appeared to be sneaking off, stiff-legged, as if ashamed.

"You're not as good at the animal for which you are named, Wildcat," Shelk observed.

"I've always had trouble with it," Tiger improvised. "I've been wondering why. It's in the wrong place: too close to the shelk and to the Sun."

"But you are in your rightful place there," said Shelk warmly. "You are the greatest artist in the land, and it was indeed a lucky day that brought you here. The Sun Pillar is finished now, and even more noble than the one I remember. Tomorrow is the day of the Sun celebration; tomorrow we'll pay you the homage you deserve."

Tiger nodded dully. He had finished his work, but he had played it false at the end, and he could not look at it without meeting the leering eye of the wildcat in the place where he knew the deadly tiger was rising in a furious assault against the shelk.

Slowly Tiger walked to his house. He knew that his work had been easy, a pleasure compared with Veyde's. While he had been working in the sunshine, in compact with the Powers and encouraged by the Master, she had been toiling in twilight and darkness, constantly afraid of detection. However much Baywillow had tried to spare her and her friends, they had been forced to do their regular work as well. All had gone well so far, but how long could they trust their luck?

THE SPIRIT OF CARIBOU LAKE

Da sprach sie schnell: Sei bald bereit,
ich wasche dir dein Totenkleid!

Heine, Buch der Lieder

The good wine comes before the poor. Thus
the Midsummer Feast started with the broaching of the
black wine of the autumn, with its deep bilberry and
whortleberry tint. Later it would be succeeded by the
raw-sap wine of the spring. Tiger drank little, for he was
waiting to see Veyde and Marten, who would arrive
when everyone's eyes were fixed on the setting sun.
With amazement and secret derision, he watched the
peculiar rites performed by the Men of the Eagle
Feather, rites drawn from various parts of the land.

Here were warriors, smeared beyond recognition with
blood and filth, stinking to heaven; they came in fours,
carrying their leaders on their backs. A knowledgeable
man at Tiger's side told him that they came from the
Land of Flints, where the horse and its Guardian were
highly honored, and that the men were eight-footed
horses, carrying their chiefs to the grave. In the Land of
Flints, he said, men spoke of a chief who vaulted onto
the back of a horse and rode away into the forest; but
sensible people did not believe in such tales.

Presently, the men threw themselves into the lake and

returned cleansed. In this way, the man continued, they believe that they wash off their ill deeds and escape their fates; they think they can cheat death. He smiled at their superstition.

But later Tiger saw the same man and several others climbing the Sun Pillar and laying their hands on the red globe. They uttered cries of blissful pain and said that their hands were badly burned.

Tiger thought this silly and childish. The artful animal dances did arouse his admiration, though. Many of Shelk's people came to him to praise his work on the pillar. Diver, clean and proper after his dip in the lake, was as proud as he would have been if he had painted the pictures himself. "You are an honor to the company," he said. Tiger flinched, feeling the scornful look of the wildcat in his back.

Later, with Hind, he walked down to the valley.

"I have wanted to talk to you, Wildcat, ever since you came here," she said. "Now, while everybody is busy, I have a chance. Why did you come here, Wildcat? I know who you are. You're the one they hate and fear more than anybody else. Yet you dare to come here. You must be a great chief with invisible powers. Did you come to strike down the Master?"

"What does Shelk mean to you, Hind?"

"What he means to me doesn't matter. What I mean to him can be said in one word: nothing. Nothing, Wildcat, as you call yourself now." She stopped and looked down. "I was meant for other things. I was meant to be the woman of a chief, a chief called Tiger. Instead I became the Master's woman—for today. Tomorrow I'll be nothing at all.

"To him I'm just a woman who might possibly give him what he wants—a son. I'm on trial, and it isn't going to work. He pours his seed into me, but it doesn't take root. He doesn't even know that it's me. His eyes are closed, and he remembers another woman. I'm nothing to him. Soon he will send me away just as he's sent the others away. And what's going to happen to me then? I who was to have been the woman of a chief? What's going to happen, Wildcat? Soon I'll be nothing to the others either. I'll go from one warrior to the next; I'll be worthless. They'll take their pleasure from me and then kick me out the moment they get tired of me. That's what will happen to me, who was meant to be Tiger's bride."

"All isn't lost yet, Hind."

"Oh yes, to me it is. I hid myself among the other women in Sunwood. The Overseers wanted me, but every day I waited for Tiger to come. Now he is here, and it's too late. The Master took me for his woman, and he changed me from a chief's bride into nothing."

"In a moon or two, Hind, you'll remember this only as a bad dream. I promise you."

"What can you do, Tiger?"

"I cannot tell you now, but I'll get you back to your father."

Hind lifted his hand to her lips. "That's all I ask."

Later, when the disk of the Sun touched the edge of the forest, Tiger was united with Veyde and Marten. The boy, who had not seen his father for so long, cried out when the bearded stranger took him in his arms. The red rims of Veyde's eyes told of hard work and little sleep, but she shrugged and laughed: "No matter! We will soon be free. Two, three days! But oh, Tiger, old Mister Silverbirch is not well."

The old man smiled happily, but he did look haggard and weak. "Dear Mister Silverbirch," said Tiger, embracing him, "are you ill?"

Mister Silverbirch denied this emphatically. He was having trouble with his food, however. He had only one or two teeth left, and the caribou meat was too tough for him. Sometimes Baywillow was able to get some fish for him. The rest of the time, his friends kept him alive by mouth-feeding, but this was hard on his stomach.

Just then Baywillow came along carrying a heavy load. That day, a gigantic beluga sturgeon had been caught in the Great River. It was the length of three men, and six men had been needed to pull it out of the water. Now it was part of the feast. Silverbirch sat down, smacked his lips, and began to munch caviar and sturgeon meat.

"The spirit of the lake is waiting for her liberation," said Veyde. "Let us know when it should be."

"Baywillow will give you the sign," said Tiger.

The sun set. The time for the poorer wine had arrived. Tern came to Tiger with a skin, but when she saw him with a Troll bitch and a small bastard child, she stopped. She stared incredulously, then ran away in a pet.

Suddenly there was a great commotion near the Sun Pillar. One of Shelk's warriors, reeling and bleeding, was brought to the Master, supported by a sentry.

"Wolf! Wolf and his gang!" he gasped.

Before the short night was over, Shelk went out with Diver's Company. Thus the feast ended. The next day dawned under cloudy skies, and soon the rain beat down.

Several days passed in sullen suspense. Tiger could hear Viper's angry commands down by the War Camp. Viper had tried to catch Wolf many times, but always in vain. This time he was not entrusted with the task.

In Sunwood the caribou were dying on their feet.

Sick people gathered around Shelk's house. The lower shamans did their best, but only the Master could heal, and he was gone.

Tern had vanished, and among the warriors

frightening rumors were told about the artist, who kept to his house.

"We're ready, Tiger," said Baywillow, but Tiger could only say, "Wait! We must wait for Shelk."

But Shelk was far away. He was standing with Diver's Company at the edge of the forest near a low, round granite hill, which had been polished by ice. The rain had stopped and the air was heavy with the fragrance of summer flowers. Three prisoners were led to him, their hands bound, ropes around their necks: Wolf, overcome at last, with two of his men.

"You've won, Shelk," said Wolf. "Make it fast, now."

The man at his side laughed. "Yes, Shelk. Hoist us into the heaven of the Trolls."

"Don't listen to him," murmured the third. "He's always in a hurry."

Shelk looked at them long and hard, and they were silent. Then he turned and walked slowly up the hill. His struggle was finished, the last enemy beaten. Now, nothing could threaten the power of the Sun, and his own power would be undisputed. There was a new warmth in his body. Everything would be all right. Perhaps at last his most ardent wish would also be fulfilled.

Shelk looked down at the rock, and *it was full of pictures.* In a great bound the black tiger rose toward the shelk!

Then Shelk knew. He cried out in pain and horror, as if the fangs of the tiger were already in his breast.

With Diver's Company and their prisoners, Shelk returned by forced marches to Caribou Lake. It took him two days and two nights, and the men were ready to drop dead when they finally arrived. They had marched through scented summer woods, with myriad singing birds, but Shelk had relived the darkest hours of his life: the time he spent in Skua's noose, the sacrifice of his finger, and above all, the day when Black Cloud left him. Just before, their happiness had been complete: her belly had grown big, and they were sure she was with child. Then the swelling went down, and Black Cloud lost all hope. Now, once more, Shelk had been betrayed by someone who had been close to him.

The four-footed beasts bolted in terror before them as they crashed through the forest.

So the story ends with Tiger's trial and judgment. For the third time he was summoned to Shelk. The first time, he came to take his oath; the second, to receive a sacred commision. Now he came as an unmasked traitor and perjurer. When he saw all the people who had gathered at the Sun Pillar, he knew what awaited him.

There were Shelk and Fox, Viper, and all of Diver's Company. There, too, were all those who knew his secret: Hind, Tern, his sister Godwit; Wolf, Beaver, and Glutton, with ropes around their necks; even Goshawk, gibbering with terror. Baywillow had been ordered to bring two witnesses from Veyde's Island: Veyde and Silverbirch. Tiger met their eyes and nodded. He took off the golden wasp, stepped up to Wolf, and hung it around his neck.

"You know its meaning, Wolf," he said, "and I have not failed you, however bad things may look now."

Wolf frowned, obviously distrustful, and Tiger cast a questioning glance at Baywillow.

"The sign has been given," said Baywillow cryptically, looking at nobody in particular. Tiger smiled. He pulled out the tiger tooth, which he had kept hidden under his shirt for so long, and let it dangle on his breast. There was a general movement, and something like a sigh. Everybody's eyes were fixed on the white crescent.

Tiger crossed his arms and looked directly into Shelk's face. Shelk raised his hand, pointing to the Sun Pillar.

"Finish it," he ordered.

Obediently Tiger went to the pillar, raised his scaffold, and started to work. Under his knife the false wildcat vanished. In its place the shape that really lived in the wood began to emerge. Everybody seemed to hold his breath, hour after hour, while the sun rose higher, and Tiger worked.

Once more there was a collective sigh, as Tiger stepped down. The pillar was finished. Now it was clear that everything else formed only a background, a garland around the two animals at the top: the shelk, in the shadow of death; the tiger, rising to it in ultimate fury. The whole pillar was transfigured by the revelation of this center of power, so that even the Sun Globe seemed eclipsed by the suspense between the two figures.

"You can kill me, Shelk," said Tiger, "but there *I* have won."

Shelk passed both hands over his face in the gesture of the Whites, yet he still spoke in the Black language.

"The magic still lives in your hand," he said, "but now I know what it's worth. Your father was a notorious unbeliever whom we had to strike down, yet he at least was honest. You have fallen lower. With perfidious cunning you insinuated yourself among us. With a false heart you took your vow. You came to kill me, did you not?"

Tiger nodded. "Cunning and perfidy are the weapons of the black tiger," he replied.

"So you have a compact with the Powers of evil. They've given you the art of confusing the minds of men with beautiful pictures and pretty speech. All the while you plot to destroy us all, as you destroyed our emissaries, with your unspeakable witchcraft. But it won't happen. You have judged yourself with your pictures and your words, and now you shall die. Seize him, Viper!''

Shelk was close to Tiger, and his eyes flashed in anger. Veyde, who had not understood much of the foreign tongue, was waiting calmly, but Silverbirch trotted up timidly and pulled at Shelk's sleeve. He began to speak, faltering, in his curious rendering of the Black tongue.

''It isn't like that, O Shelk and Master,'' he said. ''No, what really happened . . .''

Angrily, Shelk threw him aside, and Silverbirch fell. His back hit a rock, and there was a dreadful rattle in his throat as his face went blue and he fought for breath.

''The Troll ox has broken his back,'' said Beaver with interest. ''Too bad. By the Mammoth, he was a brave ox.''

Veyde threw herself down next to Silverbirch and put her arms around him. ''Dear Mister Silverbirch, are you all right?''

In the White tongue Baywillow said, ''What he was trying to tell you, Mister Shelk, was that Tiger did not kill your brother. I did. I had revenge for my father, Mister Ferret.''

''You, Buzzard?'' cried Shelk, almost choking with rage. ''Are you one of them, too?''

''My name is Baywillow. I am Tiger's brother.''

Veyde, meanwhile, was looking fearfully at Silverbirch, who was struggling for air. ''Oh Mister Skylark,'' she cried, ''come back! Come back!''

The shadow of a smile passed over the old man's face.

''He'll come round,'' said Glutton. ''You see, he's not dead yet.''

''Skylark?'' repeated Tiger, surprised.

''Yes, that is his soul-bird,'' said Veyde. ''Did you not know, Tiger?''

"Skylark?" Shelk's voice was filled with incredulity and horror. "Skylark was the name my mother took."

"Yes," said Veyde. "I have known it for a long time. But I did not want him to know. The grief would have been too much for him."

"I'd say he's as dead as a last year's grasshopper," said Beaver critically.

"That's what you say, but you don't know how tough these Troll oxen are," Glutton argued. "I've seen—"

"No!" cried Shelk in despair. "He cannot be my White father."

"He is," said Veyde, now on her feet and facing him sternly. "You have bungled everything, Mister Shelk. You may even have killed your own father. What do you think you are? The Guardian of birds? Ha! A poor raven is the only guardianship you have. The Guardian of the caribou? Just come to Sunwood and watch them die. They are starving. The wood is ravaged and the caribou have nothing to eat. They die from heat. Why have you locked them in Sunwood? Why have you not left them free to migrate to the north and south? If they are the Sun's cattle, as you say they are, then you are the Sun's enemy, Mister Shelk. And why have you shut us up there, when all we ask is to live in freedom on our island? You have given us nothing but sorrow and misery. What are your warriors but murderers and bandits? They kill ordinary decent villagers, take our property, and make us slaves. We have to toil and sweat and starve so that they can fool about with their ridiculous feathers, thinking they are our betters. You are the one who allows all this to happen, Mister Shelk. You who call yourself the Son of the Sun! But your power is coming to an end. You do not know it yet, but so it is. With these hands we have destroyed it!"

And Veyde thrust her horny hands in Shelk's face.

"By the Mammoth, that's a Troll bitch for me," said

Beaver admiringly. "I don't understand a word, but she's talked herself into the heaven of the Trolls for sure."

"Shut up," said Glutton. "Don't you see?"

Shelk dropped to his knees at Silverbirch's side, took both his hands, and studied the old man's face intently. Silverbirch lay with his eyes closed, breathing stertorously.

Viper, who had been looking from one to the other, now strode forth and lifted his spear.

"Shelk, as you call yourself," he said angrily, "you are a liar and a traitor. You're not the real Shelk, you're his shade, risen from a stinking puddle. You've fooled us all long enough. You're not the man who was like a father to me, who was my Master and shared everything with me. You sent that man to his death so that you could grasp the power yourself, so that you could fool about with the caribou—the caribou you can't even keep alive!"

Shelk looked up and said in a low voice, "Black Cloud was right, She moved with the caribou. I've shut them up. A fool I've been."

"And now you're a dead man," said Viper. "The power is mine. Tiger shall be my shaman. He's greater than you are, but I'm the greatest of all!"

Fox attacked him, but for a man of Viper's strength it took only a moment to strike Fox down.

"Why did I not find you in time?" asked Shelk, reverting to the White language, and still staring at the unconscious Silverbirch. "Perhaps you could have taught me . . ."

"He was the gentlest, most considerate man in the world," said Veyde. "Perhaps he could have taught you that. Do you think so?"

"Perhaps," said Shelk.

"Enough talk," said Viper, also in the language of the Whites. "You are finished. Viper is the Chief of Caribou Lake, and Tiger is Shaman. From now on I give the orders here."

Veyde looked at him with a grin. "No, Mister Viper, you are mistaken. It is the spirit of Caribou Lake who gives the orders, and now she is free at last. Listen!"

Viper started. There was a change in the din from the rapids; suddenly it seemed closer, and in the earth before them, there was a tremendous rumbling. The sparse birch wood shuddered as if from sudden terror. Then it started to move. The roaring of the water increased to a deafening thunder. Before their eyes the entire birch grove was snatched away, and an immense sheet of falling water came into sight. Shelk sprang up.

"The Sun Pillar!" he cried, and ran toward it.

"You won't escape me!" roared Viper, running after Shelk with his spear raised.

The moment Shelk reached the pillar, it tottered, as the rushing waters dug in beneath it. It fell and was swept away, along with Shelk and Viper.

"Go back!" cried Tiger, stooping to lift up Silverbirch, who was still unconscious. He started to run, and the others followed, in a panic. Wolf, with the rope still around his neck, with only one serviceable arm, carried Fox. Hind tripped and fell, but Baywillow saved her, and they all managed to work their way up to Shelk's solitary eyrie on the top of the hill. Behind them the Master's house was swept away by the flood. The entire lake seemed to tumble in a tumultuous white chaos down the little valley. Not a trace of the War Camp was to be seen. The spirit of Caribou Lake was free at last, and its wrath dwarfed everything around it.

THE GUARDIAN OF THE TIGER

And all those who sleep, sleep, sleep under the hills
are annihilated; Death itself is annihilated.

Gert Bonnier, Det Oförklarliga

It was Tiger who had conceived the idea of digging a new outlet for Caribou Lake, allowing it to flow
down into the valley, but Baywillow and Veyde had decided on the place. Veyde, with her Whites and with
Miss Rosebay as second in command, did the work. It
was a huge undertaking. They had nothing but sticks,
caribou antlers, and their bare hands for digging. The
work had to be done in absolute secrecy, so the ditch
was covered with branches and moss to escape detection. Fortunately, all traffic to and from Sunwood
followed a single path, which was untouched until Baywillow brought news of Shelk's return. At that moment
Veyde gave Miss Rosebay the order to break through.
Then she and Mister Silverbirch went to the gathering at
the Sun Pillar.

The results exceeded their wildest expectations. There
was only a small trickle of water at first, but as they dug
deeper the water began to detach clay and earth. At
whirling speed, the trickle grew into a great waterfall,
and Miss Rosebay and her people were barely able to
escape it.

In the Gorge the flow of water subsided, and the following day it was as dry as it had been when Mister Cornel lived there, bare and rocky. Thus the caribou were able to use their old migration route again.

Of Shelk, Viper, and the Sun Pillar, no trace was ever found, though it was rumored that some of Shelk's warriors found his body and divided it into four parts. When they set out in different directions to reach their old homes, each warrior took one part with him.

Wolf returned to Big Lake with Beaver, Glutton, and the men of Diver's Company, who swore allegiance to him. He also took Tern, who was perhaps more enamored of the golden wasp than of Wolf himself. Thus she became a chief's woman. For a short time Fox, too, lived at Big Lake with his family; later, they set out for the Salt Sea.

Wolf gave his daughter Hind to Baywillow, who had saved her life. Everybody thought it fitting that Hind should marry Ferret's eldest son after all, though he happened to be Baywillow, not Tiger. She too became a chief's woman, for Baywillow went back to reign with Veyde on Veyde's Island. Through Tiger's brotherly assistance, Hind and Baywillow were blessed with many sons and daughters, all of them Black.

Silverbirch recovered, and for years afterward he continued to set the standards of behavior on Veyde's Island. He died in peace, without ever learning the secret of Shelk's parentage. Veyde was grateful that Mister Silverbirch had been unconscious during her talk with Shelk. Not only because of the secret, but because she had been intolerably rude to Shelk. "Silverbirch would never have let me forget that day," she said.

Tiger and Veyde had many children, who grew up tall and beautiful, star-eyed, indestructible, and strangely gifted. All survived to old age, but none had a child.

Late each winter, when the sun rose high and spring was in the air, Tiger went away for a moon or more, nobody knew where. Veyde may have guessed. With a knowing smile she would look up at the Sun Pillar that Tiger had erected on the very platform where the first Shelk had once besieged them. The pillar was covered with every animal imaginable. Above them all were a shelk and a black tiger, in happy, tranquil amity.

One day a Black hunter came to Blue Lake, which was now a White village as of old. He was frightened and confused by a mysterious vision he had seen in the forest. The black God of the village received him kindly, listening to his story with interest. It was indeed an arresting tale. The man had seen a monstrous shaman—it must have been the Guardian of the tiger himself—hunting with a retinue of young black tigers. The eyes of the fat God lit up.

"That shaman is my oldest guest-friend," he said. "You came at a happy moment, my friend. I still have a skin of black wine, and I can lend you a bitch for the night. Don't thank me, the gratitude is all on my side. You've brought me news of a dear friend."

A thousand years later the ice returned to engulf their world, and the crust of the earth sagged under its weight. Even today, Veyde's Island lies at the bottom of the sea.

AUTHOR'S NOTE

I have promised a solution, but before I come to that, a few words about the setting of the story. In the time between 70,000 and 10,000 years ago, much of Europe was covered by a great inland ice-sheet, radiating from the Scandinavian mountains. But there was a warmer spell, between about 40,000 and 25,000 years ago, when the ice retreated to the north, leaving much of Scandinavia uncovered; and the story takes place in this interval. The Salt Sea is the North Sea; the Great Water, or the brackish sea, is the Baltic; and the Land of Flints is southernmost Sweden, with its flint-bearing chalk. We know that mammoth and reindeer lived in Scandinavia at the time, so I feel justified in populating the landscape of Nordic forests and skerries with an Ice Age fauna. (The reindeer is called "caribou" because the Ice Age reindeer in Europe resembled the living North American form.)

The animals are described as they may have appeared to contemporary humans. More scientific descriptions can be found in other books. But there are three animals that play a major part in the story, and I'd like to say a few words about them.

You may be surprised to see the mammoth described as black. It is usually brown in life reconstructions, for that is the color of the fur on mammoth skins preserved in the frozen ground of Siberia and Alaska. But Kenneth Oakley thinks the brown tint results from degradation of the pigment, and that the mammoth was black in life—which, I think, makes it even more impressive. (On the other hand, these mammoths of the late Ice Age were not particularly large, as elephants go.)

Then the strange "black tiger." It was not related to the living tiger, but belonged to the extinct sabertoothed cats. The scientist knows it under the name *Homotherium*, meaning "similar beast," and a more inept name would be hard to find, for apparently it looked like nothing else on earth. Its shape is described in the story. Of course, we know nothing about its color, so I was free to make it black like its favorite prey, the mammoth. (How do I know about its favorite prey? A very proper question. In a cave in Texas, many skeletons of *Homotherium* were found together with hundreds of mammoth milk teeth, so we deduce that mammoth calves formed its staple diet. One of the skeletons, by the way, had polydactylous feet.)

The "shelk," finally, is the "Irish elk," yet the animal was neither an elk nor exclusively Irish. It was probably the most magnificent deer that ever lived, and deserves a better name. This one is taken from the *Nibelungenlied,* where Siegfried kills a mythical "schelch." I hope the name will stick.

Wherever possible I have tried to base descriptive details on scientific fact or reasonable inference. As an example, Tiger, when first viewing the sea, observes gulls with white wings. I think the species in that particular setting would in fact have been the common gull, or *Larus canus*. The black-winged *Larus marinus* may have been present too, but would have been much rarer and generally farther out to sea. At the present time there are three additional species of gulls in the Baltic, but I have reasons, different in each case, for suspecting they were not present then.

The story of Cornel and the flooding of the Gorge is puzzling enough to demand an explanation, the more so as Veyde's recounting of it is hearsay and contains elements of myth. These are included to show that the story was a tradition embellished in its passage from generation to generation. (One detail, which I am not going to divulge, is a direct giveaway to an ornithologist.) But the main events are credible enough. The earth's crust, relieved from the weight of the inland ice, was rising. This rebound was in general a gradual process but occasionally occurred as a minor earth tremor. The rebound was also unequal, depending on differences in the thickness of the erstwhile ice-sheet. As a result, lake basins were gradually canted and tended to find new drainages, in this case farther south. Thus, the original eastern drainage of Caribou Lake was abandoned, and the water broke south into the Gorge and passed through it, then resumed its eastern direction. At the end of the story, Veyde digs a new channel that allows the water to bypass the long loop of the Gorge.

The bones of Neandertal man give no clues as to the color of his skin. As a rule, however, people living at high latitudes have lighter pigmentation than the inhabitants of tropical and subtropical regions. This is thought to be an adaptation to differences in the exposure to solar radiation. As the Neandertals had lived in Europe for a very long time, the inference that they were light-skinned is obvious. They could also have differentiated into local races with varied pigmentation

traits, for instance blond and red-haired. The facial
peculiarities of the "Reds," however, are modeled upon
the eastern Neandertals of the Levant.

If the sapiens emigrated from the south, they would
be likely to be darker-skinned, and we might picture
them as rather like the present-day inhabitants of India.
In the story, a southern heritage is suggested by the
name of Tiger's mother, Oriole; this bird would not be
found in the pine-clad country of the north.

Many of the rituals described, especially in the case of
the "Blacks," are documented in the Paleolithic
material. Alexander Marshack says that the thinking of
early *Homo sapiens* was very complex and surprisingly
modern. There are, for instance, sequential engravings
that can be interpreted as moon calendars. He also
found that many animal pictures were reused: repeated
engravings were made in the same contour. In the story
I suggest that this was a ritual to appease the Guardian,
or supernatural owner, of the game—who, as Ake
Hultkrantz has shown, is an important figure in the
religion of many hunting societies. Of course, other interpretations are possible.

Tiger's initiation is based on discoveries in the Basua
Cave in Savona, Italy, and the strangulation torture suffered by Left Hand was depicted at Addaura, Sicily;
both were described by Alberto C. Blanc. Ochre hand
impressions can be seen in many caves, and often a
finger or a finger-joint is missing. Perhaps sacrificed?

As an artist, Tiger is shown to rely on eidetic images
which are fixed in the brain with total recall, rather than
on conscious memorizing. He uses ochre and charcoal
for painting, but I may be guilty of an anachronism in
having him use the indigo dye extracted from the woad
plant.

In spite of the rich archaeological material at hand, it

is not easy to frame a really credible picture of the society in which Ice Age sapiens lived. When we come to the Neandertals, the problems, and the call for empathy, are much greater.

The "White" society is here described as highly ritualized and mild-mannered, probably a startling notion to anyone who has seen a life reconstruction of Neandertal man with his seemingly brutish features. A key character in the physical make-up of these men was the beetle brow. It creates an impression of ferocity, and I suspect that that was one of its main functions. A big gorilla, its eyes hooded by mighty, bony brows, looks most intimidating. This, as Dale Guthrie says, "has made it easy for writers to portray it as a dangerous beast, even though it is a vegetarian and rather shy." In nature, aggression by display is often a sham. If an intimidation stare suffices to frighten away an enemy, why engage in costly fighting? Behind his menacing mask, primitive man may well have been rather peaceable.

From this it is only a brief step to envisage a system of appeasing ritual to offset the effects of the built-in threat display. Given sufficient time, and the inventiveness of the human brain, it could even develop to seemingly absurd degrees. I do not say it did, but at any rate there is compelling evidence for the complexity and humanity of Neandertal society to support the idea of ritualization.

The demography, for instance, is surprisingly favorable. Marie-Antoinette de Lumley, studying Neandertal remains from the Cave of Hortus in southern France, noted the high incidence of old people. The fact that every fifth individual was *over* fifty years old is truly amazing in a primitive hunting society. Ralph Solecki showed that two of the old Neandertals from

Shanidar Cave in Iraq were so severely crippled that they must have been completely dependent on their fellow men for a long time. No killing of the "old and useless" here. And Erik Trinkaus and William Howells, marshaling the total evidence, point out that the longevity of Neandertal man was markedly greater than that of the succeeding sapiens. It would seem that old people were held in high respect. Probably, sages like Silverbirch were not uncommon.

Of course, many elements in the story are wholly fictitious. There is certainly no evidence for military organizations like that of Shelk, or for such early, if abortive, attempts at domestication. The first domesticated animal seems to have been the dog, but that came later, perhaps some 15,000 years before the present. And finally, there is no certain proof that Neandertals and sapiens ever met, though it appears likely.

In this story they do meet, and so I come to the model for the extinction of the Neandertals (Whites). I'm sure you have it by now, but here it is anyway. It comes in three parts.

First: The species hybrids are assumed to be sterile. Baywillow, Black Cloud, the Shelks, all are childless. At the same time, they are affected by hybrid vigor, giving them unusual resistibility, intelligence, and so on, but that doesn't affect the outcome. Even a moderate reduction of fertility would have the same effect in the long run.

Second: Both Whites and Blacks regard the Blacks as superior beings. With their less advanced technology and poorer articulation (Philip Liebermann has shown that Neandertal vocal organs probably could produce no other vowel than "ah"), the Neandertals in fact suffer from an inferiority complex. In addition, the "childlike" features of the sapient face appeal to the tender emotions of the Neandertals.

Third: The Whites in this story are matriarchal, the Blacks patriarchal. This cannot be proved, but my impression—which may be false—is that among early sapients male and female differed more in size than among the Neandertals. Could this also mean a greater difference in the sex roles—or am I poking a hornets' nest? In any case, here is the core of the model. It would lead to the offspring between White males and Black females becoming outcasts in the Black society (as happens to the Shelks), whereas the offspring of a Black male—White female mating would be honored in the White society (Baywillow). And so the great majority of the hybrids would be of the second kind: children of White mothers.

There it is. Many more White mothers than Black mothers will have hybrid children, or in other words, sterile offspring. As a result, the number of Whites will dwindle continuously even if the two kinds of humans live together in perfect amity.

The model might be compared to the use of sterilizing radiation in certain methods of biological pest control. It is, of course, an unpleasant analogy, and yet I feel tempted to stress it. Too often we have regarded groups of our fellow men as pests, thereby justifying brutal and irresponsible use of technology against them. This seems, unfortunately, to be a characteristic of the species which in its hubris calls itself *Homo sapiens*.

But I repeat, this is only one model out of many possible ones, and I don't *think* it happened just this way. *Dixi et salvavi animam meam.*

ABOUT THE AUTHOR

Björn Kurtén was born in Finland in 1924. A professor at the University of Helsinki and one of the world's leading paleontologists, he has worked extensively in Europe, Africa, and North America. Professor Kurtén has published several novels in Swedish and numerous books in English on mammals and the ice ages. He is a fellow of the Explorers Club and has held a lectureship in zoology at Harvard University.